ROAD BROTHERS

Also by Mark Lawrence

The Broken Empire
Prince of Thorns
King of Thorns
Emperor of Thorns

The Red Queen's War
Prince of Fools
The Liar's Key
The Wheel of Osheim

Book of the Ancestor
Red Sister

ROAD BROTHERS

Tales from the Broken Empire

Mark Lawrence

HARPER
Voyager

Harper*Voyager* an imprint of
HarperCollins*Publishers* Ltd
1 London Bridge Street
London SE1 9GF

www.harpercollins.co.uk

First published in hardback by HarperCollins*Publishers* 2017
1

A catalogue record for this book is
available from the British Library

HB ISBN: 978-0-00-822138-6
TPB ISBN: 978-0-00-826789-6

Set in Plantin Light by Palimpsest Book Production Limited,
Falkirk, Stirlingshire

Printed and bound in the UK by
CPI Group (UK) Ltd, Coydon, CR0 4YY

MIX
Paper from
responsible sources
FSC™ C007454

Acknowledgements

Huge thanks to Agnes Meszaros for beta-reading so many of these stories and letting me bounce ideas about this volume off her. Also to my editor at Voyager, Jane Johnson, who edited the first two Broken Empire short stories I wrote out of the kindness of her heart, and now the whole book because she's publishing it.

The cover art is the work of the late Kim Kincaid. Despite being a professional artist, Kim drew Jorg in her spare time, inspired by the books. The kind of gift every author hopes for and few receive. She was generous enough to send me a print which has hung on my wall for several years now. I'm very glad that Kim's family have granted Voyager the right to use the art, and that I had the opportunity to have it as a cover, giving it the wider audience it deserves.

I should also note the anthologies/magazines for which some of these stories were originally written: *Unfettered* anthology, *Legends 2* anthology, *Grimdark Magazine*, *Unbound* anthology, and the *Blackguards* anthology.

You will also be able to find, with a little Google-fu, free audio versions of 'Sleeping Beauty' and 'Select Mode'. They're on SoundCloud and read by authors Richard Ford and T.O. Munro respectively.

Introduction

I learned most of what I know about writing from writing short stories. They're a great place to practise the art. They are also a fine means by which to revisit a character or a world, illuminating a corner of the original tale that perhaps deserves more attention. In addition, they can be used to look back over the years, allowing us to see how our heroes and villains . . . well mainly villains if we're honest . . . came to be where we found them and what shaped them along the way.

The stories in this anthology were written over the space of a few years, mostly for other projects. They offer a mix of murder, mayhem, pathos, and philosophy, and stand on their own without the need to have read the books that inspired them. The events occur before or around the edges of those described in the Broken Empire trilogy and will contain a variety of spoilers.

I hope you'll enjoy dipping into the lives of Jorg and his brothers one more time. It was a grand tale and I was sorry to leave it behind.

Mark Lawrence
Bristol, 2017

Oh, and I've added a brief footnote at the end of each story . . . because I wanted to!

Table of Contents

A Rescue

'I spent a year hunting down the men who burned my home. I followed them across three nations.'

'I see.' The old man laid down his quill and looked up across the desk at Makin.

Makin returned the stare. The king's man had a long white beard, no wider than his narrow chin and reaching down across his chest to coil on the desk before him. He'd asked no question but Makin felt the need to answer.

'I wanted them to pay for the lives of my wife and my child.' Even now the anger rose in him, a sharpness twitching his hands towards violence, a yammering in his ears that made him want to shout.

'And did it help?' Lundist studied him with dark eyes.

The guards had told Makin the man had journeyed from the Utter East and King Olidan had hired him to tutor his children, but it seemed his duties extended further than that.

'Did it help?' Makin tried to keep the snarl from his voice.

'Yes.' Lundist set his hands before him, the tips of his long fingers meeting in front of his chest. 'Did taking your revenge ease your pain?'

'No.' When he took to his bed, when he closed his eyes, it was blue sky Makin saw, the blue line of sky he had watched from the ditch he had lain in, run through, bleeding out his lifeblood. A line of china blue fringed with grass and weeds, black against the brightness of the day. The voices would return to him – the harsh cries of the footmen set to chase down his household. The crackle of the flames finding the roof. Cerys hid from the fire as her mother had told her to. A brave girl, three years in the world. She hid well and no one found her, save the smoke, strangling her beneath her bed before the flames began their feast.

'. . . your father.'

'Your pardon?' Makin became aware that Lundist was speaking again.

'The captain of the guard accepted you for wall duty because I know your father has ties with the Ancrath family,' Lundist said.

'I thought the test . . .'

'It was important to know that you can fight – and your sword skills are very impressive – but to serve within the castle there must be trust, and that means family. You are the third son of Arkland Bortha, Lord of Trent, a region that one might cover a fair portion of with the king's tablecloth. You yourself are landless. A widower at one and twenty.'

'I see.' Makin nodded. He had disarmed four of Sir Grehem's men when they came at him. Several sported large bruises the next day although the swords had been wooden.

'The men don't like you, Makin. Did you know that?' Lundist peered up from the notes before him. 'It is said that you are not an easy man to get along with.'

Makin forced the scowl from his face. 'I used to be good at making friends.'

'You are . . .' Lundist traced the passage with his finger, 'a difficult man, given to black moods, prone to violence.'

Makin shrugged. It wasn't untrue. He wondered where he would go when Lundist dismissed him from the guard.

'Fortunately,' Lundist continued, 'King Olidan considers such qualities to be a price worth paying to have in his employ men who excel at taking lives when he commands it, or in defence of what he owns. You're to be put on general castle duty on a permanent basis.'

Makin pursed his lips, unsure of how he felt. Taking service with the king had seemed to be what he needed after his long and bloody year. Setting down roots again. Service, duty, renewed purpose, after his losses had set him adrift for so long. But just now, when he had thought himself cut loose once more, bound for the loneliness of the road, he had, for a moment, welcomed it.

Makin stood, pushing back the chair that Lundist had directed him to. 'I will attempt to live up to the trust that's been placed in me.' He thought of the ditch. Cerys had had faith in him, a child's blind faith. Nessa had had faith, in him, in his word, in God, in justice . . . and her trust had seen her pinned to the ground by a spear in the cornfield behind her home. He saw again the blue strip of sky.

Lundist bent to his ledger, quill scratching across parchment.

As Makin turned to go, the tutor spoke again. 'The need for vengeance feels like a hunger, but there is no sating it. Instead it consumes the man that feeds it. Vengeance is taking from the world. The only cure is to give.'

Makin didn't trust himself to speak and instead kept his jaw locked tight. What did a dried-up old scribe know of the hurts he'd suffered?

'There's a gap between youth and age that words can't cross,' Lundist said. He sounded sad. 'Go in peace, Makin. Serve your king.'

'The Healing Hall is on fire!' A guardsman burst through the door into the barracks.

'What?' Makin rolled to his feet from the bunk, sword in his hand. He'd heard the man's words. Saying 'what' was just a reflex, buying time to process the information. He glanced at the blade in his grasp. An edge would rarely help in fighting flames. 'Are we under attack?' No one would be mad enough to attack the Tall Castle, but on the other hand the queen and her two sons had been ambushed just a day from the capital. Only the older boy had survived, and barely.

'The Healing Hall is on fire!' The man repeated, looking around wildly. Makin recognized him as Aubrek, a new recruit: a big lad, second son of a landed knight and more used to village life than castles. 'Fire!' All along the barracks room men were tumbling from their beds, reaching for weapons.

Makin pushed past Aubrek and gazed out into the night. An orange glow lit the courtyard and on the far side tongues of flame flickered from the arched windows of the Healing Hall, licking the stonework above.

Castle-dwellers scurried in the shadows, shouts of alarm rang out, but the siege bell held its peace.

'Fire!' Makin roared. 'Get buckets! Get to the East Well!'

Ignoring his own orders, Makin ran straight for the hall. It had once been the House of Or's family church. When the Ancraths took the Tall Castle a hundred and twenty years previously they had built a second church, bigger and better, leaving the original for the treatment of the sick and injured. Or, more accurately, to repair their soldiers.

The heat brought Makin up short yards from the wall.

'The Devil's work!' Friar Glenn's voice just behind him.

Makin turned to see the squat friar, halted a few yards shy of his position, the firelight glaring on the baldness of his tonsure. 'Is the boy in there?'

Friar Glenn stood, mesmerized by the flames. 'Cleansed by fire . . .'

Makin grabbed him, taking two handfuls of his brown robe and heaving him to his toes. 'The boy! Is Prince Jorg still in there?' Last Makin heard the child had still been recuperating from the attack that had killed his mother and brother.

A wince of annoyance crossed the friar's beatific expression. 'He . . . may be.'

'We need to get in there!' The young prince had hid--den in a hook-briar when the enemy had come for him a week earlier. He had sustained scores of deep wounds from the thorns and they had soured despite Friar Glenn's frequent purging in the Healing Hall. He wouldn't be getting out on his own.

'The Devil's in him: my prayers have made no impression on his fevers.' The friar sank to his knees, hands clasped before him. 'If God delivers Prince Jorg from the fire then—'

Makin took off, skirting around the building toward the small door at the rear that would once have given access to the choir loft. A nine-year-old boy in the grip of delirium would need more than prayers to escape the conflagration.

Cries rang out behind him but with the roar of the

fire at the windows no meaning accompanied the shouts. Makin reached the door and took the iron handle, finding it hot in his grasp. At first it seemed that he was locked out, but with a roar of his own he heaved and found some give. The air sucked in through the gap he'd made, the flames within hungry for it. The door surrendered suddenly and a wind rushed past him into the old church. Smoke swirled in its wake, filling the corridor beyond.

Every animal fears fire. There are no exceptions. It's death incarnate. Pain and death. And fear held Makin in the doorway, trapped there beneath the weight of it as the wind died around him. He didn't know the boy. In the years Makin had served in King Olidan's castle guard he had seen the young princes on maybe three occasions. It wasn't his part to speak to them – merely to secure the perimeter. Yet here he stood now, at the hot heart of the matter.

Makin drew a breath and choked. No part of him wanted to venture inside. No one would condemn him for stepping back – and even if they did he had no friends within the castle, none whose opinion he cared about. Nothing bound him to his service but an empty promise and a vague sense of duty.

He took a step back. For a moment in place of swirling smoke he saw a line of brittle blue sky. Come morning this place would be blackened spars, fallen walls. Years ago, when they had lifted him from that ditch, more dead than alive, they had carried him past the ruins of his home. He hadn't known then that Cerys lay within, beneath soot-black stones and stinking char.

Somehow Makin found himself inside the building, the air hot, suffocating, and thick with smoke around him. He couldn't remember deciding to enter. Bent double he found he could just about breathe beneath the worst of the smoke, and with stinging, streaming eyes he staggered on.

A short corridor brought him to the great hall. Here the belly of the smoke lay higher, a dark and roiling ceiling that he would have to reach up to touch. Flames scaled the walls wherever a tapestry or panelling gave them a path. The crackling roar deafened him, the heat taking the tears from his eyes. A tapestry behind him, that had been smouldering when he passed it, burst into bright flames all along its length.

A number of pallets for the sick lined the room, many askew or overturned. Makin tried to draw breath to call for the prince but the air scorched his lungs and left him gasping. A moment later he was on his knees, though he had no intention to fall. 'Prince Jorg . . .' a whisper.

The heat pressed him to the flagstones like a great hand, sapping the strength from him, leaving each muscle limp. Makin knew that he would die there. 'Cerys.' His lips framed her name and he saw her, running through the meadow, blonde, mischievous, beautiful beyond any words at his disposal. For the first time in forever the vision wasn't razor-edged with sorrow.

With his cheek pressed to the stone floor Makin saw the prince, also on the ground. Over by the great hearth one of the heaps of bedding from the fallen pallets had a face among its folds.

Makin crawled, the hands he put before him blistered and red. One bundle, missed in the smoke, proved to be a man, the friar's muscular orderly, a fellow named Inch. A burning timber had fallen from above and blazed across his arm. The boy looked no more alive: white-faced, eyes closed, but the fire had no part of him. Makin snagged the boy's leg and hauled him back across the hall.

Pulling the nine-year-old felt harder than dragging a fallen stallion. Makin gasped and scrabbled for purchase on the stones. The smoke ceiling now held just a few feet above the floor, dark and hot and murderous.

'I . . .' Makin heaved the boy and himself another yard. 'Can't . . .' He slumped against the floor. Even the roar of the fire seemed distant now. If only the heat would let up he could sleep.

He felt them rather than saw them. Their presence to either side of him, luminous through the smoke. Nessa and Cerys, hands joined above him. He felt them as he had not since the day they died. Both had been absent from the burial. Cerys wasn't there as her little casket of ash and bone was lowered, lily-covered into the cold ground. Nessa didn't hear the choir sing for her, though Makin had paid their passage from Everan and selected her favourite hymns. Neither of them had watched when he killed the men who had led the assault. Those killings had left him dirty, further away from the lives he'd sought revenge for. Now though, both Nessa and Cerys stood beside him, silent, but watching, lending him strength.

'They tell me you were black and smoking when you crawled from the Healing Hall.' King Olidan watched Makin from his throne, eyes wintry beneath an iron crown.

'I have no memory of it, highness.' Makin's first memory was of coughing his guts up in the barracks, with the burns across his back an agony beyond believing. The prince had been taken into Friar Glen's care once more, hours earlier.

'My son has no memory of it either,' the king said. 'He escaped the friar's watch and ran for the woods, still delirious. Father Gomst says the prince's fever broke some days after his recapture.'

'I'm glad of it, highness.' Makin tried not to move his shoulders despite the ache of his scars, only now ceasing to weep after weeks of healing.

'It is my wish that Prince Jorg remain ignorant of your role, Makin.'

'Yes, highness.' Makin nodded.

'I should say, *Sir* Makin.' The king rose from his throne and descended the dais, footsteps echoing beneath the low ceiling of his throne room. 'You are to be one of my table knights. Recognition of the risks you took in saving my son.'

'My thanks, highness.' Makin bowed his head.

'Sir Grehem tells me you are a changed man, Sir Makin. The castle guard have taken you to their hearts. He says that you have many friends among them . . .' King Olidan stood behind him, footsteps silent for a moment. 'My son does not need friends, Sir Makin. He does not need to think he will be saved should ill befall him. He does not need debts.' The king walked around Makin, his steps slow and even. They were of a height, both tall, both strong, the king a decade older. 'Young Jorg burns around the hurt he has taken. He burns for revenge. It's this singularity of purpose that a king requires, that my house has always nurtured. Thrones are not won by the weak. They are not kept except by men who are hard, cold, focused.' King Olidan came front and centre once more, holding Makin's gaze – and in his eyes Makin found more to fear than he had in the jaws of the fire. 'Do we understand each other, Sir Makin?'

'Yes, highness.' Makin looked away.

'You may go. See Sir Grehem about your new duties.'

'Yes, highness.' And Makin turned on his heel, starting the long retreat to the great doors.

He walked the whole way with the weight of King Olidan's regard upon him. Once the doors were closed behind him, once he had walked to the grand stair, only then did Makin speak the words he couldn't say to Olidan, words the king would never hear, however loud-spoken. 'I didn't save your son. He saved me.'

Returning to his duties, Makin knew that however long the child pursued his vengeance it would never fill him, never heal the wounds he had taken. The prince might grow to be as cold and dangerous as his father, but Makin would guard him, give him the time he needed, because in the end nothing would save the boy except his own moment in the doorway, with his own fire ahead and his own cowardice behind. Makin could tell him that of course – but there are many gaps in this world . . . and there are some that words can't cross.

Footnote

Makin has always been an interesting character for me, a failed father-figure if you like. He should be Jorg's moral touchstone but too often finds himself swept along by the force of Jorg's personality and by the chaos/cruelty of the life he's entangled in. We root for him to recover himself.

Sleeping Beauty

A kiss woke me. A cool kiss pulled me from the hot depths of my dreaming. Lips touched mine, and deep as I was, dark as I was, I knew her, and let her lead me.

'Katherine?' I spoke her name but made no sound. A whiteness left me blind. I closed my eyes just to see the dark. 'Katherine?' A whisper this time. Damn but my throat hurt.

I turned my head, finding it a ponderous thing, as if my muscles strove to turn the world around me whilst I remained without motion. A white ceiling rotated into white walls. A steel surface came into view, gleaming and stainless.

Now I knew something beyond her name. I knew white walls and a steel table. Where I was, who I was, were things yet to be discovered.

Jorg. The name felt right. It fitted my mouth and my person. Hard and direct.

I could see a sprawl of long black hair spread across the shining table, reaching from beneath my cheek, overhanging the edge. Had Katherine climbed it to deliver her kiss? My vision swam, my thoughts with it – was I drunk . . . or worse? I didn't feel myself – I might not yet know who I was, but I knew enough to say that.

Images came and went, replacing the room. Names floated up from the back of my mind. Vyene. I had a barber cut my hair almost to the scalp when I left Vyene. I remembered the snip of his shears and the dark heap of my locks, tumbled across his tiled floor. Hakon had mocked me when I emerged cold-headed into the autumn chill.

Hakon? I tried to hang details upon the void beneath his name. Tall, lean . . . no more than twenty, his beard short and bound tight by an iron ring beneath his chin. 'Jorg the Bald!' he'd greeted me and fanned out his own golden mane across his shoulders, bright against wolf-skins.

'Watch your mouth.' I'd said it without rancour. These Norse have little enough respect for royalty. Mind you neither do I. 'Has my beauty fled me?' I mocked sorrow. 'Sometimes you have to make sacrifices in war, Hakon. I surrendered my lovely locks. Then I watched them burn. In the battle of man against lice I am the victor, whilst you, my friend, still crawl. I sacrificed one beauty for another. My own, in exchange for the cries of my enemies. They died by the thousand, in the fire.'

'Lice don't scream. They pop.'

I recalled the bristling of scalp beneath palm as I

rubbed my head trying to find an answer to that one. I tried now to touch the hair spread out before me across the steel but found my hands restrained. I made to sit up but a strap across my chest held me down. Straining, I could see five more straps binding me to the table, running across my chest, stomach, hips, legs, and ankles. I wore nothing else. Tubes ran from glass bottles on a stand above me, down into the veins of my left wrist.

This room, this white and windowless chamber, had not been made by any people of the Broken Empire. No smith could have fashioned the table, and the plasteek tubes lay beyond the art of some king's alchemist. I had woken out of time, led by dreams and a kiss to some den of the Builders.

The kiss! I flung my head to the other side, half-expecting to find Katherine standing there, silent beside the table. But no – only sterile white walls. Her scent lingered though. White musk, fainter than faint, but more real than dream.

Me, a table, a simple room of harsh angles, kept warm and light by some invisible artifice. The warmth enfolded me. My last memories had been of cold. Hakon and me trudging through the snow-bound forests of eastern Slov, a week out from Vyene. We picked our path between the pines where the ground lay clearest, leading our horses. Both of us huddled in our furs, me with only a hood and a quarter inch of hair to keep my head from

15

freezing. Winter had fallen upon us, hard, early, and unannounced.

'It's buggery cold,' I said unnecessarily, letting my breath plume before me.

'Ha! In the true north we'd call this a valley spring.' Hakon, frost in his beard, hands buried in leather mittens lined with fur.

'Yes?' I pushed through the pine branches, hearing them snap and the frost scatter down. 'Then how come you look as cold as I feel?'

'Ah.' A grin cracked his wind-reddened cheeks. 'In the north we stay by the hearth until summer.'

'We should have stayed by that last hearth then.' I floundered through snow, banked along a break in the trees.

'I didn't like the company.'

I had no answer for that. Exhaustion had its teeth in me and my bones lay cold in white flesh.

The house in question had stood implausibly deep in the forest, so isolated that Hakon had been convinced the tales of a witch were true.

'Don't be stupid,' I'd told him. 'If there's a witch living in the forest and she eats children then she's going to want to live on the edge, isn't she? I mean how often does a little Gerta or Hans come wandering this far in?'

Hakon had caved beneath the undeniable weight of my logic. We'd gone to ask for shelter, and failing it being offered, to take it. The door stood ajar – never a good sign in a winter storm, and the snow in front of the porch lay heavily trodden, covered with a fresh fall that obscured detail.

'Something's not right.' Hakon unslung his axe, a heavy, single-bladed thing with a long cutting edge, curved to bite deeper.

I'd nodded and advanced, silent save for the crump of fresh snow beneath my boots. Reaching out with my sword, I pushed the door wider. My theory about little girls and the middle of forests didn't survive the hallway. A child lay sprawled there, golden curls splashed with crimson, arms and legs at broken angles. I advanced another step, my nose wrinkled against the stink. Blood, the reek of guts, and something else, something rank and feral.

A hand clamped my shoulder and I nearly spun to hack it off. 'What?'

'We should leave . . . the witch—'

'There's no witch living here.' I pointed at the corpse. 'Unless she's got teeth big enough to bite a girl's face off, a taste for entrails, and a nasty habit of shitting in her own hallway.' I pointed to the brown mound by the foot of the stairs, which, unlike the girl's guts, was still steaming ever so slightly.

'Bear!' Hakon released my shoulder and started to back away. 'Let's run.'

'Let's,' I agreed.

A big black head thrust out from beneath the stairs

as we retreated to the horses. I saw another bear, larger still, through the broken shutters to the side of the house, licking out a bowl in the kitchen. And, as we reached our steeds and started to hurry away, a cub watched us from the attic bedroom, its wet muzzle thrust out between the winter boarding, teeth scarlet.

Why did it have to be bears? If it had been a witch I'd have stuck my sword through her neck and moved in. Bears though . . . Better to run, even if it's out into the killing cold.

Each step sapped my strength as the heat left me, stolen a scrap at a time, squandered into the night air with every breath.

I plodded on, deep in myself, refusing exhaustion. It had been time to leave Vyene, whether winter was approaching or not. I might regret it now, freezing in the pathless forest, but I'd stayed too long. Sometimes the dream of a place sucks you in and before you know it you're part of that dream too. In a city as grand and as old as Vyene the dream is one of glory, steeped in history, but like all dreams it's an illusion that will use you up while grass grows under your feet, while thorns spring up, dense on all sides, and hem you in. A kiss had woken me there too. Elin, leaving with her brother, Sindri, to their halls and duties in the north. Hakon had wanted to stay, but he'd had enough of the ancient capital and wanted to see the provinces, to slum it with the King of Renar. And so we'd left, escaped the trap of intrigue and politicking that was Vyene, shook ourselves free before its soft jaws closed entirely around us, and moved along.

Full night and a bitter moon found us some miles further on, breaking from the treeline and setting out across a snowfield where the land turned stony and started to rise. Snow began to fall once more, large-flaked, ghostly, ponderous at first, then rushing as the wind picked up again.

I lay on the steel table remembering – seeing lost days unfold. The dreams that had wrapped me still clung, leeching away urgency and care. It occurred to me that some drug pulsed in my veins, some sleeping draught to keep me dull. I jerked my body within the bands that kept me on the table. Nothing moved. The thing must be bolted to the floor.

Each strap had a buckle. One free hand and I'd be out of there. So all that truly held me was the binding on my wrists. I strained to break a hand free but the bands weren't made for breaking.

'Fuck.'

I stared around the room. In the top corner, opposite me, a glass eye watched, a short black cylinder ending in a dark lens.

The tubes that ran, from bottles on a steel stand to needles in my arm, hung tantalisingly close. Straining until my neck screamed and my vision blurred, I could almost touch the nearest of the trio with the tip of my tongue. Close! But 'close' can be the difference between cutting a throat and slicing air.

I stared at the tubes, hating them, trying not to let the drugs drag me down again. I felt myself sinking, the whiteness of the ceiling filling my mind.

Sinking.

I had felt myself sinking into a white embrace when we left the trees behind. The snow crust lay too thin to hold my weight and beneath it, cold soft depths where a man could flounder. In the drifts a man would lose the last of his heat quick enough, and find at the limits of his strength that the snow became almost warm, a cradle into which he might relax, and perhaps sleep, just for a moment, to recover himself.

'Here!' Hakon held the haft of his axe for me to grab hold and hauled me onto firmer ground.

'Why did we leave the woods, again?' I asked the question with numb lips, the words coming out blunt-edged. At least my teeth had ceased to chatter, which seemed as if it should be a good thing. The wind scoured the hillside. In the forest the trees had muted it.

'Nothing beats a cave for shelter.' Hakon pushed me on.

'Cave? Where?' I could see little past swirling snow and darkness.

I'd promised Sindri to send his cousin back alive after his trip to Renar. So far it looked as though it was Hakon keeping me alive. 'And where's my damn horse?'

'Back in the trees with mine. I saw a light. We're checking it out. You'll remember when you're warmer. Let's get to the cave.' Hakon kept up a steady pace and I stumbled after him.

'Cave? There'll be bears!' I remembered something about a baby bear with a red muzzle, and a girl with golden locks and no face. Swords and axes aren't a match for a bear's strength. Put a length of steel through one and the beast will still kill you before it realizes it's dead.

'Bears don't carry lanterns.' Hakon scrambled up a boulder. 'There! I see it. A light.' He slid back down. 'Doesn't look like a fire though.' A note of concern creeping in amid the excitement.

'Hell if I care.' I pushed past him, weaving a path up the slope.

In the end he followed. What choice was there other than to freeze to death? The bitter weather had come on us unexpectedly, a vicious early bite of winter at the tail of a mild autumn.

It's the simple things often as not that lay us low. It's the everyday world intruding on our little dreams of power and glory that kills us. For all my cunning and deathly swordplay a prince of Ancrath could die coughing up the flu, or choking on a fishbone, or frozen on a lonely slope by a freak snowstorm, same as any other man.

The light and the promised cave both came into

view over the next rise. The sight arrested me. The light burned at the back of a yawning cavern but as we approached a second glow began to spread across the slope ahead of us. A luminous mist. The spirit rose from the ground as a swimmer breaks the surface of a river. She moved across the snow-covered rocks. Back and forth before the cave mouth, illumination bleeding from each line, her face a death mask, jawbone gaping. She drifted closer, straggles of pale hair and tatters of dress unmoving despite the wind that tore across the hillside. The snow lit beneath her, each curious lump and bump of it commanding black shadows, revolving to point away from the spirit as she moved, as if indicating the many directions in which we might flee.

I felt Hakon shift behind me, turning to run. 'Stay,' I told him. 'I've met ghosts before. None of them with a bite meaner than their bark.'

The white skull tilted on its vertebrae, cocked to the side whilst the empty orbits considered me. 'Better run, boy. Death waits inside.' Her voice was a cracked thing that set my teeth on edge.

'No,' I said.

'My curse is on you.' A bony digit marked me out as her target. Madness wavered in her words, and strain, as if each utterance were gasped out past some unbearable agony. 'Run and you might outpace it.'

'I'm too tired to run, ghost. I'm going inside.'

She drifted closer still, surrounding me with a light that held no whisper of warmth. 'Needles and death, boy, there's nothing in there for you, just needles and death.' A gasp.

Something about being threatened lit a fire in my belly and, although the cold seemed all the more bitter for it, I felt more myself.

'Needles? Might I prick myself on one? That's probably the silliest curse I've heard in a long while – and men are seldom eloquent when sliding off my sword so I've heard some stupid curses in my time.'

'Fool!' The phantom's voice built to a piercing shriek, the glow of her bones growing more fierce by the second. 'Run while you—' And just as swiftly she was gone, torn to shreds on the wind, her light extinguished.

I stood for a long moment, blind, pinched by the gale's icy fingers. The moon peered through a wind-torn rip amid the cloudbanks and found the slope again before either of us moved to speak.

'Well,' I said. 'That was unusual.'

'Odin keep us.' Hakon's wisdom on the subject.

'He's as likely to keep us as the White Christ is.' I had no bone to pick with heathen bone-pickers. One god or many, none of them ever seemed to like us much. 'What did she think to terrify us with? Needles?' I started in toward the cave.

'What are you doing?' Hakon caught my arm. 'She said we'd die.'

I knew Norsemen took their evil spirits seriously but I hadn't expected one deranged ghost to unman my axe-wielding barbarian so much. 'If we see a needle we'll avoid jabbing ourselves with it. How about that? We'll go around.' I drew my sword and waved him on. 'Does she have some demonic sewing kit in there? Will the thread assault us? The thimbles hurl themselves upon me? Bobbins—'

'She said—'

'We'll die. I know. And what will we do out here?' Something tugged at my foot as I made to take another step. I crouched and brushed at the snow and my hand came away dark with blood though I'd felt no bite. A gleaming coil of wire lay exposed, emerging from the stony ground, covered in thin blades sharp as razors. Hakon crouched beside me to look.

The wire was a thing of the Builders. None today could make such steel and have it sitting out in the wilds, still sharp, untouched by rust. I looked at the blood blotting into my wrappings then eyed the uneven terrain with new suspicion. The Builders made their own ghosts too – not echoes of emotion or shadows of despair such as men of our time might leave behind, but constructs built of data and light, powered by dry machinery where cogs turned and numbers danced. I mistrusted such monstrosities more than mere phantoms.

'Perhaps we should build a windbreak among the trees,' I said. 'Try the tinderbox again and, if we can get a flame, build a fire big enough to put a boat-burning to shame.'

As I spoke the snow where the ghost had fallen apart began to glow and a second spirit rose through it, taking all the light for herself. There could be no confusing this one with the departed curse-maker. Mouldering bones and a death's head grin had been replaced with alabaster limbs spun about with gossamer, her face ivory perfection, all compassion and kind eyes.

'The cave is warm and safe.' Golden tones pulsating through the light. 'A place of sanctuary against the night. My sister's madness does not rule there – though her curse lingers. I can't break it but I can bend it. Even if a needle should prick you, you won't die, only sleep a while.'

I made a courtly bow, there on the hill in the teeth of the gale and on the edge of my endurance. 'Sleep sounds fine and good, but if it's all the same to you, fair spirit, I'd rather slumber on my own terms.' I held my hand and its red bandages out toward her. 'Without needles. I've bled enough tonight already.'

'If you see a needle . . . go around.' She offered her suggestion with a hint of a smile and vanished, not breaking apart as the sister did but fading like a footprint on wet sand where the waves wash. I hesitated still but the thought of warmth pulled at me.

'Come on.' And I led the way forward, placing each foot with care and encountering no more razored wire.

Inside the cave the wind fell away within the space of three steps. It still shrieked and moaned outside but, where we stood, the dry flakes could manage no more than a lazy swirl about our boots. My ears rang with the near-silence after so long filled with that relentless howl, and almost immediately my head began to ache and my body burn. Pain is life's signature. Sheltered at last, we stopped dying and started to hurt.

I returned to myself as if rising from the depths, reaching for a distant surface. The white ceiling greeted me. The table, the tubes, the straps. How long had I dreamed? Was Katherine still here or had her kiss grown cold upon my lips?

I thrashed in my bonds, sacrificing any shred of pride against a remote chance of escape. I stopped moments later, sweaty and with my hair strewn across my face. I spat out black strands and looked at those tubes and the clear liquids within. The drugs still pulsed in my veins, waiting to drag me back into sleep.

Flinging my hair back from my face, I banged my head against the table. 'Fuck.' It hurt and the dull clank might alert my captors but even so, I did it again, the other way this time, slinging the length of my locks back across my face and raising my head until the bones in my neck screamed.

It took seven attempts but finally my hair draped the bundled tubes and at the utmost lunge I caught some of the spare ends between my front teeth, ensnaring the whole bundle. I pulled down and, with my head against the table managed to get my teeth around one of the tubes itself.

In the ceiling corner a small red light began to wink above the glass eye that watched me.

It took several moments to feed the tubes through my teeth until they made a taut line to my wrist. I paused one time at a distant noise, a mechanical clunking that sounded once, twice, and fell silent.

With the tubes tight in my mouth, I shot a venomous look toward the watching eye and jerked my head. A sharp pain flared in my wrist as the needles tore free, followed by a dull ache and wetness – blood? Liquid from the tubes?

I started to pull my hand free. The pain of ripping the tubes clear proved nothing next to the agony that followed. It helped to think that if I didn't escape then endless torments might be heaped on me whilst I lay trapped.

The hand is made of many little bones. I've seen them often enough, exposed in cut flesh or revealed by rot. With sufficient pressure these bones give. They will rearrange and, if necessary, crack, but there are no constraints the size of a wrist that will prevent a hand from being drawn through them . . . if you are prepared to pay the price.

My hand came free with a snap. The cost of freedom included broken bones, considerable lost skin, and agony.

Without the lubrication from the fluids that had spilled out as the tubes came free, and my own blood, the price would have been steeper. Even so, my sword hand would not be fit to hold a sword for quite some while.

A loud clang, closer than before. A metal door opening.

On the stand that held the vials and tubes red lights began to blink and a high-pitched call rang out like the cry of some alien bird, repeating again and again.

Undoing tightly buckled straps with a broken hand and slippery fingers is difficult. Doing it fast, expecting at any second to hear the approach of footsteps, is still more difficult. In an ecstasy of fumbling I managed to get my other wrist unbound, cursing in pain and frustration.

The door that opened was not the one I imagined to lie somewhere behind my head but a small and thus far unsuspected hatch high in the wall to my left. The thing that emerged from the darkness behind the little door had too many legs, possibly ten, all gleaming silver and cunningly articulated. A bulbous glass ovoid comprised the bulk of its insectoid body, and within it a red liquid sloshed. Where the creature's mouthparts should have been a single long needle protruded.

I started to unbuckle the first and topmost of the six belts holding me flat against the table.

The darkness of the cave mouth had been less profound than that of the night outside. A light had burned at the back of it. Hakon and I edged in deeper, axe and sword gripped in frozen hands.

The light still blinked and now we saw that it sat beneath the legend 'Bunker 17' and above a rectangular doorway set into the back of the cavern.

'A Builder light.' The cold circle of illumination had no hint of flame about it.

Hakon made a slow rotation, checking the shadowed margins. I glanced back at the falling snow, lit by the glow of the Builders' light. White legions racing silent across the cave mouth. I wondered at the ghosts we'd seen. Spirits of those who failed to do correctly that last thing anyone ever has to, and die properly, or something older still . . . the minds of long-dead Builders trapped within their machinery and projected in some game of puppetry and shadow. I'd met both kinds before and had thought these ones to be true ghosts, but now my suspicions grew.

'We should stay here,' I said, turning and stepping away from the doorway.

As I did so a wave of warm air followed me, thick with the scent of roasting meat. I turned back to face the corridor leading away into the hill. 'It's a trap. And not a subtle one.'

'In the north we take what we need.' Hakon lifted his axe and advanced, already swallowing as the juices ran in his mouth.

My stomach rumbled. With a shrug I followed him in. 'We do that in the south too.'

Lights went on ahead of us down the length of the corridor. Maybe one in seven of the white glass discs on the ceiling still worked but together they provided better illumination than any torch or lantern.

Fifty yards on and a heavy steel door blocked the way, but only partially. The thickness of it lay curled around the force of some unimaginable blow and it stood propped against the frame, heavier than an armoured warhorse but with room to slide past. Just beyond, through the gap, I could see a gleaming and many-legged insect, silver in the ancient light, needle-mouthed, its body a clear chamber filled with red venom.

'I've seen the needle,' I said, not turning away. 'Going around might be difficult . . .' I kept my eye on it against the possibility it might scuttle forward and sting me through my boot. 'But I think if I beat it with my sword the problem should go away.' It's a technique that works on a lot of problems.

'Uh,' said Hakon. Not exactly the encouragement I'd been hoping for but I shrugged it off.

'You hold the door. I'll go through and stick it.'

'Uh.' Followed by the clatter of axe hitting floor.

I turned to see Hakon sprawled, five of the metal insects on his back, their needles deep in his flesh.

'Shh—' Something small and sharp stabbed me in the hollow of my back, '—it!' I spun, trying to dislodge the thing but it clung with a dozen clawed feet. Warmth spread up my spine. 'Bastard!' I threw myself back, crushing the thing against the door. Others scurried out from little hatches in the wall beside the door. The ones on Hakon withdrew their needles and scuttled toward me.

I wrecked several with my sword, shearing off legs and shattering bodies but I went down with needles in my thigh, hip and foot before I got them all, my strength flowing away like water from a broken gourd.

'I remember you, you little bastard!' I snarled it at the needle-bug as it descended from the now-invisible hatch. My hope that it might not be able to scale the table waned somewhat at seeing its speed over the smoothness of the wall.

The first of the six bands came loose and I started on the next. The dry click of metal feet reached me as the insect vanished beneath the table. For all I knew there were holes under my back through which it could stick me. I worked on, fingers slipping across the next buckle. If the thing had any intelligence behind it, it would come up out of reach by my feet.

The click of small claws against the steel leg of the table told me it was climbing the far end. The thing must have lodestones for claws: no creature the size of a rabbit could find purchase on the metal otherwise.

I freed the second band and started on the third . . . paused . . . looked about. Two silver legs hooked over the far end of the table. I leaned back and reached out for the stand holding the drug flasks, their tubes hanging loose now, contents leaking upon the floor. The needle-bug pulled itself over the lip of the table with a quickness that made my skin crawl. It turned its head toward my bound calf, needle pointing, a bead of clear liquid glistening at its tip . . . And with a roar I hauled the stand overhead, lifting it as far as the bands allowed, and crashed the haft of it into the needle-bug's glassy body. Fragments flew everywhere and the twitching carcass slithered over the edge, landing with a brittle crunch.

With feverish concentration I unbuckled the remaining straps, scanning the walls as I did so for the arrival of more needle-bugs.

A minute later I set two bare feet to the cold floor and found my legs reluctant to take the weight of me, skinny as I was. Blood still dribbled from my wrist where the tubes had fed their filth into me. Skin flapped, raw flesh glistened.

The table lay bare save for some clear and squidgy pads that must have kept it from wearing sores into my back. A vent ran the length of it and a drain below. They must have sluiced away my filth as I lay unconscious. A pure hatred ran through me. I would hurt whoever did this to me, and then I would end them.

A door stood behind me, silvery-steel like the table. I looked about for weapons but the room was bare save for the corroded carcasses of ancient machinery. Gripping the drug stand like a spear, I advanced on the door. There would be larger foes outside. The bugs hadn't lifted me onto the table or buckled me down.

I stood with a hand to the door for a moment, trying to clear my head. Had Katherine truly been here? Had she wakened me? A kiss seemed unlikely – the princess hated me, and with good reason. A knife to the heart seemed a more realistic greeting. Even so, something had woken me from what must be months of slumber, years even. And Katherine had once kept the company of a dream-witch, so why not her? Perhaps she thought letting me sleep my days away here, safe from nightmares, was too kind an end for me.

Remembering that I was watched, I left the door and stood before the eye peeping at me from the high corner with its little red light flashing.

'I'm coming for you and death will not hide you.' I swung the stand at arms' length, smashing the box from its stand. It hit the wall, then the floor, and when the lens rolled free I crushed it beneath the stand's metal foot. A grand speech perhaps for a man with no clothes, no weapon, and no plan, but it lit my fire and it never hurts to sow the seeds of unease in your foe's mind.

The destruction of Builder machines is of course a terrible waste of knowledge and wonder beyond our imagination. There is, however, an undeniable thrill in doing it.

The door opened for me, the locking mechanism corroded, the metal degenerating into curious white powder – a good thing as I would not have been able to force it. The most surprising thing about the works of the Builders is always not how broken they are but just how many of them still function. After the slow passage of the eleven centuries since the Day of a Thousand Suns I would have expected them all to be dust. Certainly nothing built in the first three hundred years to follow that conflagration now survives.

The corridor beyond lay thick with dust, the corpse of a needle-bug disarticulated and strewn along the margins. Stairways led left and right, both blocked with rubble, the ceiling collapsed. I advanced further, to a point where a door opened to either side. To the left a domed steel machine glowing gently through small portals. Dozens of needle-bugs and others of similar design – but with cutting wheels or opposing thread-laced jaws in place of the needle – scattered the floor, most in pieces. The least damaged of them huddled close to the dome as if seeking sustenance from it. Several twitched towards me as I looked in, but none made it more than half way before the light died from their eyes and they ceased to move.

To the right, a room that radiated cold and contained several large chests, white, rectangular and without ornament or lock. Goosebumps rose across me as I entered the room. Perhaps just from the cold. It's hard to be naked in a place that wants to hurt you. A layer of cloth would offer me little protection but I would have felt far more brave. I read in Tacitus that the Romans when they came to the Drowned Isles faced Brettan men who charged them wearing nothing but blue dye. The Brettans died in droves and surrendered their lands, but I can respect their courage, if not their methods.

A steel cylinder, thicker than my arm and half as long, stood between the chests. A long strap of dark and woven plasteek ran from top to bottom. I picked it up: heavier than I imagined. The legend stamped upon it was in no alphabet I recognized. I slung it over my shoulder. A looter decides on worth once he's out.

I raised the lid of one of the chests using the metal stand. Freezing mist escaped with a soft sigh. The space within lay filled with frost, and with organs wrapped in clear plasteek: hearts, livers, eyeballs in jelly, and other pieces of man-tripe beyond my vocabulary. A second chest held glass vials bound top and bottom with metal rings and stamped with the plague symbol – triple intersecting crescent moons. This I knew from a weapons vault I once set on fire beneath Mount Honas.

I reached in and took three vials at random, so cold they stuck to my flesh. I put them on the ground, tearing skin to be free of them, then bound each with the plasteek tubes to the foot of the stand. I didn't know what plague they might contain nor whether it was still virulent but when the only weapon you have is an awkward metal stick sporting blunt hooks you take whatever you find.

Turning to leave, I found the spirit in the doorway: Miss Kind-Eyes-and-Compassion, flickering now like the Builder-ghost I'd seen nearly a year earlier, and wearing a long white coat, almost a robe but without fold or style.

'You should put those back, Jorg.' She pointed to the vials at the end of my stand.

'How do you know my name?' I walked toward her.

'I know a lot of things about you, J—'

I walked through her into the corridor. Often as not conversation is a delaying tactic and I'd waited long enough on that table.

'—org. I know what is written in your blood. I could remake you whole from the smallest flake of your skin.'

'Interesting,' I said. 'Where's Hakon?'

I came to a large door at the end of the corridor. Locked.

'You should listen carefully, Jorg. It's difficult to maintain this projection so far from—'

'Your name, ghost.'

'Kalla Lefarge. I—'

'Open this door, Kalla.'

'You must understand, Jorg, mechanisms have finite duration. I need biological units to carry out my work. To carry me even. Projection has its lim—'

'Now,' I said, and banged the vials against the metal.

'Don't!' She held out a hand as if that might stop

me. The very first thing she said to me was to put them down. It pays to notice priorities. She'd said it as if they were of no great importance . . . but she said it first.

'Or what?' I clonked the end of the stand against the door again and the vials clinked together.

'If a class alpha viral strain contaminates this facility it will be purged. I can neither override that protocol nor allow it to happen.'

A flicker of concern over those perfect features. Builder-ghosts were woven from the story of a person's life – every detail – extrapolated from a billion seconds of scrutiny. This one I felt had drifted far from its template, but not so far it couldn't still know fear.

'Purged?'

'With fire.' Kalla's face flickered briefly to a look of horror, returning to its customary serenity a moment later. I wondered from what instant that look had been stolen and what had set it on the face of the real Kalla – flesh and blood and bone like me, dust these many centuries. Had the creature before me grown far from its roots or had Kalla shared this madness? 'Enough fire to leave these halls hollow and smoking.'

'Better open the fucking door then.' And I banged the stand in earnest.

'Careful!' A hand flew to her mouth. 'There! It's open!'

The hall beyond lay crossed with shadow and lit by irregular patches of light bright enough to make me squint. Steel tables lined each wall. A stench of rot filled my nose, along with something sharp, astringent, chemical. Corpses lay on every table. Some in pieces. Some fresh. Some corrupt. Organs floated in glass tubes running from ceiling to floor, threaded with bubbles – hearts, livers, lengths of gut. Behind the table closest to me a metal skeleton, or some close approximation, leaned across yet another corpse. Despite lacking muscle or flesh the thing moved, the cleverly articulated fingers of one hand swiftly driving the needle of a drug-vial into vital spots all across the cadaver before it. The other hand moved from unstrapping the remains to depressing raised bumps on certain mechanisms that replaced sections of the body such as the elbow joints. It finished by turning a dial on some engine sunk deep into the chest cavity.

I held the stand out between us, vials clinking, ready to fend the thing off if it jumped me.

'This is the last of my medical units,' the ghost said, voice wavering between two pitches as if unable to settle. 'I'd ask you not to damage it further.'

As the skeleton straightened to regard me with black eyes bedded in silver-steel sockets, I noted across its bones the white powdery corrosion that I'd seen back on the lock to my sleeping chamber. The thing stepped away from the table, favouring one leg, a gritty sound accompanying each movement of its limbs. Only the nimble fingers seemed unaffected by the passage of a millennium.

The corpse, on the other hand, moved with far more surety and only the slightest whine of mechanics as it sat up between us.

'Hakon.'

They'd done something to his eyes, rods of glass and metal jutting from red sockets; his hair and beard had been shaved away, but his smile was the same.

In my moment of hesitation Hakon, or his remains, took hold of the stand. I tugged at it but his grip had no give.

'This one nearly succeeded,' he said. Or rather it was the ghost's voice, but firmer, and sounding from the box in his chest. 'He can support me, but his brain degenerates under fine control and the degree of putrefaction about the implants is too great to be sustained in the longer term.'

'And I was to be your next . . . steed?' I tugged at the stand again.

'You still will be,' Kalla said, her voice coming distractingly from both the ghost and the box in Hakon's chest. 'The last faults have been analysed. This time it will succeed. Nor will your life be forfeit. Even this one isn't dead – not truly.' Hakon slipped from the table and stood before me, both hands tight about the stand. 'Carry me for long enough to complete three alternate hosts and I'll send you on your way with nothing but a few stitches.'

'Why me?' I glanced around, looking for the way out. 'Get some new bodies to play with.'

'You've broken my last sedation units.'

'Mend them—' I lunged forward and tore one of the vials free.

Releasing the stand, I stepped away, holding the vial overhead, ready to smash it.

'Don't—'

'Who was the other one? The ghost who put on the skull-and-bones show for us, tried to scare us off?'

'A colleague at this facility, also copied and stored as a data echo. She . . . disapproves of my work here. We're isolated in this network. Security they called it.' She made a bitter noise. 'Our research too classified to risk a leak. And so until I find a way to have our data physically carried to another portal we're cut off from the deep-nets. Just us two . . . arguing . . . for a thousand years. I have the upper hand now though, especially in here. The outer part of the station collapsed long ago and our projection units are outside. She lacks the power to interfere for long.'

I spotted a door and backed rapidly toward it. The ghost winked out but Hakon followed me, carrying the stand like a quarterstaff, a touch awkward in his gait. I wondered if he was still in there, fighting her, or were the important parts of his brain floating in some jar on a high shelf?

'Where's Katherine?' I asked it to keep Kalla occupied, though perhaps when a machine does your thinking for you distraction is impossible. Maybe all my parameters were already calculated within the Builders' engines, wheels turning through each possibility like the math-magicians of Afrique, the odds sewn tight against me.

'So you did have help?' A flicker of annoyance in the voice, though Hakon's face revealed no emotion. 'It was a subtle thing, detected only after analysis. A manipulation at sub-instrumental levels. Sleep psionics of advanced degree . . .'

I found the door and tugged at it. Hakon took three quick steps and I set both hands to the vial, making to twist the top. 'Do it and I'll open Pandora's Box here and we'll see what ills emerge.'

'If you leave I am finished,' Kalla said, flexing Hakon's hands.

'Not at all.' I hooked the door open with my bare foot and retreated through it. 'If I break this, you're finished. If I leave you still have a chance. Use Hakon, steal another subject. Some chance is better than no chance.'

'You don't seem to accept that logic yourself.' Kalla kept pace with me as I backed down the long corridor.

I smelled fresh air but didn't risk a glance back as I retreated. 'I'm not afraid to die, ghost.' I spoke the truth. 'You've spent a thousand years cheating death. That kind of dedication is built on fear. I've spent much of sixteen years hunting it. We're very different, you and I.'

I passed a great and twisted door, propped against the corridor wall. The remains of needle-bugs told me I'd reached the point where they first took me. A breeze played against my neck, back, thighs, reminding me of my nakedness. My hand hurt, almost as much as when I first ripped it free – the feeling in it perhaps woken by the scent of the green world outside.

I saw my sword, still lying there in the dust by the broken door, as if it held no value. I'd no time to pick it up and little good it would do me in my left hand. Even so it pained me to leave it as I carried on down the corridor.

Hakon held back, allowing the yard between us to grow into two, three. 'Take a look, Jorg.'

I glanced over my shoulder. The cavern opened out behind me . . . onto a sea of tangled green, deeper than a man is tall. Small red flowers peppered the curls and hoops of the briar.

'You know thorns, Jorg: that much was written on you when you came. Perhaps it was this variety that marked you so? The hook-briar?'

I looked down at my chest, arms . . . 'Gone?' The scars had vanished. I'd borne them so long but it took until now to notice they had gone. I felt more naked than ever. The scars had been an armour of sorts. An account of my personal history set down in blood and permanence. The scars were to be with me forever – taken to the grave. The loss unsettled me more than eyeballs in frozen jelly or the reanimated corpse of a friend. Those I'd seen before. 'How?'

'This is a medical facility, Jorg. Look in the skin-flask.'

'The what?'

'It's on your back. Depress the third, seventh, and sixth button.'

I took the cylinder from my shoulder and set it down before me by its strap. I knelt and pressed the numbered bumps as directed, glancing down only briefly, expecting to be rushed. I leapt back as the lid began to unscrew along a previously unseen seam. The top fell away with a hiss and I leaned forward to peer at the contents.

'Pink slime.' For some reason my stomach rumbled, reminding me I hadn't eaten in . . . well, a very long time. 'Does it taste as bad as it looks?'

'Nu-skin. Touch it to your hand.' Hakon turned his head, the ugly array of rods emerging from his eyes now pointing at my injury.

I didn't trust Kalla but knowledge can be power and my half-flayed hand hurt badly enough to stop me concentrating. With my good hand I dipped a fingertip into the muck and felt it writhe, the sensation similar to holding a slug. I touched the slightest smear of it to the raw flesh of my other hand, still tight around the plague vial. The effect came within seconds, the livid pinkness of the slime flowing into something more skin-coloured, spreading, thinning, the feeling of insects crawling . . . and finally, a patch of new skin little wider than a fingerprint.

'If you help me you can walk away with many such treasures. Wonders of the old world. I could explain them to you. A man with that kind of magic on his side could rule—'

'I already have a kingdom, ghost.' I sealed the cylinder and set it over my shoulder again.

'Is it enough?' she asked, Hakon immobile, her voice rising from his chest. The sweet smell of rot hung about him. A fly buzzed about his head, settling by the corner of an eye.

'Nothing is ever enough.' Habit led my fingers to the old burns across the left side of my face, still rough and puckered. 'You didn't want me pretty? Or doesn't your gloop heal burns?'

'It was made for burns. Burns are its speciality. But that injury is curiously resistant. There's an exotic energy signature . . . If our physics laboratory were operational then . . .'

I backed toward the mouth of the cave and the green riot of hook-briar. The drone of bees reached me now, the call of birds. High summer outside, the seasons had turned whilst I slept.

'There's no escape that way, Jorg.' Kalla followed. 'Hook-briar was one of our works.'

'Yours?'

'Well, not mine. But from this facility. This was a big place once. Three hundred people worked here. Chamber upon chamber, waiting now for a man with enough vision to excavate them. Hook-briar – a cheaper, self-renewing razor wire. Highly effective engineering. For warmer climes than this of course if you want all-year protection. They never did get a strain that wouldn't die back in the winter.'

'And your . . . "projector" is out there?' I tilted my head toward the midst of the thorns. 'You're not worried I might call on you in person?' I gave her my dangerous smile. I hadn't felt like smiling since I woke but now the edge of an idea sliced through the fading fog of Kalla's drugs.

Hakon nodded. 'It's safe enough from you even if you wore armour and carried shears. Naked and without weapons you pose no threat. I tell you this to show you how hopeless your situation is. Work with me and power beyond your dreams could be—'

'I've dreamed enough, ghost,' I said. 'Time to die. Goodbye, Brother Hakon.'

His lips twitched, a snarl of effort, and words stuttered out. 'B-b-beauty. S-s-sacrifice.' His own voice, free of Kalla's control. The mutterings of a broken mind. Or perhaps his memory of our joking in Vyene about the price we'd pay to see our enemies burn.

I set my strength to untwisting the top of the vial.

'No!' Hakon started forward, Kalla shouting from his chest unit.

The lid came free and I flung the container over his head, back along the corridor. Kalla had said it held death, a plague that might scour mankind from the world. I'd called it Pandora's Box. I turned and ran, shrugging Hakon's reaching fingers from my shoulder. I built up speed, barefoot across the stony cavern floor.

I'd released Pandora's ills and back along the corridor

a klaxon sounded, wailing like a thousand banshees. Angling toward the extreme left of the cave mouth, I reached the impenetrable wall of thorns, and leapt, high as I might, diving forward.

'Purging. Repeat – level 0 viral breach. Repeat. Full Purge!'

Pandora's Box held all the world's troubles . . . but at the bottom of it, last to emerge, trapped among nightmares, lay Hope.

The hook-briar gave before my weight, thorns snagging at my skin, slipping in, tearing, slicing deeper, holding, until at last they arrested my advance and I hung among them. Trapped as I'd been trapped years before, pierced by the same sharp and sudden pain, but this time by my own volition.

I heard rather than saw the hot white tongue of fire that roared from the cave mouth, a spear of incendiary rage surrounded by billowing flame that spilled to either side, spreading, engulfing.

The klaxon felt silent, leaving only the roar of flames, the crackle of burning, and my screaming as the margins of the inferno reached me, naked amongst the thorns.

Unconsciousness is a blessing in such times, but horrifically late in coming. I felt my skin crisp, saw my hair shrivel and burn as the hot breath of the fire blew around me. I saw the skin melting from my hands before the heat took my sight.

Unconsciousness is a blessing, but only a temporary one.

I found myself amid a forest of blackened coils, thorn-toothed, stark against the blueness of the sky.

Rolling my bald and weeping head, I saw with blurred eyes a corridor cut through the midst of the hook-briar where only fine white ash remained. The silver-steel of the cylinder lay beneath me, scorched but unharmed. I jabbed at the buttons with sticky fingers, some welded together with molten skin, clumsy in a pain that admits no description.

Three times I tried the numbers. I would have wept but I'd gone past tears. At last, infinitely slow, the lid rotated off and I dipped my hands into the nu-skin. I daubed the slime across each finger. As the stuff writhed across them I held each digit wide, despite the pain. I smeared slime across my face, into my mouth, into each eye, down across my body as far as the remaining thorns would let me.

Whatever science or enchantment the nu-skin held it proved to be powerful. The unguent worked different wonders depending on where it found itself, repairing my sight, flowing down my windpipe and healing my lungs to the point where I could scream once more, building new skin across my arms while the dead stuff sloughed away.

I tore free of the thorns, only to snare myself on new ones, but allowing the application of my dwindling stock of slime to new areas, groin, legs, back. The skin's work drew on my own strength, an exhaustion rising through me that dragged me into a torpor despite the crawling agony of it all.

At last a light rain woke me. I stood, caught amid the skeletal remains of the briar, impaled on black thorns, smeared with ash, but unburned, clad in a new hide.

Even burned and brittle the hook-briar took its toll on me as I struggled through. By the time I reached the corridor of ash I ran with blood from a hundred wounds, the last of the nu-skin exhausted early in the escape. The rain came heavy now, but warm, sluicing down across my body in a crimson wash. I stood in the mud and ash and let it clean me.

I returned to the cave, finding it still hot, the stone ticking as it cooled, no trace of Hakon save a stain around the blackened drug stand. Wincing at the heat beneath my bare and bleeding feet I made my way along the dark corridor and found my sword. And thus dressed I left the bunker.

At last, before my strength failed once more, I picked my way around ancient remnants of razor wire and came to where the top of a sunken pillar of Builder-stone emerged from the mud. The stone had been cracked by the fire's heat and a little less than a foot of it lay exposed. Despite the weathering and corrosion it took more effort than I thought remained in me to slide the top to one side. The hollow interior stretched down beyond sight, the inner surface crowded with myriad crystalline growths, all interconnected with a forest of silver wires, some thick, some finer than spider silk. Many of the crystals lay dark, but here and there one glowed with a faint light, visible only in the shadow.

'Found you.'

'Don't.' Kalla's voice, weak and pulsing from the interior.

I pried a rock from the muck about me. A heavy chunk of what might once have been poured stone. Grunting with effort I lifted it to the lip of the column. It would fit down the inside with an inch or two to spare.

'I can't end. Not like—'

'A thousand years is too long to live.' And I let the rock fall. It dropped with a prolonged and continuous sound of shattering, ricocheting from one wall to the other, tearing away the guts that had let Kalla echo for so long within the last works of the Builders.

I looked at my hands, torn and empty. A great weariness washed through me, a desire to lie myself down in the mud and let sleep claim me. All that stopped me was the memory of a kiss, the hint of her scent.

'No. I've slept long enough.'

A kiss had woken me and I'd found, as we so often do, that the world had moved on without me. And that's the riddle of existence for you. When to move and when to stay. Dwell too long and we become the prisoner of our dreams, or someone else's. Move too fast, live without pause, and you'll miss it all, your whole life a blur of doing. Good lives are built of moments – of times when we step back and truly see. The dream and the dreamer. There's the rub. Does the dream ever let go? Aren't we all only sleepwalking into old age, just waiting, waiting, waiting for that kiss?

Bleeding, smeared with muck and ash, I staggered down the hill, all that survived the purge of Bunker 17. I might be counted one more ill to be visited upon the world, for I could hardly be called its hope. But, hope or horror, I had endured. I had been delivered from the thorns in fire and pain and set free.

I ran a hand across the baldness of my scalp and felt my mouth twist in its old smile, a bitter one to be sure – but not only bitter.

'Sleeping beauty, woken by the princess's kiss,' I said.

And so I set off to find her.

Footnote

This was the first Broken Empire short story I wrote, prompted by a reader daring me to do a Jorg/fairy-tale mash-up. It's framed around Sleeping Beauty but has a nod to Goldilocks and even Rapunzel! Chronologically it takes place between the two threads in Emperor of Thorns, *before the Wedding Day thread in* King of Thorns, *on Jorg's return to Ancrath from his first visit to Vyene. Hakon is a character seen in The Red Queen's War trilogy.*

Did Katherine wake Jorg using her dream-magic, or was it just a failure of the ageing machinery? That's for the reader to decide.

Bad Seed

At the age of eight Alann Oak took a rock and smashed it into Darin Reed's forehead. Two other boys, both around ten years old, had tried to hold him against the fence post while Darin beat him. They got up from the dirt track, first to their hands and knees, one spitting blood, the other dripping crimson from where Alann's teeth found his ear, then unsteadily to their feet. Darin Reed lay where he had fallen, staring at the blue sky with wide blue eyes.

'Killer,' they called the child after that. Some called 'kennt' at his back and the word followed him through the years as some words will hunt a man down across the storm of his days. Kennt, the old name for a man who does murder with his hands. An ancient term in the tongue that lingered in the villages west of the Tranweir, spoken only among the greyheads and like to die out with them, leaving only a scatter of words and phrases that fitted too well in the mouth to be abandoned.

'You forgive me, Darin, don't you?' Alann asked it of

the older boy a year later. They sat at the ford, watching the water, flowing white around the stepping-stones. Alann threw his pebble, clattering it against the most distant of the nine steps. 'I told Father Abram I repented the sin of anger. They washed me in the blood of the lamb. Father Abram told me I was part of the flock once more.' Another stone, another hit. He had repented anger, but there hadn't been anger, just the thrill of it, the red joy in a challenge answered.

Darin stood, still taller than Alann but not by so much. 'I don't forgive you, but I wronged you. I was a bully. Now we're brothers. Brothers don't need to forgive, only to accept. If I forgave the blow you might forget me.'

'Father Abram told me . . .' Alann struggled for the words. 'He said, men don't stand alone. We're farmers. We're of the flock, the herd. God's own. We follow. To stray is to be cast out. Strays die alone. Unmourned.' He threw again, hit again. 'But . . . I feel . . . alone here, right among the herd. I don't fit. People are scared of me.'

Darin shook his head. 'You're not alone. You've got me. How many brothers do you need?'

Alann fought no more battles, not with his first wreaking such harm. They watched him, the priest and the elders, and hung about by his guilt the boy stepped aside from whatever small troubles life in the village placed in his path. Alann Oak turned the other cheek though it was not in his nature to do so. Something ran through him, something sharp, at the core, not the dull anger or jealous loathing that prompts drunks to raise their fists, rather a reflex, an urge to meet each and any challenge with the violence born into him.

'I'm different.' Spoken on his fourteenth name-day, out in the quiet of a winter's night while others lay abed. Alann hadn't the words to frame it but he knew it for truth. 'Different.'

'A dog among goats?' Darin Reed at his side, untroubled by the cold. He swept his arm toward the distant homes where warmth and light leaked through shutter cracks. 'With them but not of them?'

Alann nodded.

'It will change,' Darin said. 'Give it time.'

Years fell by and with the seasons Alann Oak grew, not tall but tall enough, not broad but sturdy, hardened by toil on the land with plough and hoe. He walked away from his past, although he never once strayed further than Kilter's Market seven miles down the Hay Road. He walked away from the whispers, from the muttered 'kennt', and all that came with him from those days was Darin Reed, the larger child but the smaller man, his fast companion, pale, quiet, true.

The smoke of war darkened the horizon some summers, and once in winter, but the fires that sent those black clouds rising passed by the villages of the

Marn, peace still lingering in the backwaters of the Broken Empire just as the old tongue still clung there. Perhaps they lacked the language for war.

Sometimes those unseen battles called to Alann. In the stillness of night, wrapped tight by darkness, Alann often wondered what a thing it would be to take up sword and shield and fight, not for any cause, not to place this lord or that lord in a new chair – but just to meet the challenge, to put himself to the test that runs along the sharp edge of life. And maybe once or twice he gathered his belongings in the quiet after midnight and set off from his parents' cottage – but each time he found Darin, sat upon the horse trough beside the track that joins the road to Melsham. Each time the sight of his blood brother, pale beneath the moon, watching and saying nothing, turned Alann back the way he came.

Alann found himself a woman, Mary Miller from Fairfax, and they married in Father Abram's church on a chill March morning, God himself watching as they said their vows. God and Darin Reed.

More years, more seasons, more crops leaping from the ground in the green storm of their living, reaped and harvested, sheep with their lambs, Mary with her two sons, delivered bloody into Alann's rough hands. As red as Darin Reed when he lay there veiled in his own lifeblood. And family changed him. The need to be needed proved stronger than the call of distant wars. Perhaps that was all he had ever looked for, to be valued, to be essential, and who is more vital to a child than its ma and pa?

Time ran its slow course, bearing farm and farmer along with it, and Alann watched it all pass. He held his boys with his calloused hands, nails bitten to the quick, prayed in God's stone house, knowing every hour of every day that somehow he didn't fit into his world, that he went through the motions of his life not quite feeling any of it the way it should be felt, an impostor who never knew his true identity, only that *this* was not it. Even so, it was enough.

'None of them see me, Darin, not Mary, not my sons, or Father Abram. Only you, and God.' Alann thrust at the soil before him, driving the hoe through each clod, reducing it to smaller fragments.

'Maybe you don't see yourself, Alann. You're a good man. You just don't know it.' Darin stood looking out across the rye in the lower field.

'I'm a bad seed. You learned that the day you came against me.' Alann bent and took up a clod of earth, crumbling it in his hand. He pointed across the broken earth to where Darin's gaze rested. 'I sowed that field myself, checked the grains, but there'll be karren grass amongst the rye, green amongst the green. You won't see it until it's time to bear grain – even then you have to hunt. But come an early frost, come red-blight, come a swarm of leaf-scuttle, then you'll see it. When the rye starts dying . . . that's when you'll see the karren grass

55

because it may look the same, but it's hard at the core, bitter, and it won't lie down.' He dug at the ground, then, turned by some instinct, looked east across the wheat field. Two strangers approaching, swords at their hips.

'It's a bad day to be a peasant.' The taller of the two men smiled as he walked across the field, flattening the new wheat beneath his boots.

'It's never a good day to be a peasant.' Alann straightened slowly, rubbing the soil from his hand. The men's grimy tatters had enough in common to suggest they had once been a uniform. They came smeared with dirt and ash, blades within easy reach, a reckless anticipation in their eyes.

'Where's your livestock?' The shorter man, older, a scar threading his cheekbone leading to a cloudy eye. Close up both men stank of smoke.

'My sheep?' Alann knew he should be scared. Perhaps he lacked the wit for it, like goats led gently to their end. Either way a familiar calm enfolded him. He leant against his hoe and kept his gaze on the men. 'Would you like to buy them?'

'Surely.' The tall man grinned, a baring of yellow teeth. Wolf's fangs. 'Lead on.'

For a heartbeat Alann's gaze fell to the soldiers' boots, remnants of the fresh green wheat still sticking to the leather. 'I've never been a good farmer,' he said. 'Some men have the feel for it. It's in their blood. The land speaks to them. It answers them.' He watched the strangers. Conversations carry a momentum, there's a path they are expected to take, a cycle, a season, like the growing of a crop. Take the rhythm of seasons away and farmers grow confused. Turn a conversation at right angles and men lose their surety.

'What?' The shorter man frowned, doubt in his blind eye.

The tall man twisted his mouth. 'I don't give a—'

Alann flipped up his hoe, a swift turn about the middle, sped up by kicking the head. He lunged forward, jabbing. Instinct told him never to swing with a long weapon. The short metal blade proved too dull to cut flesh but it crushed the man's throat back against the bones of his neck and his surprise left him in a wordless crimson mist.

Without pause, Alann charged the soldier's companion, the shaft of his hoe held crosswise before him in two outstretched hands. The man turned his shoulder, reaching for his sword. He would have done better to pull his knife. Alann bore him to the ground, pressing the hoe across his neck, pinning the half-drawn blade with the weight of his body.

Men make ugly sounds as they choke. Both soldiers purpled and thrashed and gargled, the first needing no more help to die, the second fighting all the way. When soldiers poke a hole in a man and move on, leaving him to draw his last breaths alone, there's a distance. That's battle. The farmer though, the death he brings is more personal. He gentles his beast, holds it close, makes his cut, not in passion, not with violence, but as a necessary thing. The farmer stays, the death is shared, part of the cycle of seasons and crops, of growing and of reaping. They name it slaughter. Alann felt every moment of the older man's struggle, body to body, straining to keep him down. He watched the life go out of the soldier's good eye. And finally, exhausted, revolted, trembling, he rolled clear.

Getting to all fours, Alann vomited, a thin acidic spew across the dry earth. He rose to his knees, facing out across the next field, rye, silent and growing, row on row, rippling in the breeze. It hardly seemed real, a dead man to either side of him.

'You should get up,' Darin said. Solemn, pale, watching as he always watched.

'. . . they called me kennt.' Allen's mind still fuzzy within that strange and enfolding calm. 'When I was a boy, the others called me kennt. They knew. Children know. It's grown men who see what they want to see.'

'You can walk away from it.' Darin looked down at the dead men. 'This doesn't define you.'

'Forgive me then.' Alann got to his feet, drawing the sword the soldier had failed to pull and taking the dagger that he should have reached for instead.

'You need to forgive yourself, brother.' Darin offered him that smile, the only one he ever had, the almost smile, sadder than moonset. The smile faded. 'You have to go to the house now.'

'The house! They came from the house!' Even as Alann said it he started to run up the slope toward the rise concealing his home. He ran fast but the sorrow caught him just the same, a chokehold, misting his eyes. His life had never fitted, his wife, his children, always seeming as though they should belong to someone else, someone better, but Mary he had grown to love, in his way, and the boys had taken hold of his heart before they ever knew how to reach.

Alann ran, pounding up the slope. The flames had the house in their grip by the time he cleared the ridge. The heat stopped him as effectively as a wall. Some men, better men perhaps, would have run on, impervious to the inferno, impervious to the fact that nothing could live within those walls, too wrapped in grief to do anything but die beside their loved ones. For Alann though, the furnace blast that blistered his cheeks and took the tears from his eyes, burned away the mist of emotion and left him empty. He stepped back from the crackle and the roar, one pace, three paces, five until the heat could be endured. He dropped both weapons and stared into his empty hands as if they might hold his sorrow.

'I'm sorry.' Darin, standing at his side, untouched by the heat, untroubled by the run.

'You!' Alann turned, hands raised. 'You did this!'

'No.' A plain denial. A slow shake of his head.

'You brought this curse . . . you never forgave me!'

'It didn't happen for a reason, Alann. These things never do. Hurt spills over into hurt, like water over stones. There's no foreseeing it, no knowing who it will touch, who will be left standing.'

Alann knelt to take up the sword and the knife.

'You've got to get to the village, warn the elders. There needs to be a defence—'

'No.' Alann's turn to offer flat refusal. He turned and walked toward the shelter where the sheep huddled against winter storms. Kindling lay stacked in the lee of the dry-stone wall, and in a niche set into its thickness, wrapped in oil-cloth, an old hatchet, a whetstone alongside. Alann thrust sword and dagger into his belt and took the hand-axe, and the stone to set an edge on it.

'There's another side to this, Alann. It's a storm like any other, the worst of them, but it will end—'

'You want me to rebuild? Find a new wife? Make more sons?' Alann scanned the distant fields as he spoke, his hands already busy with the whetstone on the hatchet blade. He could see the lines where the soldiers had set off through the beet, angling towards Warren Wood. Robert Good's farm lay beyond, and Ren Hay's, the village past those. Alann pocketed the stone and set off after his prey at a steady jog.

Darin was waiting for him at the wood's edge.

'You'll die, and for nothing. You won't save anyone,

won't get revenge. You'll die as the man you never wanted to be. God will see you—'

'God sent the soldiers. God made me a killer. Let's see how that turns out.'

'No.' And Darin stepped into his path, careless of the hatchet in his brother's hand.

'It's over.' Alann didn't pause. 'And you're just a ghost.' He stepped through Darin and went on into the trees.

Six soldiers rested at the base of one of the old-stones, monoliths scattered through the Warren Wood, huge and solitary reminders of men who lived off these lands before Christ first drew breath. They had insignias beneath the grime of their tunics but Alann wouldn't have known which lord they took their coin from even if the coat of arms had flown above them on a new-sewn banner. He slipped back through the holly that hid him and in the clearer space behind drew the sword he had taken. It would serve him poorly in the close confines beneath the trees and he had never swung one before. He stepped around the bush, breaking through the reaching branches of a beech, the sword held in two hands over his shoulder.

The soldiers started to rise as he emerged into the clearing around the old-stone. He threw the sword and it made half a turn in the ten yards between them, impaling a bearded man through the groin. Alann pulled the hatchet and knife from his belt and charged, arms crossed before him.

The quickest of the patrol came forward before he covered the ground, one with sword in hand, helm on head, the other bare-headed, his knife in his fist, shield awkward on his arm. At the last moment before they closed Alann threw himself to the ground before the pair, feet first, sliding between them through the dirt and dry leaves. He swung out with both arms, hatchet to the back of one knee, knife to the other. A farmer butchers his own meat, he knows about such things as tendons and the purpose they serve.

Alann's slide ended at the base of the old-stone, taking the feet from under a third soldier as he stood. He rolled into space and threw himself clear as a sword struck sparks from the monolith just above his head. He ran, sure-footed, a tight circle around the base of the old-stone, thicker than a pair of grandfather oaks. Two soldiers gave pursuit but were yards behind him as he came again upon the three felled men and a fourth seeking to help one of the injured men up. Alann powered through the cluster, a quick hatchet blow to the back of the standing man as he bent over, followed by a knife slash across the neck of the groin-stabbed man as he gained his feet.

A tight turn around the monolith and Alann spun about, crouching low. The two soldiers thundered round the corner, swords before them. Alann launched himself into the foremost, beneath the man's sword, both legs driving him forward and up, shoulder turned to take the impact against the man's belly. The two of them crashed back into the third, taking him down. Four quick stabs to the man's abdomen at the tempo of a fast clap. Alann clambered over him, pinning his sword arm beneath his knee, and lunging, brought his hatchet down into the face of the soldier behind. The man had been scrabbling away on his backside to get clear, but too slow.

Alann drove his dagger through the throat of the gut-stabbed man then wrenched it out. Dripping with blood he stood and jerked the hatchet from the face of the second twitching soldier. It came free with a crack of bone.

A wounded animal is only at its most dangerous because that's when it's likely to attack you. A man who was already attacking you is considerably less dangerous when wounded. Alann walked around to finish the two hamstrung men.

He stood from the task, scarlet with other men's blood. Darin watched from the gloom beneath the trees, silent, ghost-pale, his limbs translucent, little more than suggestions of the light and shade.

'You've killed evil men,' Darin said.

Alann looked around at the red ruin he'd made. 'There's evil in most men – just waiting for its chance.'

'They were evil. You did God's work.'

'God didn't make me to kill evil men – he made me to kill, like the knife is made to cut.'

Shouts rung out deeper in the woods, more soldiers, from several directions. Alann raised his hatchet.

Darin slid from the shadows, almost invisible when he stood in the sunlight. 'We're brothers, Alann, come back with me. There's still a life for you here.'

'The choice has been made. By me, or for me. There's no going back. Not anymore.'

The shouts grew closer.

Alann spoke again. 'There's only one thing you can do for me now, Darin.'

A silence hung between them, golden in the light.

'I forgive you, brother.'

And saying it Darin stepped back into the shadow, indistinct even there now, his features smoothed into some blur that might be any man. Around him others rose, pale ghosts, eight more, crowding close so that Alann could no longer be sure which was Darin. They stood there, nine wraiths, the shadows of his kills. His new crop.

Three soldiers burst into the clearing, blinking in the light, and Alann threw himself among them.

He couldn't say how long he fought or how many he killed beneath the green roof of the forest, only that it was long and many. At last he stood red-clad and panting, his back to a tall rock, and found himself where he started, at the old-stone, more corpses before him.

A slow hand-clap made him lift his head though exhaustion weighed it down. A man walked from the trees, lacking the soldiers' urgency though moving with more care. Others emerged behind him, all armed, not soldiers though. Bandits, road men, the scum that roamed the borders of any war, picking at the wound. Alann looked from one face to the next. Hard men all. Each different from the next, short and tall, young and old, dirty and clean, but he recognized something in each one. Every man a killer born.

Their leader stopped clapping. A young man, tall, wild, a dangerous look in his eye. 'You cut men like an art-form, brother. I watched the first six . . . magnificent.'

Alann wiped his mouth and spat, the copper taste of blood across his tongue. 'You watched?'

The man shrugged. He was younger than Alann had first thought. 'Some men just want to watch the world burn.' He grinned.

'I'm the fire.'

'That you are, brother, and which of us is worse?'

Alann had no answer to that.

'How do they call you, brother?' The sound of a horn in the distance. Another, closer. More soldiers.

'Kennt.' A dozen men and more watched him now. 'They call me kennt.'

'Brother Kent.' The young man drew his sword, a glimmering length of razored steel. 'Red Kent I'll call you, for you come to us bloody.'

'Red Kent.' Muttered up and down the line. 'Red Kent.' The welcome of the pack.

'The baron's men are coming, Brother Kent.' The

youth pointed with his blade out into the Warren Wood. 'Will you fight beside us?'

Alann shrugged away from the old-stone. He looked once more across the ragged band before him, a family of sorts, pack rather than herd, a band of brothers who knew what lay at the core of him because they shared it, killers all. He looked down at the crimson weapons in his crimson hands and knew that moment of peace that happens when a thing surrenders to its nature.

'I will.'

Footnote

Red Kent has always been a reader favourite despite getting very little 'screen time'. There's a tradition in fantasy that the 'hero' is a great swordsman, and an implicit connection between quality of character and martial talent. Red Kent started off as a play on that, a character with great weapons skill but no corresponding gravitas, vision, strength of character etc. A man of 'average' character who just happens to be lethal in combat.

The Nature of the Beast

Screams tore the night, underwritten by the crackle of fire in thatch. The smoke itched at Sabitha's nose, invading beneath the door. She saw glimpses of flame, orange through the cracks in the shutters.

When the door burst in, flying off its leather hinges, Sabitha didn't turn from the table or the work that occupied her hands.

'Take a seat, I'll be with you in a moment.' She let flow what little enchantment she had. It never took a woman much magic to earn herself the title 'witch' and after that the power of suggestion did most of the work. People are a suggestible lot, providing you choose the right words.

'I'll take more than a seat, old woman!' He made a strange noise, a kind of 'hur hur hur' that she supposed must be laughter.

'Of course you will.' Sabitha turned and found herself amazed by the size of the man who now sat on the three-legged stool beside her stove. He was a foot taller than Ben Wood, who in turn stood a foot taller than Sabitha, even before age bowed her. And Sabitha had never thought of herself as short. 'Would you take a cup of ale to start with?' The man wore ragged chainmail over a padded tunic and despite his great size no part of him was clean. Blood spattered a broad forehead, a raw cheekbone, and a blunt chin. Soot stained his shoulder and side, mud smeared his hip and leg, filth of many kinds clumped around his boots.

'Who's that?' He nodded toward the table, narrowing pale eyes.

'A patient,' Sabitha said. 'I treat the sick, heal the injured. She has the Wasting Grey. I've done my best but I doubt she'll wake again. It's in God's hands now.'

'Huh.' The man made to spit, then scowled. 'You're a witch then.'

'A healer. They call me Mother Sabitha. And you are?'

'Rike.' He spoke it like a bark. The stool was too short for him and his knees were almost at his chest. The dull, bloodstained sword across his lap looked to be nearly as long as Sabitha was tall. The man's brow beetled in confusion, and at a scream from outside he started to rise.

'Had me an old yellow dog once.' Sabitha took a wooden mug from its hook on a rafter and went across to the small keg where she kept her ale. 'Stayed with me for years. Loyal, honest – well, as honest as any dog ever is – then one day he upped and bit me. Out of nowhere

'. . . bit me and wouldn't let go.' She held Rike's gaze, narrow and full of unfocused malice. 'You can never know what moves a beast to action. Even the simplest of them will surprise you. Surprise themselves too, often as not.'

She held out the mug of ale, dark stuff with scattered islands of suds. Rike reached out and took it, scowling as if his arm were betraying him. 'I don't care about your dog.'

'My sister, Chella, now she *is* a witch. A black-hearted one at that. Had herself a grey dog, vicious thing. Would go for anyone that so much as looked at it.' Sabitha watched the raider, his blunt, scarred fingers tight around the untouched ale. She drew on him as she spoke, pulling away what she could of his fury, snagging a memory here and there. The memories floated in her head like fragments of nightmare. Ugly pieces of an ugly life. She smiled her warmest smile. 'The funny thing about those dogs—'

'I don't care about your sister's dog either.' Rike seemed to overcome his inhibitions and spat upon the floor. 'Where's your valuables, woman?'

'Funny thing about them dogs, Rike, was that they were brothers. Bitch whelped 'em one after the other, grey then yellow.' Sabitha cracked her knuckles. It relieved the ache just a little. Outside, figures ran this way and that, glimpsed for a moment in the open doorway, then gone. 'You got a brother, Rike?'

'Price.' Rike nodded. 'Out there.'

69

'Every family has a price.' Sabitha grinned at her joke. 'We don't ask for them, we don't choose them, but they come with a price.' She took another mug and started to fill it. 'The thing about that grey dog was that years after I had to take a rock to my yellow hound a wolf came into the village. Big beast it was, all ribs and foam and teeth. Had the dry-sickness you see, gone mad. It caught me out by Jenner's barn. I was coming back from the woods, basket of mushrooms under one arm, my stick in the other. It would have taken more than an old woman's stick to stop that wolf though.'

A red-face appeared in the door, eyes wild, soot-smeared. The wild eyes fixed momentarily on Rike and the head withdrew.

'That wolf wasn't going to leave much of my insides on the inside. But old Grey comes charging out of my sister's house and leaps right at him. They went down together, all teeth and fur. Only Grey came up in the end.' She raised her ale to her lips and took a long sip. Outside someone was sobbing. 'The wild ones are like that. You can never know them, or what they'll do.'

'Huh.' Rike shook his head and put down the ale untouched.

A raider burst in through the open doorway, a lanky man with long hair in black rat-tails, clad in leather armour with wolfskins thrown over, still sporting the legs and trailing paws. He held a spear levelled at Sabitha. Whether he saw Rike by the stove she couldn't say but it would be hard to miss so large a man. In any event the large man didn't miss the smaller one. Rike surged up and clouted the newcomer around the head, so hard that he fell bonelessly to the floor and lay there without motion, blood spreading on the dirt floor beneath his head.

'Thank you, Rike. I do believe that wolf meant me harm.'

Outside, the shouts and screams were becoming fewer and the crackle of fire more steady. By dawn the village of Jonholt would be ashes. A light rain had begun to fall. Wet ashes.

'You've been cut, Rike.' Sabitha pointed to Rike's wrist where something had sliced him, leaving an ugly gash a couple of inches long.

Rike blinked at the injury in surprise.

'I could tend it for you,' Sabitha said, her voice a sing-song, calming and rhythmic. 'It could sour if not, and that's no way for a warrior to end his days.'

Rike scowled then nodded. Sabitha took her bag from the shelf above her cot and knelt before him, drawing his wrist closer. She fished out her needle and thread along with the pot of ointment she used for wounds, black ginger and thyme in a little oil. Rike growled as she set the first stitch.

'Wasn't there a woman on that table?' He peered over her shoulder.

'No.' Sabitha set another stitch.

Another man appeared in the doorway, fat this one,

jowly with it, dripping with the strengthening rain. 'Come on! We're going. Can't stay.'

'Bugger off, Burlow!' Rike glared at the man, then as he turned to go, added, 'And take Kevtin with you.' The fat man barged in, grumbling, and took hold of the fallen man's ankle. He dragged him out into the rain, the legs of Kevtin's wolfskins trailing.

Sabitha continued her stitching, tsking at Rike when he flinched. 'A great big warrior like you scared of a little needle.' She took her time, waiting for the other raiders to leave. She had the big man under her glamour. All that weight of muscle and so little brain to drive it. He truly was like one of the dogs in her story, though that had had no more truth to it than anything else she'd told him, except about her sister – Chella would make a short end of Master Rike if she were here.

At last Sabitha tied the thread off and stood up. 'There.'

Rike sucked his teeth and inspected the work, still seeing the wound that wasn't there. He took on a sly look. 'I suppose I'll have to pay you then. So it won't get jinxed.'

Sabitha smiled inwardly. She would need as much coin as she could get. She doubted Rike's friends had left much of the village standing or many of its inhabitants alive. She would have to move on, set up somewhere new. 'Gold is the best seal.'

Rike muttered to himself and fished in his pocket.

Coin chinked against coin and he drew out several gold pieces, selecting the smallest of them before returning the others. 'There!' He placed it in her hand.

'Thankee.' She resisted the urge to bite the coin and turned instead to put it away. 'Drink your ale, Rike.' She let the remnants of her power flow around the suggestion.

Leaning over her cot, she tapped the coin on the wall-post and let it slip in. A glamour stronger than any she could cast hid the slot it passed into. Her sister's work, though where that evil crone might be now she couldn't say. Chella had taken to necromancy long ago and followed where it led.

'RIKE!'

The shout whirled Sabitha round towards the door. An enormous man, possibly even larger than Rike, stood outside, stooping to look in under the lintel. 'Get out here! The others are already on the road!'

Rike got up, also stooping to prevent putting his head through the roof. He held his sword in the hand of the arm the old woman had stitched. 'Coming.'

With a lazy thrust he skewered Sabitha through the stomach. It hurt more than she imagined such a thing might and she folded around the cold iron, spitting curses in the old tongue.

'Can't trust a dog any more than you can trust a witch.' Rike twisted the blade and the old witch screamed.

'You should have done that before, when there was

time.' His brother Price withdrew his head and started to walk away.

'Had to wait for you to show me where the gold was, didn't I?' Rike pulled his blade clear and let Sabitha fall. 'Witches always have the best loot.' He drew back his sword for a swing. 'But they hide it so well!' He hacked at the wall-post. It splintered, spilling gold and silver from its hollow interior.

Sabitha could see nothing but the floor now, her strength flowing from her. She could smell smoke and hear the crackle of flame. The other brother must have managed to fire the thatch despite the rain. Above the sound of the roof burning Sabitha could hear Rike's chuckles and the chinking of her coin as he scooped it into his pockets. His laughter had a certain innocence to it, something kept over from a childhood rather than the humourless sound he'd made when he had first sat down.

The witch lay on her floor, bleeding, dying, while the man stole all that she owned. She had often pondered death, though unlike her sister she had never come to terms with it. It surprised her to find that now, with a sword hole through her middle, her thoughts were not of the journey ahead but firmly on the moment, rooted in revenge. She couldn't allow this man to triumph over her so casually, to take her gold and forget her before it was even spent. Sabitha had never been much of a witch, but the dying curse of a witch, even a weak one, holds power. How to curse this brute though? He wasn't old, not yet thirty, practically a boy. He had no great fear of death. She was glad he hadn't drunk the ale. Poison would have been too easy. Even that poison.

Sabitha bled and chewed on her revenge. Rike hadn't the imagination for great fear. He had nothing he cared for, no one whose loss would touch him. He stood literally beyond her revenge, incapable of feeling any sorrow deep enough to compensate her. If his brother fell dead in the next hour the brute would shrug and loot his corpse.

Rike rose, patting jingling pockets and strode toward the door. All about him the smoke coiled, the flames above starting to bite. Sabitha saw only his boots and muttered her curse from numb lips.

'You'll learn to care. It might take a lifetime, but you'll learn. You'll find someone you can call brother and mean it. And you'll lack the words to let him know or any quality to make him care. And at the last . . . you will *fail* him. And then *my blood* will take him from you.'

Rike left the hut and the smoke closed behind him. Sabitha lay around her hurt and felt the heat of the fire. Hell waited for her. Her life had not been a good one and she would leave nothing behind. Nothing but her curse.

It wouldn't take effect immediately. It might take

years, for the brute's skin was thick and her powers weak. But one day . . . one day . . . it would make him deep enough to hurt. And then hurt him.

And perhaps Chella might even be the one to strike that blow.

Footnote

Readers expressed interest in a story about Rike. I've shied away from using him as the point-of-view. I think there's more to be learned from the outside.

The witch's curse comes to pass at the end of Emperor of Thorns. *Rike fails to do the last thing Jorg asks of him, and we can imagine that it's because Jorg means something to him. Moments later Sabitha's sister ends the matter.*

The Weight of Command

In the first glow of a summer's day the barn held an almost cathedral silence, penetrated only by shafts of light exposing every chink in its walls and turning the motes of dust within to dancing gold.

Ropes hung slack from rafters, sacks stood piled in flaccid heaps, plough and scythe waited patient beneath their covers, one with its job complete, the other sharp with anticipation of a distant harvest.

Birdsong had preceded the light and echoed now in the raftered vaults where sparrow and martin battled one tune against another for territory.

Hay in heaps, barrels caulked and content, planks and fencing posts, raw timbers waiting to be shaped, a chaos with sufficient order for the farmer to find his way.

Birds, two swift rats, a sloe-eyed cat, smoke-grey and suspicious. Nothing else stirred beyond the timeless golden waltz tracking the light's slow progression across mud floors.

At last, beneath one sprawled pile of sacking, motion.

Something larger than expected. A veritable earthquake, shedding sackcloth. In dark corners the rats froze. The cat turned from his hunt and climbed toward an escape beneath the eaves.

A groaning accompanied the heaving. Seismic tones as a mountain rose. A grubby hand exposed, fingers plump as sausages groping for salvation.

'My head.' Spoken in the smallest of voices by a person of monumental proportions. The heap of sacking revealed itself as a heap of man beneath a skin of sacks. Dark and deep-set eyes squinted suspicion at the barn's interior from an over-stuffed face.

The man gained his feet through a painful set of manoeuvres, battling gravity, his own bulk, and the fact that every movement seemed to be the source of considerable distress. He glanced around once more, patted the broadsword hanging from his belt and staggered to the doors.

Shielding his eyes, he peered out into the day. The air lay sharp with the stink of ash and char. Smoke still wafted across the field.

'Oh. You. Bastards.'

The man groaned and held his head in both hands, compressing it as if concerned it might split in two.

Seized by sudden panic, he hastened back to his nest beneath the sacks, kicking one way and the other until he unearthed a battered leather travel pack of the kind commonly strapped behind a saddle. A massive sigh escaped him, the tension easing. Another groan as he stooped to heft the bag to a shoulder.

'Bastards.' He turned toward the doors once more.

In the hayloft above something moved. A grey and sinuous something. Not a cat though, too large by far. With no more than a rustle it escaped the hay's depths and slid over the edge of the boarded rafters, disdaining the ladder. A hang, a drop, a silent landing, and the boy rose behind the fat man.

'Burlow.'

The big man rotated on the spot, reaching for his sword, a turn led by his head and twisting through his bulk, feet last to follow. 'God's blood, Sim! I told you not to do that! My heart can't take it.'

Sim yawned, rubbing a hand across his face, bleary-eyed. 'I should wear bells to warn you?'

Burlow waved the idea away. 'They've left us behind. Again.'

Sim stretched. Arms behind his head, all manner of cracks and pops accompanying the motion as if he were threatening four score years rather than shy of his first. 'Horses?'

'Not that I can see.'

'What time is it?' Sim asked.

'Coming to noon.' Burlow went to the corner and began to relieve himself. 'I think I drank a barrel of that ale by myself.'

Sim's turn to grunt. 'Mouth tastes like something

crawled into it last night and died.' He pressed fingers to forehead, testing his pain. 'I was doing fine until Makin found that wine.'

'We'd best be going. The word will be out. Won't be long before there's peasants come to pick the place over. Militia following. Wouldn't do to be found here alone.' Burlow patted his sword again and crossed to the doors, peering out.

'We're neither of us alone,' Sim said.

Burlow grunted. 'Good to know I'm not the only one that gets left behind.' He shouldered through the doors. 'I'll be having a word with young Jorg when we catch up.'

'Who said I got left behind?' Sim crossed to the door, brushing hay from his trousers and shirt, both black, stolen from some lordling's wardrobe. 'Perhaps I chose to stay to make sure you didn't get lost.' A narrow smile. 'Or Jorg asked me to stay, to make sure you did?'

Burlow shook his head, irritated by Sim's good humour. 'I wouldn't have woken up if you wanted to play knife.' He stepped out into the day.

'True.' Sim shrugged and followed.

The main holding had been put to the torch and the fires had burned tracks through the wheat field, soot-black fingers reaching perilously close to the barn. A few goats browsed among the beets, a lone sow wallowing in the pond before the smoking spars of the nearest building.

'Nothing here,' Sim said. 'We should go to Perryville.'

Burlow scowled at the ruins. The plan had been a

sound one. Attack Sol Tarron's compound, seize his coin. The merchant was said to have a hoard of enough gold to buy a throne. Go in hard and fast, all at once. A tried and tested approach favoured by the brothers since Price had brought them together. Enough screaming and fire will bring chaos to the most ordered defence. Price might have fallen but Burlow saw no reason to change tactics. 'Jorg wants to lead us. Undermining my authority, that's what this is.'

Sim shrugged. 'You're a decent leader, Burlow. Cleverer than most. Firm but fair. But . . .'

'But?' Burlow knew the 'but'. The boy, Jorg, was something else. Jorg hadn't wanted them to rush the place last night. He'd said Sol Tarron's guards would see them coming, the merchant would escape. And somehow, goddammit, he had. With his money! A tunnel to the woods behind the big house. All the brothers got was ale, wine, and access to a well-stocked kitchen. And blood of course. Plenty of that. Brother Rike had murdered a dozen by himself, at least.

Burlow led off toward the road that would take them to Perryville. The town wouldn't hold a welcome for road brothers but just the two of them, unhorsed, would pass as footsore wanderers, still doubtless treated with suspicion but unlikely to be strung from a tree.

'You think Jorg's plan would have worked?' Sim asked, following on behind.

'Probably.' Burlow grunted the admission. He'd flat

out refused to consider the boy's objection. 'Whether it would have worked isn't the point though. Once the leader has set out his plan, that's the plan. I could hardly change track at that point, could I?'

Jorg had wanted to send a brother or three in by themselves, unsupported.

'Let them get captured,' Jorg had said. 'Let Sol Tarron come out and poke them a bit. The whole place will turn its eyes inward. That's the time to strike. Come in fast and silent.'

'And what idiot is going to volunteer for that?' Burlow had asked.

'You,' Jorg had said. 'It has to be the leader. The leader and someone dangerous.'

Burlow had snorted at the suggestion. 'Me? You'd love that wouldn't you, boy? Let Sol Tarron murder old Burlow and then try to take the brothers for your own!'

Jorg had just shrugged. 'I'd be coming with you. I could ask someone else to go if you prefer.'

Burlow had just laughed. 'Let me know how that goes!'

Burlow looked back at Sim, pacing the road behind him, another boy, though at least this one had a few more years on him than Jorg. A deadly one too, not that there was much to look at, a pretty face, no meat on his limbs, but fast, faster than thinking with those knives at his hips. 'Jorg's plan might have worked with the merchant but he didn't want just one merchant, did he?' Burlow shook his head in disgust. Jorg had wanted to take a whole town. Not one merchant but dozens. Gold, horses, armour, weapons, hostages. 'Should we reach up and take the moon from the sky next?'

Perryville lay a good ten miles down the Western Road and Burlow missed his horse within the first few hundred yards.

'Bastards.'

After nine miles his feet hurt, his legs hurt, his shoulders hurt, and he let the world know it.

'Not a walker then, brother?' Sim seemed untroubled by the miles.

'I'll walk from the fire to my fucking horse. After that I expect to be carried from one place to the next.'

'We could always take a couple of horses . . .' Sim nodded ahead to three riders approaching along a distant curve of the road, escorting a small group of wagons.

Burlow shook his head. 'Don't want to draw any attention. Not with the ashes of Sol Tarron's place still hot, and him out there somewhere. He's probably put prices on our heads already.'

Burlow plodded on, sweating beneath a sun too hot for the season.

The last mile brought them to the gates of Perryville. The brothers would not be there of course but it was a place where news of their exploits would arrive and spread. Burlow and Sim had only to lie low, bide their time, spend stolen coin on ale and good food, and in a day or three the word from the road would lead them back to the troop. What would be waiting for him then though Burlow didn't know. Jorg would spend each day tightening his grip on the brothers. Burlow snarled into the straggles of his beard as he came into the shadow of the town's palisade. Only Jorg's youth held him back. Even with the Nuban and Makin to back him up there were some among the band who couldn't yet put their faith in anyone with so few years beneath their belt. One big victory, though. One big score would clinch it.

The town of Perryville hugged both banks of the River Perry, a waterway too narrow for any serious traffic but too wide to be called a stream. A palisade of stout timbers, grey with age, encircled the main town though a tail of a few hundred ramshackle huts spilled out beyond the wall, following the Perry upstream. The old town boasted a few dozen good stone-built houses, most of them merchants' mansions surrounding the manse of Lord Hetton. The lord being Perryville's ageing master, a military man of some repute.

Burlow, still dogged by the echoes of the morning's hangover, led the way to River Street where a good handful of taverns and bawdy-houses lured people from the road and sat them to drink their ale with a view across the water.

'You don't think we're too close still?' Sim asked when Burlow stopped beneath the faded sign of the Royal Stag.

'Damned if I'm going another yard on foot. Next town's Wheeldon, and that's a sight more than five miles further. Look.' Burlow scraped a circle in the mud with his heel. He put a dent at the centre. 'That's where we came from. That circle's twenty miles across. How many square miles is that?'

Sim shrugged.

'It's a lot is what it is. I read in a book how to figure it. You take Pi—'

'Pie?' Sim shot him a narrow look laden with suspicion. The brothers had never taken kindly to his education. The leather-bound tomes in his travel bag he kept well-hidden and read only in private. 'What kind of pie?'

'Forget it,' Burlow grunted. The boy who learned his letters had lived long ago and far away. The young scribe he became had weighed a third of what Burlow weighed now and had introduced himself as Callum ver Lowe. Burlow had left him far behind. Life on the road is an exercise in choice. A man is made of what he chooses to take with him from one day into the next, and by what he chooses to leave behind. On the road it's easy to leave parts of yourself behind. Sometimes too many of them. 'The point is that there are a lot of miles in that circle and no good reason for trouble to find us in Perryville.'

'Here then?' Sim looked up at the tavern sign. 'You've the coin for it?'

Burlow shook the heavy saddle roll he'd been labouring beneath all day. A faint jingle rewarded him. 'I have.' He had his hand on the door. He could smell the sourness of the ale, hear the voices raised in amiable conversation. Already his mouth watered at the thought of mutton and potatoes, gravy pouring from the jug, buttered swede, fresh bread . . .

'You there! Stop!'

Burlow pushed at the door.

'You! The fat man!' The tramp of approaching feet accompanied the man's shout.

Burlow swung about. A dozen men-at-arms were closing on him, coming from both directions.

'Run!' Burlow ripped his sword clear with an oath. He would have doubted Perryville had a dozen regulars, let alone a dozen patrolling River Street. 'Run!'

'Do not run!' A crossbow bolt hammered into the doorpost beside Burlow's head. The armoured captain waved his men forward.

To Burlow's surprise Sim, who he would have bet on being through the door and lost in the tavern crowd within the moment, raised his arms. Two men tackled the lad, and in Burlow's moment of hesitation he found himself likewise grappled to the floor.

Not long afterward, bloodied, beaten, and caked with mud, Burlow found himself in the grand square before Lord Hetton's manse, hemmed in on three sides by the houses of noted merchants, their pillared porticos thrust before them.

Three men had dragged him there. Just one had been needed to wrestle Sim along. Rope burned against the raw flesh of Burlow's wrists, securing his hands behind his back. The boy was tied the same way, both of them trussed like pigs for slaughter. Behind them a score of additional guards traipsed along for the show, regulars from their patrols and the household men-at-arms in service to the high families of Perryville. Outnumbering the guards were the highborn themselves, or at least those now raised by golden ladders from whatever elevation birth had chanced to give them. The lord and his lady, various sons and daughters, merchants in their finery, their families behind them, some scowling, some delighted, all of them fascinated by their two captives.

'Sometimes justice strikes almost as swiftly as it should do!' A bald and grey-bearded merchant stood before them, ivory buttons in the black velvet of his tunic. Burlow noted the marks of travel on the cape that the wind wrapped around the man. This one hadn't just stepped out of his house for the show.

'Who the hell are you?' Burlow tried to shake free of the men who held his arms. It took four of them to arrest his progress toward the bald man.

'Listen to the fiend!' The man spread his arms, turning to the crowd. 'His band raze my home and water my fields with the blood of my servants and he doesn't even recognize me. I am Sol Tarron, the man whose house-guard left your command in tatters before they fell.' He returned the ferocity of his gaze to Burlow. 'Did you think when you fled the ruins of my home that you could restore your fortunes by following me here? Did you really imagine you would pass the gates unnoticed?'

Burlow opened his mouth, hot with retort, but surprise stole his words. He'd been recognized? He hadn't imagined himself so famous. The brothers did have quite a reputation . . . and he was the leader . . . but even so, they kept on the move . . . He knew a moment's pride then, even if they were about to kill him. Brother Burlow – famed and fearless leader!

Lord Hetton came forward, no mistaking him, an elderly man held erect by the discipline of his office and the blood of old royalty that ran thin but definite in his veins. A circlet of pale gold threaded the white wispiness of his hair, the blue eyes beneath watery with age but cold and hard even so. Despite his years he held the attention of the square, the guards' gaze on him, waiting for direction. He stopped before Burlow, of a height with him, though half his width.

'You were seen on the road from Gowland and identified by your bulk, scoundrel. A toothless ancient reported you to the guard within moments of your passing the gates.'

'I'm not the man you're looking for, my lord. Just an innocent traveller!' Burlow tried to look both innocent and outraged. He wasn't sure he managed either.

Lord Hetton shook his head. 'You'll be put to torture

until you furnish descriptions of your fellow outlaws who survived the attack on Master Tarron's home.'

'Torture!' A cold terror twisted Burlow's gut. He struggled for freedom again, failed again, and spat. 'No need for that. Won't take a hot iron to get the names of that faithless crew from me.'

Lord Hetton offered a thin smile. 'Well, at least the matter of your guilt is settled beyond doubt.' A glance toward Sim. 'This one we can kill now.' The old man crossed to stand before the boy. 'Unless he's anything interesting to say?'

Sim did something then that Burlow's eyes couldn't quite follow. Something that was part slump and part jerk. Somehow it got him free of both ropes and restraining hands. Where he got the blade from Burlow couldn't tell. His hair perhaps. Just a small piece of sharp iron, but enough to cut an old man's throat.

Burlow, knowing the end would be quick now, threw himself forward with an animal roar. He had always been strong – you have to be strong to throw a decent weight around. The guards before him went down like skittles. It would do him no good but he felt better for it. Die angry not scared. That's what they said on the road.

A guardsman with more wit than the rest stood his ground, steel bared, timing his swing as Burlow barrelled towards him.

Chooom

The man's neck seemed to explode to the side, a

welter of blood bursting into the air. He dropped without protest. The swordsman behind him wiped crimson from his face and as he pulled his hand back an arrow sprouted from his chest. It was hard to know which of them was more surprised. Within moments feathered shafts were appearing all around, the air full of the hiss and thunk of travel and arrival. Sol Tarron turned to run, cloak swirling about him. A spear transfixed him. Burlow followed the line of it back and saw upon the roof ridge of Lord Hetton's manse half a dozen figures, bows in hand. One reaching for another spear from the bunch stacked against the closest chimney.

The square's other rooftops proved to be similarly adorned, and charging from the tree-lined road to Perryville's great church came Brother Rike, Red Kent, Hendrik, Emmer and others in their wake, axes and swords raised high.

The routing of an entire town took far less time than Burlow had ever imagined. It helped that the core of its defence had gathered in Jorg's killing field and turned their backs upon his archers. It also made a difference that the massacre began at the heart of the town. The people understood themselves defeated from the outset and sought only to run. If the brothers had thrown themselves at the walls or gates the town would have rallied behind their defences to repulse the intruders. But when the foxes are in the hen house, the hens' only thought is to leave.

Burlow came to Lord Hetton's grand reception room dirty, wet with the blood of others, burdened with the bone-deep exhaustion that follows any slaughter. The stink of burning followed him: a pall of it hung over Perryville, half the town already aflame.

Jorg and the brothers had made a feasting hall of the great chamber, and a tavern of it, and a brothel, splashing ale across fine tables and rugs, smearing grease and worse over moulded plaster walls, removing with knife and hammer anything that took their fancy. Jorg himself sat in the lord's chair, regarding the brothers' revels past his booted feet, raised before him on a delicate occasional table. Brother Gains had a whole pig roasting in the hearth. Rike sat before a heap of treasure, the sum total of gold, gems, and silver from half a dozen grand homes, watching it as jealously as if his heart surmounted it. Red Kent, Grumlow and Sim were engaged in competition, throwing knives at the portrait of the late Lord Hetton's wife, answering each other's calls for an eye, an ear, or 'on the nose'.

Tired as he was, sated with killing, pockets heavy with stolen gold, Burlow had little appetite for argument. Little that was until his eyes returned to rest upon Jorg, slouched in Hetton's tall ebony chair, and suddenly an anger woke in him, as fierce as it was unexpected, the wrath of the old stag when he turns to see a young buck fresh to his antlers parading among the does he had counted his own.

'Jorg!' A roar rather than a word, swelling from deep

within him. Burlow's fingers wrapped the hilt of his broadsword. 'What in hell—'

'It went very well,' Jorg cut through Burlow's outrage. They had the brothers' attention now in that guarded sideways manner in which men watched such encounters on the road.

'It what?'

'It went very well,' Jorg said. 'When I told you my plan yesterday morning you laughed and asked me to let you know how it went. It went well.' He waved a hand at the treasure piled before Rike. 'I said we'd need to send our leader in, together with someone dangerous.'

'What?' Burlow looked around left, then right, noting the Nuban's unsmiling eyes upon him, Makin's grin, Row's quiet speculation. 'What? Nobody sent me anywhere! You abandoned me! Us. You abandoned Sim and me! Stole our horses!'

Jorg raised his brows. 'All part of the plan. Did Sol Tarron's ale wash it away? Sim? Was I unclear?'

Brother Sim stepped around Jorg's throne – Burlow named it for what it was, a throne. 'No, brother,' Sim answered. 'Very clear.'

'You see, Burlow? I gave you a wanderer's disguise and aimed you after Sol Tarron, straight at Perryville—'

'You?' Burlow's growing confusion burst out. 'Nonsense. Nobody aimed me! I chose to come here. I—' He bit the word off. Had he chosen Perryville? Or had it been Sim who first named the town, back when he was saying what a good leader Burlow was? 'How would you know Sol Tarron would come here?'

Jorg swigged ale from a golden cup. 'Best place to get justice. Lord Hetton's the sort to raise a posse, *noblesse oblige* and all that. Time was that Hetton led armies in King Amon's name. A greybeard now, but still sharp.' Another swig and he put the cup down. 'Besides, Tarron was just the cherry, Perryville the cake. We offered up our leader and watched them turn inward. While the gate guard were busy hurrying after you we were busy hurrying in after them.'

'But . . .' Burlow let go of his sword. 'I was recognized. You can't time something like that. An old man . . .'

Brother Elban stood up, wine flask in hand, offering a smile, all wrinkles and gums. 'That man just ahead of me, guard cap'n sir? I know that man! He's the famous outlaw leader. Fat Burlow. King o' the Brothers he is! I'll swear it on my mother's grave, sir. A demon of a man, sir!'

'If we'd not put Lord Hetton down and quickly it could have turned out very different.' Jorg nodded to Brother Sim. 'If they'd got themselves organized and realized how few we were . . . But "if" is a big word, is it not Burlow?'

Jorg stood up from Lord Hetton's chair. 'Well done, Brother Burlow. You stepped into the lion's den. None of us could ask more from a leader.' Jorg's eyes found Burlow's and narrowed. 'Or less.' He waved at the seat behind him. 'Perhaps you're famous already, but if not

I can swear that before too long everyone west of Vyene will know the name of the leader of our band. A man who leads from the front and dares any danger that bars the path to greatness, whatever the cost.'

Burlow stared at the empty throne. Just hours earlier he'd been standing before Lord Hetton, disarmed, hands tied, expecting only torture and death. His glance flickered to the gleaming pile of coins and jewellery. Close by, Makin pushed out the chair beside his and gestured with a leg of roast lamb to the rest of the beast on the table.

Burlow frowned. His mouth watered as the scents of meat and ale reached past his fading anger. The late lord's throne looked as narrow and uncomfortable as the man himself. He met Jorg's eyes, dark and unreadable, the empty throne beside him, both an offer and a dare. 'Piss on it. It's too far to walk. I'll sit with Makin. I've marched enough miles today already.'

And with that he settled himself between Brother Makin and Brother Maical, feeling that whilst his horse might not notice it on the morrow, a great weight had been lifted from his shoulders.

Footnote

Burlow has never seemed to be a readers' favourite but I thought I would let him march across the pages without the immediate burden of Jorg. The world isn't divided between leaders and followers. There are people who will take on the burden of command if it falls their way. But someone more hungry for it always comes along, and it seldom ends well!

Select Mode

They call me a monster and if it were untrue the weight of my crimes would pin me to the ground. I have maimed and I have murdered and if this mountain stood but a little higher I would cut the angels from their heaven. I care less for accusations than for the rain that soaks me, that runs down every limb. I spit both from my lips. Judgment has always left a sour taste.

'Keep moving!' And he strikes me across the shoulders. The staff is thick and polished from hard use. I imagine how he'll look when I make him eat it. Avery, they call him.

There are five left to guard us now, twenty when they found us on the Orlanth Road. A man like the Nuban doesn't give up easy but two against twenty are poor odds, especially when one of the two is a child. He surrendered before the Select had even drawn their horses up around us. It took me longer to reach the same decision, hampered by my pride.

'Pick it up!' The stick catches me behind the knee and I stumble, loose rocks scattering beneath my feet, rolling away down the steep path. Rope chafes at my wrists. We exchanged our weapons for rope, but at least the odds have narrowed. They sent only five men to take us into the mountains for judgment. Two against five are the best odds I've had in a while.

The Nuban is ahead of me, huge shoulders hunched against the downpour. If his hands were unbound he could throttle four of them while I fed Avery his staff.

Back on the Orlanth Road the Nuban had shrugged off his crossbow and let it fall. Set his short sword on the ground, leaving only the knife in his boot against the chance of discovery.

'One black as the devil and the other's not thirteen!' Avery had called out when they surrounded us, horses stamping, tails flicking.

A second rider leaned from his saddle and slapped Avery, a cracking blow that set the white print of his hand on a red cheek.

'Who judges?' A thin man, grey, but hard-eyed.

'The arch, Selector John.' Avery pushed the words past clenched teeth, his scowl on me as if it were my handprint on his face.

'The arch.' Selector John nodded, looking from one man to the next. 'The arch judges. Not you, not I. The arch speaks for heaven.' He rode between us. 'And if the man, or this boy, are Select then they will be your brothers!'

And now the pair of us walk, soaked, freezing, beaten toward judgment on the mountain, wrists bound. With Avery's staff to encourage us on, and four more of the Select to see we don't stray from the path.

I choose each step, head down, rain dripping from the black veil of my hair. I wonder at this arch of theirs, puzzle how an arch could judge, and what it might say. Certainly its words have power. The power to bind Selector John's disparate band together and hold them to his command.

'If you are Select you will ride with me,' he had said.

'If not?' the Nuban rumbled.

'You won't.'

And that seemed to be all that underwrote the Select, feared across the north counties of Orlanth, famed for their loyalty and discipline. Men taken at random from the road and judged in secret, bound by nothing but the good word of some arch, some relic of the Builders no doubt, some incomprehensible toy that survived their war.

The water runs in rivulets between my boots, their frayed leather black with it.

'Hell—' Avery's cry turns into something inarticulate as his slip turns into a sprawl. Even his staff can't save him. He lies for a moment, embracing the mountainside, stunned. As he starts to rise I skip forward and allow myself to fall, letting the whole of my weight land behind my knee as it hits the back of his neck. The sound of bone breaking is almost lost in the rain. With my bound hands pressed to his shoulderblades I manage to stand before the others reach me. Avery does not stand, or move, or complain.

Rough hands haul me back, a knife at my throat, colder than the wind. John stands before me, a hint of shock in pale eyes unused to such expression.

'You murdered him!' he shouts, fingers on the hilt of his sword, closing on it, opening, closing.

'Who judges?' I shout back and a laugh rips out of me.

I slept until my ninth year, deep in the dream that blinds us to the world. The thorns woke me. They gave me sharp new truths to savour. Held me as my little brother died, embraced me for the long slow time it took my uncle's men to kill my mother. I woke dark to the world, ready to give worse than I got.

'I will see this arch and listen to its pronouncement,' I say. 'Because if it speaks for heaven then I have words of my own to speak back.'

Deep in the cloudbank lightning ricochets, making the thunderheads glow, a flat light edging the slopes for a heartbeat. The rain hammers down, pricked with ice, but I'm burning with the memory of those thorns and the fever they put in my blood. No absolution in this storm – the stain of sin is past water's touch. The wounds the thorns gave turned sour, beyond cleansing. But heaven's arch waits and suddenly I'm eager to let it speak of me.

The hand on John's sword spasms open. 'Let's go.' A curt nod, scattering water, and he strides off. I follow, impatient now, the slope seeming less steep. Only the Nuban spares a backward glance for Avery, still hugging the mountainside, and a second glance for me, watchful and beyond reading. The glow of my small victory fades, and not for the first time it's the Nuban's silence rather than his words that makes me want to be better than I am.

Another of the Select takes up the rearguard. Greb, they call him. 'Watch your footing,' I say. 'It gets slippery.'

We crest the lip of a valley and descend into shadows where the wind subsides from howls to muttered complaint. The light is failing but where the trail snakes down the slope I can see something is wrong. I stop and Greb stumbles into me, cursing.

'There's something wrong with the rain.' I stare at it. Across a wide swathe the rain seems to fall too slowly, the drops queuing to reach the ground and making a grey veil of falling water.

'Slow-time,' John says, not turning or raising his voice.

Greb kicks my calf and I carry on. I've heard of slow-time. Tatters of it wreath the Arcada Mountains, remnants from when the Builders broke the world. We discovered the same thing, the Builders and me: if something shatters your world then afterward you find the rules have changed. They had the Day of a Thousand Suns. I had the thorns.

I follow the Nuban into the slow-time, a band of it two or three yards wide. From the outside the rain within seems to fall at its leisure. Passing into the region all that changes is that now *only* where I'm walking are things right. Ahead and behind the rain powers down as if each drop had been shot from a ballista and would punch holes in armour. And we're out. Greb's still wading through it behind me, moving like a street-mummer, slower than slow, until he's free and starts to speed up. The slow-time sticks to him, reluctant to release its prisoner, as if for ten yards it's still clinging to his skin before finally he's walking at our pace once more.

We advance and a shoulder of rock reveals the strangest sight. It's as if a bubble of glass, so clear as to be invisible, has been intersected by the mountainside. Rain streams off it, turned from its path by unseen currents. At the heart of the half-sphere, close to the ground, a wild blue light entices, part diamond, part promise. And all around it statues stand.

'Idiots.' John waves an arm at them as we pass. 'I can understand the first one being trapped, but the other seven?'

We're close enough to see they're not statues now. Eight travellers, the closest to the light dressed in fashions seen only in dusty oil paintings on castle walls. Flies in amber, moths drawn to the light of the fire in which we burn. What world will be waiting for them when they think to turn around and walk back out?

'Do all time-bubbles have a handy warning light at the centre?' I wonder it aloud but no one answers.

I glance back once before the distance takes them. All of them held there like memories while the days and months flicker past outside. I have time-bubbles in my head, places I return to over and again.

When I killed my first man and left the Healing Hall in flames, sick with poison from the wounds the hook-briar gave, they tell me it was Father Gomst who found me, unconscious, black with smoke. I escaped from Friar Glenn's care again within the hour, and again it was Father Gomst who found me. Memory takes me to that tower-top where I leaned out, watching the flames spiral and the lanterns moving far below as Father's guards hunted me. We stand on that tower, trapped in those minutes, we two, and often I pass by, pausing to study it once more, and learning nothing.

Father Gomst raises both hands. 'You don't need the knife, Jorg.'

'I think I do.' The blade trembles in my grip, not from fear but from what the fever puts in me. A sense of something rushing toward me, something thrilling,

101

terrible, sudden . . . my body vibrating with anticipation. 'How else would I cut?'

'Give it to me.' He doesn't reach for the knife. Around his neck a gold cross, and a Builder talisman, a fone, the ancient plasteek fractured, part melted, chased with silver like the church icons. He says God hears him through it, but I sense no connection.

'The thorns wouldn't let me go,' I tell him. Sir Jan had thrown me into the middle of the briar. The man had slabs of muscle, enough to tear the carriage door off and throw me clear before my uncle's soldiers caught us. A strong man can throw a child of nine quite a way.

'I know.' Father Gomst wipes the rain from his face, drawing his hand from forehead to chin. 'A hook-briar can hold a grown man, Jorg.' If he could truly speak to God he would know the judgment on me and waste no more words.

'I would have saved them.' The thorns hid me in their midst, held me. I had seen little William die, three flashes of lightning giving me the scene in frozen moments. 'I would have saved them.' But the lie tastes rotten on my tongue. Would anything have held William from me? Would anything have held my mother back. Anything? All bonds can be slipped, all thorns torn free. It's simply a matter of pain, and of what you're prepared to lose.

Greb jabs me and I'm back on the mountain. The stink of him reaches me even through the rain. 'Keep moving.'

It's as if he didn't just see me kill Avery for the same damn thing. Judgment . . . I'm ready for it.

'Here.' John raises his hand and we all stop. At first I don't see the arch, and then I do. A doorway rather than an arch, narrow and framed by the silver-steel of the Builders. It stands on a platform of Builder-stone, a poured surface still visible beneath the scatter of rocks. Twenty yards beyond is a pile of bones, an audience of skulls, some fresh, some mouldering, all cleaned of flesh by the dutiful ravens. 'What happens if we're not Select?' Dead men's grins answer the Nuban's question.

John draws his sword, an old blade, notched, the iron stained. He goes to stand beyond the arch. The other three men take position around it, and Greb, who took over Avery's position as Jorg-poker, draws his knife. 'You, big man. You're first.'

'When you pass through stand still and wait for the judgment. Move and I will kill you, without the mercy of the ritual.' John mimes the killing thrust.

The Nuban looks around at the faces of the Select, blinking away raindrops. He's thinking of the fight, wondering where his chance will come. He turns to me, making a single fist of his bound hands. 'We have lived, Jorg. I'm glad we met.' His voice deep and without waver. He walks to the arch of judgment. His shoulders almost brush the steel on either side as he passes through.

'Fail—' The arch speaks with a voice that is neither male nor female, nor even human.

'Move aside.' John gestures with his blade, contempt on his face. He knows the Nuban is waiting his chance, and gives him none. 'You next.' The Nuban is secured by two Select.

I step forward, watching the reflections slide across the Builder-steel as I approach. I wonder what crimes stained the Nuban. Though he is the best of us you cannot live on the road and remain innocent, no matter the circumstance that put you there. With each step I feel the thorns tearing at me. They can't hold me. But they held me on that night the world changed.

'Judge me.' And I step through. Ice runs down my spine, a cold fire in every vein. Outside the world pauses, the rain halts in its plunge for an instant, or an age. I can't tell which. Motion returns almost imperceptibly, the drops starting to crawl earthward once more.

'Faaaaaiiiiilllllllu—' The word stretches out for an age, deeper than the Nuban's rumble. And at the end it's snatched away as if a knife sliced the throat it came from.

I believe in the arch. I deserved to fail, because I am guilty.

Even so.

'Join your friend.' John waves his sword toward the Nuban. His voice is wrong, a touch too deep.

'The rain is too slow,' I say. The quick-time is fading from me but still the arch's effects linger. I step back through the silver doorway. God made me quick in any event, God or the Devil, and the Builders made me quicker. This time the arch has no comment, but before the Select can close on me I step through once more.

Again the cold shock of transition. I ignore the arch's judgment and dive forward, wrapped in quick-time, trailing it with me. John hardly flinches as I sever the ropes around my wrists on the sword he is so kind as to hold steady for me.

'Sssssseeeeeellllect m—' While the arch speaks I take John's knife from his belt and cut him a new smile. And before the blood comes I'm off, sprinting toward the Nuban. I'm still quick, but less so as I reach him and stab the first of his guards through the eye. I twist the blade as I pull it free, grating over the socket. The Nuban breaks the second man's face with the back of his head.

I chase Greb down. He runs although he has the bigger knife, and he thinks I'm as old as thirteen. My arm aches to stick John's blade into the man, to sink it between his shoulders and hear him howl. But he sprints off a drop in the half-light before I reach him. I stop at the top and look down to where he sprawls at broken angles.

Returning to the arch, I take slow steps. The rain comes in flurries now, weakening. The cold is in me at last, my hands numb. The Nuban sits upon a rock by the bone-pile, checking his crossbow for damage. He looks up as I draw near. It's his judgment that matters to me, his approval.

'We failed.' He nods toward the arch. 'Maybe the Builders have been watching us. Wanting us to do better.'

'I don't care what they think of me,' I say.

His brow lifts a fraction, half-puzzled, half-understanding. He puts the crossbow across his knees. 'I'm as broken a thing as my gods ever made, Jorg. We keep bad company on the road. Any man would look good against them.' He shakes his head. 'Better to listen to the arch than me! And better to listen to neither of us.' He slaps a hand to his chest. 'Judge yourself, boy.' He returns his gaze to his work. And more quietly, 'Forgive yourself.'

I walk back to the arch, stepping around the corpses of the Select. I wonder at the ties that bound them, the bonds forged by the arch's judgments. Those bonds seem more pure, more reasoned than the arbitrary brotherhood of the road that binds me to my own band of rogues, links forged and broken by circumstance. A yard from the arch I can see my reflection warped across the Builder-steel. The arch called 'fail' for me, condemned me to the bone-pile, and yet seconds later I was Select. Did I validate myself in the moments between?

'Opinions are well and good,' I tell it. I have a rock in my hands, near as heavy as I can lift. 'Sometimes it's better not to speak them.' I throw the rock hard as I can and it slams into the cross support, breaking into jagged pieces.

I set a hand to the scar left on the metal.

'FAILure to connect,' the arch says.

And in the end the arch has the right of it.

Footnote

There are many opportunities in Jorg's story for seeing elements of our world through new eyes. You'll see old buildings repurposed, everyday objects venerated. Here, standard messages from our age: 'Failure to connect' and 'Select mode' become the basis for a brotherhood not dissimilar to Jorg's. The idea reflects on the arbitrary nature of so many loyalties, friendships, and loves.

The theme of brotherhood is written through the Broken Empire trilogy. Brothers by birth, leading into the larger issue of family. Brothers by association, leading to the issues of belonging, groups, and leadership. Brothers through friendship, leading to issues of loyalty and duty.

And here we have the Nuban, whose comparative moral superiority seems to be integral to the man, and Father Gomst, who represents religious ideals and at the same time the difficulty men with no great strength of character have in embodying such ideals. Two very different kinds of father-figure, both playing a role in the life of a young man whose own father leaves much to be desired.

Mercy

'Serve revenge hot or cold, it will never sate you. It's a hunger that only grows the more you feed it.'

'Very lyrical.' The angular young woman on her sway-backed mare rubbed the hollow of her stomach. 'I could do with a meal right now. A good chicken soup would do. Like my mother used to make.' She smacked her lips. 'But very lyrical.'

'I took to reading while my wound kept me abed, Sister Ellen.' Makin found his fingers touching the place where the sword had entered his back. 'It seems I'm treading a path that's been trod before. The wise have a lot to say about it.'

'Vengeance is mine, saith the Lord.' Ellen crossed herself. The tail of Makin's stallion swished before her and she slowed her mount. 'That's what they taught us in the convent. Mother Superior had it written in bible-black on the wall behind her desk.'

'So I'm stealing from God?'

'If you're going steal, you might as well steal from

whoever has the best stuff. If you're breaking one of the ten commandments why not go the whole hog?' Ellen glanced out into the darkness, her eyes defocused.

Makin shivered, the girl saw through things. Darkness was the least of it. She saw through men too. The second sight wasn't something they'd taught her at the convent. They'd tried to drown her for it. That had been a mistake.

'Here will do.' He pulled on his reins. 'They say that an eye for an eye will leave the whole world blind. That's another one the wise are fond of.' He turned and slipped the knot securing the blanket-wrapped bundle across the back of his horse. It fell and landed with a thud, accompanied by the kind of 'ooof' that a man makes when the air has been driven from his lungs. 'They say that revenge is a sweet poison that ruins a man even as he craves it.' Makin nodded to his retainer. 'Sister Ellen, if you please.'

The woman nodded and pushed aside lank yellow hair. She drew her knife from her belt, a cruel piece of iron blackened with age, as thin and wicked as its owner. Just the line of its edge caught the moonlight. She went to one knee and cut the cord binding the blanket about their prisoner. 'Kill him if you must, but let's be quick about it either way. This is a bad place.'

'Indulge me, Ellen.' Makin set a boot to the prisoner and with a grunt of effort set him rolling. A journey of a yard or so across the close-cropped grass proved sufficient to unwrap the young man who came to rest lying on his back, wide eyes fixed on the warrior's face.

Makin drew his sword and squatted down, heels to haunches, the gentle sounds of a summer night pressing around him from the dark fields. 'You know who I am?'

'My father is Lord Bucey.' The man tried to roll, tried to sit up, but with hands and feet tied that wasn't easy. He lay back. 'He'll pay—'

'I asked if you knew who *I* am. Not who your father is. And if there's paying to be done tonight it's you who will be paying, Gorlan.' Makin set the point of his sword to the lad's chest.

'W-what have I done?' White-faced.

'If you didn't know the answer to that then you wouldn't have been hiding in Merdith Fort four hundred miles from your father's holdings, now would you?'

'You're Makin Bortha.' The man tested his bonds, pulling hard enough to bleed around the cords, but not hard enough to break them.

'I am. You burned my home. I've crossed three nations to find you, Gorlan.'

'It wasn't me.' He managed to sit and started to shuffle backward. 'The others—'

'The others are all dead.' Makin allowed Gorlan to retreat from his sword. 'I found Captain Orlac on the edge of the Ken Marshes. It took me six months to heal and another two to track him down, but I was still raging, was I not, Ellen?'

'You were.' Ellen spoke from behind Gorlan. The lad whipped his head around to stare up at the figure at his back, lean and ragged, her narrow face unreadable. 'You hung that one by his own guts. A slippery business. The worst part was finding a tree. They're thin on the ground in marshland.'

Makin stood and thrust his sword into the turf between Gorlan's scrabbling legs. He left it standing there. 'Sergeant Elias Smith we found in Orlanth, in Hollor Town, a busy place. He knew he was being hunted but he didn't quite believe it even so. He thought if he put enough miles between us he could live a normal life, find work, drink in taverns, chase girls. If he'd known what was coming he'd have found a cave in the mountains and lived off rabbits and rainwater.'

'I had nothing to do with it! I swear!' Gorlan stopped his pointless retreat and looked up at his captors. 'I didn't even get off my horse.'

'And yet you were their leader,' said Makin. 'Gorlan Bucey, the lord's son. And as their leader, you led them. To my house. My wife was called Nessa. She was clever and kind. Good with her hands – she could embroider a scene that made you think you were looking through a window . . . A terrible cook, mind.'

'I didn't—'

'They ran her down behind the house. Stuck a spear through her. I was lying in a ditch at the time, bleeding to death. Someone ran a sword into my back while I was fighting off your men. I still remember that ditch, the sky through the weeds and grass, very blue and very calm, and the shouts as your men fired the roof.

'I put a spear through Sergeant Smith in the Red Lion tavern in Hollor. When you do a thing like that everyone watches and no one moves. Except for the sergeant – he tried to get up as I was walking back out into the street, but a spear's an awkward thing to carry around at the best of times and he got tangled up in various chairs and what-have-you. You'd think a spear would kill you quick enough, but if you know how to place it it can take days.' Makin glanced across at Ellen. 'Cut his bonds.'

The woman hunkered down behind Gorlan and began slicing.

'You don't have to do this.' Gorlan twisted to look at Ellen. 'Have mercy! You were a nun—'

'A novice. And not by choice.'

'I have money.'

'You're on the right track there.' Makin offered a smile in the darkness. 'Sweet Ellen's a mercenary soul. I hired her to track you and your officers down. Not that the rabble you brought to my home was really an army . . . but you called yourself one, and when you named your-selves its commanders you gave me a place to aim my vengeance. Find the right price and she's yours.'

'My father could give you five hundred in crown gold . . .'

112

'But you recall how I said Nessa couldn't cook?' Makin said.

'Nessa?' Gorlan yanked his hands before him, free of their bonds now but white things, lifeless until the blood returned to them.

'My wife. Pay attention or I might grow angry.' Makin squatted down again, his sword standing between them. 'We had a nanny, a gardener, four hands for the fields, a stableboy . . . a whole household. Our cook, Drusilla, was meaner than a sick dog, but she could work miracles with the plainest fare. Made the best pies I've eaten. Chicken soup too – to die for. And your men killed her in the kitchen.'

'My mother.' Ellen stood, the lad's bonds loose in her hand.

'Her mother,' Makin said. 'She ran from that convent and came looking for her dear old ma, only to find her buried by the ruins of my house. Still, offer her enough gold and I've no doubt that Ellen will consider the deal. She's only here because I'm paying her. She's told me to let it go more times than I can count. Perhaps that's what some old nun taught her. Everything has its season, and seasons pass?'

Gorlan looked up at Ellen, eying the blade in her hands. 'I'm sorry about your mo—'

'I hated the old witch.' Ellen shrugged. 'She put me in that place. Said I was a disgrace to the family and to God. I came back to discuss the matter with her . . .'

Makin kicked Gorlan's foot. 'We're here to discuss me and mine. So pay attention.'

'I'm sorry—'

Makin cut across him. 'I don't even think there was any particular malice in the attack. It was, after all, just a little skirmish over who owned what, which boundary ran where. The house Nessa's father gave us was just in an inconvenient spot. Men die in wars every day, and this wasn't even big enough to be called a war.'

'That's what I've been trying to say.' Gorlan flexed his numb hands and wiped his mouth. 'I didn't even see your wife die. I had fifty men and an objective. Take the manor.'

'And men die in war every day,' said Makin. He rolled his shoulders, feeling the ache in his back and ribs. The sword hadn't hurt going in. His lung hadn't hurt as it filled with blood. The pain had moved in days later, seemingly to stay. 'And women too!'

'What?' Gorlan flinched at the suddenness of Makin's addition.

'And women,' he repeated. 'Women die in wars every day.'

Gorlan spread his hands, looking younger than his years. He couldn't have been more than twenty. 'I didn't tell anyone to—'

'Objectives are secured, people die. I understand how it goes. Ellen understands better. She says the hunger for revenge eats a man up. She says killing doesn't fill that hole. It just makes it echo.' Makin rubbed beneath his ribs, trying to press out the ache of that sword wound, nearly two years old now. 'She's right too. Hanging Captain Orlac with his own guts, impaling Elias Smith on a spear . . . it didn't ease what's inside me, didn't loosen the teeth of it none. It made me hungrier for the rest of you, made me think that if I just got you all then I could sleep, I could rest, I could close my eyes without seeing them.

'That's the problem though, Gorlan. I don't want to stop seeing them.' Makin peered across at the younger man. 'You're trying not to ask. You're thinking *"them?"* but you don't want to say it in case it leads somewhere bloody. Ellen will tell you.'

Ellen cleared her throat, looked down at her knife, then up at the moon. 'There was a daughter. Little girl.'

'I'm sorry . . .' Gorlan glanced at the sword standing unguarded from the ground between his knees, then out into the night as if sizing up his chances if he ran.

'Cerys. Three years old. Pretty as a flower. Sweet as— but she doesn't need my broken poetry. She was a child, my little girl. When you make a new life . . . see her brought into the world . . . see her grow . . . you change as quickly and profoundly as the baby. You watch the world through fresh eyes, from a different place. My heart beat for her . . . do you understand me, Gorlan?'

'Yes,' he said, though his eyes denied it. It's not

something most young men can fathom. He flexed his hands, less white now, and waited.

'She ran into the house and hid. Her mother told her to. A lot of children that age would have panicked and clung to their mother's skirts. They would have died together then.' Makin drew a deep breath and steadied the waver in his voice. 'She hid, but the fire found her. The smoke first most likely, strangling her before the flames came seeking. A kindness really.' His hands made fists and each knuckle creaked. 'We found Sergeant Devid in a fleapit of a village on the borders of Renar. He knew we were coming for him. It should be easy to lose yourself in this Broken Empire . . . but everyone's hungry for coin and we all have eyes on us.' Makin drew a deep breath. 'I threw whisky on Devid and let him burn. He screamed something awful. I don't know if it was him that ordered the fire set . . . I told myself it was. And when the whisky burned off and he lay there black and red and groaning, I looked at him and I felt worse. I thought it would close a door . . . but I stood there and knew they were watching me, Nessa and Cerys, and I felt dirty. I put my sword through him and rode off hard. Took Ellen two days to find me, and she's good at finding people. She's got the sight and nobody can hide from her for too long.

'So here we are, Gorlan. I understand that you were just a lord's boy put in charge of a band of levies, doing what you were told. I understand that killing you won't make this right, or make me feel better. I know that men follow this same path every day, despite knowing all that I know . . . because they can't find it in themselves to let the person who wronged them live.'

'S-so you're going to kill me?' Gorlan asked, shivering despite the warmth of the night. 'Is that why the sword's there? You want me to reach for it, to make it easier for you?'

Makin nodded. 'It would be easier if you did.' He looked around. 'Do you know what this place is?'

Gorlan shook his head. 'No.'

'They call it the Coney Meadows. That's what keeps the grass short, rabbits. You'd think it would be a fine place for cows, what with the soil.' Makin dug his fingers in and turned the sod, deep and rich and black. 'But in the old days, way back when, in the times when men had sharper means of killing than a sword point . . . they fought here and buried their bombs. Thousands of them. Millions. Walk your cattle out here and before the day's done half of them will be scattered in small red chunks, each bit smoking.'

'You brought horses,' Gorlan said.

'I know the paths. Ellen can see what lies beneath, remember? She can see past your bones.' Makin smiled. 'You'll be able to follow our trail for a way in the morning but it goes across stony ground soon enough and you'll lose it there.'

'You said you didn't want to kill me . . .'

'Oh, I want to kill you, Gorlan. That fire burns too hot to go out . . . but it's not raging so fierce now that I can't see past it. I'm going to leave you here. You'll make it home by yourself or you won't . . . and I won't ever know. I can't kill you, not and stay whole, not and keep my daughter's memory a pure thing inside me. But I can't forgive you either. I can't just let you walk away from this. So there it is. As close to mercy as I can come.'

Makin stood. He gestured to the sword, waiting to see if the boy would take it.

Gorlan shook his head. 'I saw you fight that day. For a while I wasn't sure I'd brought enough men.'

Makin pulled his blade from the ground and, wiping it on his cloak, returned it to its scabbard. He stepped into his stirrup and mounted the black stallion he'd ridden in on.

'Don't forget their names.'

'Cerys, and Nessa.'

'And don't ever let me see your face again.'

Makin rode off. Ellen mounted her sway-backed mare with equal grace and followed him, sparing a single and unreadable glance backward. The night swallowed them both.

Dawn found Gorlan shivering in the blanket they'd left him. He got up in the first grey light, mist coiling about his ankles, and began to follow the trail the pair had left behind them. Even in the gloom and mist the marks of hooves on soft turf weren't difficult to spot.

He walked on, hardly caring that any stray step might see him blown apart by fires from beneath the ground. Sir Makin had haunted his dreams for the better part of a year. Always drawing closer – reported here, reported there – a trail of dead men in his wake, each death more ghastly than the one before. And now . . . Gorlan felt himself reborn. He'd regretted attacking the manor almost as soon as they rode out of the vale. His father had told him to convince Makin Bortha to leave. Somehow it had got out of hand, and quickly. He hadn't got off his horse but it was his spear that impaled the wife. A red day – but one that had finally ended.

The sun showed bloody on the hills to the east and the mist drew back as if inhaled. The ground grew dry and stony, gorse bushes encroaching on the moorland. Gorlan had to look harder for the hoofmarks, bending to study each patch of grass.

'Hello.' A knife blade slipped under his chin, a hand to the back of his head.

'Wait!' Gorlan held deathly still. It had been a woman's voice, mouth close to his ear. 'He said he wouldn't—'

'Ah, men say a lot of things, especially high-borns. The nuns used to like to talk everything through six ways before breaking fast too. We weren't a silent order, more's the pity. Over-thinking I call it.'

'Please don't.' The blade rested icy against his neck. 'Your mother—'

'I didn't hunt you for her!' She laughed. 'The thing is – you were very difficult to find, Gorlan. I've ridden a thousand miles to find you and your friends, and I didn't much enjoy it.' Fingers tightened in Gorlan's hair. 'Now one of these days that good man is going to say, "I've changed my mind. Fetch Ellen to me. We're going to track down that Gorlan and kill him proper this time."'

'You'll never hear my name again. I swear it. By my mother's—'

Ellen jerked her arm and pressed hard against Gorlan's head. Ice turned to fire and warmth flooded his chest.

'And I'll say, "I can save you a trip, good sir, because I absolved the young man of his sins that first morning."' Ellen let Gorlan fall to the hard earth. 'Besides, it doesn't do to call on your ma when dealing with a woman whose own mother you put in the grave. You stole that particular bit of revenge from me, and theft is a sin. A deadly one in this case.'

Gorlan felt no pain, only sorrow, his limbs seeming to float, the voice growing distant.

'I do miss her soups though. Having found you I would have slit your throat just for that. Some men hunger for vengeance and yet it offers them no comfort – me though? I like the taste. It feels as warm and filling as a good hot bowl of chicken soup.' She smacked her lips. The last thing Gorlan saw was her left boot heel as she walked away.

Footnote

Revenge is a theme throughout the Broken Empire books. Here we see that the Ancraths don't hold exclusive rights to it. Jorg is characterized in part by a lack of restraint. That can take you to bad places even though each step on the path is attractive. The pursuit of revenge is one such path where restraint is the only real way out.

A Good Name

The scars of his name still stung about his neck and shoulders. The sun beat down on him as it had always beaten, as it would continue to beat until the day came at last for the tribe to put his bones in the caves beside those of his ancestors.

The young man held his name tight, unwilling even to move his lips around the shape of it. He had won both manhood and a name in the heat and dust of the ghost plain. Long Toe had led him out a nameless child. He found his own way back, bleeding from the wounds of a thousand thorn pricks. Long Toe had patterned him with the spine of a casca bush. In time the scars would darken and the black-on-brown pattern would let the world know him for a man of the Haccu tribe.

'Firestone, fetch me water.' Broken Bowl rose from his bower as Firestone approached the village, dusty from his long trek.

Broken Bowl watched his cattle from the comfort of his shaded hammock most days. Men would come to buy, leaning on the twisted fence spars, chewing betel until their mouths ran bloody, spitting the juice into the dust. Half a day spent in haggling and they would leave with a cow, two cows, three cows, and Broken Bowl would return to his hammock with more cowrie shells for his wives to braid into his hair.

'I'm a man now. Find a boy to bring you water.' Firestone had known Broken Bowl would test him. Many of the new men still fetched and carried for him as they had when they were boys. Broken Bowl might only have worn his scars for five years but he had wealth and he could wrestle a cow to the ground unaided when the time came to bleed one. Besides, his father led the warriors to battle.

'Don't make me beat you, little man.' Broken Bowl slid from his hammock, and stood, tall, thick with muscle, honour-scars reaching in bands from both shoulders nearly to the elbow.

'I'm not making you.' Firestone had carried Broken Bowl's water and been his 'little man' for years. He was neither little now nor ready to carry another gourd from the well. On the ghost plain Long Toe had tested him, broken him nearly, left him dry long enough to see the spirits hiding in the dust, hurt him bad enough to take the sting from pain.

Broken Bowl rolled his head on his wide neck and stretched his arms out to the side, yawning. 'End this foolishness, Firestone. The young men bring me water.

When you have fought alongside the warriors, when you have Hesha blood on your spear, or a braid of Snake-Stick hair on your wrist, the young men will carry for you too.'

'You are still a young man, Broken Bowl. I remember when you came back with your scars.' Firestone's heart beat hard beneath the bone of his breast. His mouth grew dry and the words had to be pushed from it – like ebru forced from cover before the hunters. He knew he should bow his head and fetch the water, but his scars stung and his true name trembled behind his lips.

Broken Bowl stamped in the dust, not just ritual anger – the real emotion burned in his bloodshot eyes. Two men of Kosha village turned from the cattle pens to watch. Small children emerged from the shade of the closest huts, larger ones hurrying after. A whistle rang out somewhere back past the long hall.

'Do you remember why they call you Firestone?' Broken Bowl asked. He sucked in a breath and calmed himself.

Firestone said nothing. He knew that Broken Bowl would tell the story again for the gathering crowd.

'Your brother found you bawling your eyes out, clutching a stone from the fire to your chest.' Broken Bowl rubbed his fists against his eyes, mocking those tears. 'Your father had to take the stone from you and he cursed as it burned him.'

Firestone felt the eyes of the children on his chest.

The scars there had a melted quality to them. One of the Kosha men laughed, a lean fellow with a bone plate through his nose.

'Your name is a lesson, Firestone. About when to put something down and walk away.' Broken Bowl cracked his knuckles. 'Put this down. Walk away.'

Firestone carried no weapon; he had a spear in his father's hut, warped, its point fire-hardened wood. Broken Bowl had a bronze curas at his hip on the leather strap that held his loincloth. The larger man made no move to draw it though. He would beat Firestone bloody but do no murder. Not today. Even now Firestone could fetch the water and escape with nothing more than a slap or two.

'Harrac.' Firestone whispered his true name, curling his lips around the sound. Every prick of that casca spine lanced again through his skin as he spoke his name – all of them at once – a thousand stabs, a liquid pain. He threw himself forward, the lion's snarl bursting from him.

Perhaps he was faster than he had thought – and he had thought himself fast. Perhaps Broken Bowl hadn't taken him seriously, or had expected threats and stamping. Either way, when Harrac leapt, Broken Bowl reached for him too slowly, fumbled his grapple, and the top of Harrac's forehead smashed into Broken Bowl's cheek and nose.

They went down together, Broken Bowl hammering

into the dust, Harrac on top, pounding the edge of his hand into Broken Bowl's face. Broken Bowl threw him off. The man's strength amazed Harrac but didn't daunt him. In two heartbeats he was back on his foe. Broken Bowl managed to turn onto his side but Harrac threw his weight upon the man's back as he tried to rise. Harrac drove his elbow into the back of Broken Bowl's neck, brought his knee up into his ribs, pressed his face into the ground with his other hand. A red fury seized him and he didn't stop pounding his foe until the men of the village pulled him off.

Harrac sat on the ground, sweat cutting paths through the dust caking his limbs, the crowd around him an indivisible many, their words just noise beneath the rush of his breathing and the din of his heart. Out of the corner of his eye he saw five men carry Broken Bowl toward the huts. Later his father came, and Broken Bowl's father, and Carry Iron in his headman's cloak of feathers, and Long Toe, Ten Legs, Spiller . . . all the elders.

'I am a man,' Harrac said when he stood before them, with the village watching on. 'I have a name. I have a man's strength.'

'Then why do you not use it as a man?' His own father, three of Harrac's grown brothers at his shoulders.

'I would not carry water for him,' Harrac said.

'Maybe nobody will have to carry water for my son

again.' Red Sky made the sign of sorrow, his hand descending on a wavered path. 'There is no disputing your right to fight him. But you fought as though he were our enemy, not a brother.'

'I . . .' Harrac drew in a long breath. 'There is only fighting or not-fighting. Fight or do not. He didn't ask me to dance.'

A muted ripple of laughter through the children, but the men exchanged glances. Red Sky turned to look at Harrac's father. Carry Iron looked too, the blackwood club in his hand.

'You must go to Ibowen, Firestone. Tell the king what you have done. He will send you back to us, or he won't.'

It made no sense. Why would Harrac's own father try to steal his victory? Were they jealous? Just three days a man and already he had humbled Broken Bowl. Harrac felt the red tide of anger rising in him again. He set his jaw and looked Carry Iron in the eye. 'I will go to the king.'

He turned and started walking, knowing they all watched him, knowing the stories and talk around the fires tonight would be his. Pride and anger bubbled in him, a bitter taste in his mouth. He spat his own blood as he walked, red as betel juice.

A mile on Harrac stopped by the marula trees, anger, pride, bitterness gone, as if it had leaked from him, colouring his footprints. He crouched in the shade wondering what madness had taken him, sore in every limb. He carried no food, no water, he didn't even know the way to Ibowen. West, past the River Ugwye. Not the best of directions. Lion country too. No place for a man alone.

He sat for a long time, staring at his hands, the same hands that had beaten Broken Bowl. He remembered the looks shot his way as the men had carried Broken Bowl toward the huts. A mix of disgust and horror, as if he were a rabid dog rather than a warrior. Harrac's eyes prickled with tears, though he couldn't say who they might be for.

Three days he'd carried his name before disgracing it. One day recovering, two days walking, and just minutes beneath the eyes of his village. Long Toe had said there were deeper secrets to a man's name but that the elders did not teach them, only pointed the way across the years – they were learned, or not, as a man carried his name beneath the sun. Long Toe said the secrets lay in the Haccu songs and stories, and in the way men lived, laid out in full view. Harrac wondered what the king-of-many-tribes would say. If he was sent away he would never know the full truth signified by his true name, earned in pain and suffering.

Ragged Tail, the eldest of Harrac's three younger brothers, came to him as the sky shaded red in the west. He brought a hard slab of bread-cake, a grass bag of lebo nuts, and a gourd of water.

'Broken Bowl has woken.' Ragged Tail watched his brother with wide eyes as if he were a wild creature off the yellow grass, seen for the first time. 'He has broken ribs but Long Toe thinks he will recover.'

'Ribs?' Harrac didn't even remember hitting him in the side. He drank from the heavy gourd. 'You fetched me water, 'Tail.'

'You're my brother.' He didn't sound entirely sure.

Harrac put his hand on Ragged Tail's shoulder. 'Fetch water for whoever asks you. Make all men your brother.' He took the gourd, the bag, and the bread-cake then started to walk.

'You're not coming back?' 'Tail called after him.

'I'm a man now. I can't just say sorry. I have to do what Carry Iron told me to do.'

Ibowen lay further from Harrac's village than he had ever imagined, and the city itself lay further beyond his imagination still. First he discovered a road – a trail beaten into the ground by the passage of many feet, marked with stones, rutted with wheels. Then came the houses. It seemed that a thousand villages had gathered together. It started as clusters of huts made from mud and straw, though taller than those of the Haccu, but before long the buildings became mud-brick, hard-angled, longer than the long hall, taller than a man holding his spear above him. Harrac walked through a wholly alien landscape, without grass, without views to the distance, hardly a tree, everything edges and windows, noise, strangers, multitudes, none of them interested in his arrival. They spoke strange languages here, or familiar ones with strange voices.

At length, following the directions of a man who recognized his Haccu scars, Harrac came to the high mud walls of the king's palace. He circled, tracking around the perimeter, passing dozens of houses that put Carry Iron's hut to shame. The palace gates stood taller than an elephant, thick timbers bound with an extravagance of iron, gates that would stand against a hundred men.

A multitude camped around the entrance: naked children, men in loincloths, priests with bird-skull necklaces and the ia-lines painted red across their arms and chests, warriors with spears and so many honour scars they almost lacked the skin for more.

Two warriors, splendid in leopard skins, ostrich feathers in their woven hair, iron-tipped spears, curved iron swords at their hips, stood by the gates. A man stood in conversation with one of the pair, his back to Harrac as he worked his way through the seated crowds. Where the man wasn't covered in folds of white linen he had the palest skin Harrac had ever seen, white as fish meat on his hands, an angry red on his forearms. And his hair – a white mass of it beneath a broad-brimmed hat of woven grass.

Harrac came closer still and realized how huge the

man was. Head and shoulders above the guardsmen, but both of those were as tall as any man Harrac knew, and this man stood thick with muscle, far broader across the shoulders than Broken Bowl, a white giant.

The man turned as Harrac approached. 'A boy fresh in off the grassland.' The white man grinned down at him, his teeth showing amid a thick beard, cut close to his chin. He watched for a reply then narrowed his pale blue eyes. 'Did I say it wrong? You look Haccu to me.'

'I am Haccu.'

'What's your name, boy?'

Harrac found himself on the point of speaking his true name to a stranger. 'Firestone. I'm a man of the tribe.' He turned to the closest of the plumed guards. 'My headman sent me to speak with the king.'

The guardsman nodded unsmiling toward the crowd. 'Wait.'

Harrac looked back. The people seemed settled in for a stay of days or more, food supplies heaped beside them, shelters erected to provide shade. 'For how long?'

The guardsman stared ahead as if no longer seeing anyone before him. Harrac felt his name-scars sting, his pride pricking him even in this strange place of walls and iron. He stood immobile, held between the angry heat in his blood and the cold fact of his station. Older and more important men than him sat waiting by the roadside: the doors belonged to the king-of-many-tribes. And still he couldn't walk away.

'Ha! The boy doesn't like to wait.' The huge foreigner grinned still more broadly. 'And who does? Especially in this damned heat!' He reached out to slap Harrac's shoulder.

Harrac caught the white man's wrist. He felt ridges of scar tissue beneath his fingers. 'I am a man.'

'Of course you are. Firestone wasn't it?' The man looked surprised, though with his face half covered in beard it was hard to tell. 'I'm Snaga ver Olaafson. May I have my arm back?'

Harrac released Snaga's wrist and the big man made a show of rubbing it. The scars there were ugly – nothing ritual about them – and matched those on the other wrist.

'Snaga?' Harrac asked. 'Why do they call you that?'

'It's my name.' Again the grin, infectious. Harrac found an unwilling echo of it on his lips.

'Your true name?'

Snaga nodded. 'We don't view it the same where I come from. A man wears his name. None of this hiding it.'

'You are from the north. Across the sea. The lands of Christ, where men are pale.' Harrac felt pleased he had listened to the wisdom of the elders at circle and remembered enough of it to keep him from seeming ignorant before this stranger.

'Ha!' Snaga nodded to the side and led off into the shadow of the wall, raising a hand toward the two guards.

132

'I'm from the utter north. Across two seas. My home is a place of snow and icy winds and our gods are many just as yours. The men of Christendom call us Vikings, axemen, and they fear us.'

'Snow?'

Snaga sat cross-legged and patted the ground for Harrac to join him. 'You have to learn to trust me before I tell you about snow. I wouldn't want you to call me a liar.'

Harrac crouched, wary, eyes on the straight iron sword now laid across Snaga's lap. 'You don't have an axe.' All Broken Bowl's cattle and cowrie shells might buy him an iron sword, but not one as long or heavy as this.

'I left my axe with my son.' Snaga's smile became thin. 'A good lad. Big. He'd be about your age, Firestone. When I sailed from home – oh, it was autumn some . . . four years ago now. Odin take it. Four years . . . ?'

Harrac didn't know 'autumn' or 'Odin' – they didn't sound like Haccu words – but he knew about listening.

'Anyway, when I sailed I consulted a vol— a witch, and she told me if I sailed in that season I wouldn't return to the shores of the Uulisk. So I left my axe, Hel, with my son. My father wielded that axe, and his father. I didn't want it to be gone from our people.'

'Why did you sail then?' Harrac had never seen a sea, or even a lake, but he knew the Nola pond that came in the rainy season and it seemed no great leap of imagination to picture it many times as wide with men crossing the waters on wooden rafts. 'If the witch said—'

'A man can't live by prophecy. I had a duty to my clanmates. How many of them might not have come home if I stayed in my hut? How would my son have valued me or my axe then?' Again the smile. 'Besides, I might go back yet!'

'What happened?'

'Sailed too far, into warm seas, lost too many men, got taken captive, taken south, sold as a slave, taken further south.'

Harrac's eyes returned to the scars on Snaga's wrists. The Snake-Stick tribes dealt in slaves with the Moors beyond the north mountains. Took men captive too sometimes. Only the ghost plain stood between the Haccu and the Snake-Sticks with their ropes and markets where men were sold like cattle.

'Did you escape?'

'Your king bought me for his guard. The Laccoa.' He nodded back at the wall.

Harrac knew a dozen stories about the Laccoa. If there were a more dangerous band than the king-of-many-tribes' elite the elders of the Haccu had no knowledge of them.

'The Laccoa has slave-warriors?' Harrac knew they had men from many tribes and even lands beyond the king's domain, but he hadn't heard of any enslaved to fight.

'Not any more.' Snaga patted the sword across his

knees. 'I won my freedom after our first battle. Salash from the deep Sahar had taken a desert town. We took it back.'

'The Salash—'

'There's a better question you should be asking.' Snaga cut across him.

Harrac sat back on his haunches. He looked across at the waiting crowd. Old men playing mancala with wooden boards and shiny pebbles. Tribal warriors hunched under their spears, chewing betel, merchants seated on cushions beside their mounded wares.

'Why is a warrior of the Laccoa sitting to talk with me?'

Snaga nodded. 'Because you have fire in you.' He gave Harrac a narrow look. 'Why did you come here?'

'I beat a man. My father sent me to tell the king.' Harrac felt more guilty saying it out loud before a stranger than he had before the people of his village.

'Was he an enemy? This man?'

'The son of the leader of our warriors. A warrior of repute and a rich man.'

'What was it that made you attack him?' Snaga asked.

'He told me to fetch him water.'

'What really made you attack him?'

'He told me—'

'No.' Snaga slapped Harrac across the face, a heavy, casual blow, so unexpected that even Harrac's speed couldn't help him.

Harrac surged up, toward the Northman, but Snaga planted a hand on his scarred chest and pushed him back without apparent effort. 'Why?'

'Because he was there. Because he was big.' Harrac's face burned with the blow.

'Now you know why I'm sitting with you, Firestone.' Snaga stood, brushing the dust from his robes. 'Because I saw the killer in you.'

Harrac stood too, willing himself not to rub his cheek. 'I'm sorry for what I did. I hope Broken Bowl gets better. I don't want to be a killer.'

Snaga shrugged. 'Perhaps you're not. I was the same at your age, too ready to put my fist into someone's face for looking at me wrong. Full of fire and anger, without reason or anything to aim it at. Young men show the world a fierce face, and behind it? Confusion. Lost angry boys not knowing their place in the world yet. That's just how some of us grow – most grow through it, some die, some are stuck with it. Those are the true killers, blood to bone.

'Killers who fight against what they are make better soldiers than those who don't. Marry a killer's instinct to a conscience and you may not get a happy man, but you get a useful one.' He started walking back toward the gates. 'Come on. We'll see if you've got enough in your arms to match what's in your head and heart.'

'But—' Harrac hurried to catch up. Snaga waved at the guards to open the gates for them both. 'I need to speak with the king. Then go home.'

'Better to serve first – speak later. Our king is not a kind man.' Snaga led the way through the gates. 'His justice tends toward . . . harsh. Go to him once you've wet your spear in his service though and you'll get a more reasonable judgment. Oomaran appreciates warriors.'

Harrac stopped, with the gates closing behind him, narrowing away the world he knew, the path home. 'I'm not a killer . . .'

Snaga came back, put his hand to Harrac's shoulder to steer him. 'My life didn't end the day they put chains upon me. I endured. So will you. Perhaps we'll both go home in the end.'

Harrac looked up at the giant. 'Why don't you? Go, I mean. You're free.'

'Free and a thousand miles from the coast. Lacking money or the skills to travel these wilds. But most of all? I'm a Northman.' He held out his arm and pulled back the sleeve of his robes. Harrac wasn't sure if he was more shocked by the skin, white as the linen itself, or the sheer amount of muscle heaped upon the bone. 'It's dangerous for a Haccu to travel out beyond the tribes he knows. Even in the lands that pay tribute to the king-of-many-tribes there are villages where you would be speared or find an arrow in your back. For me – ten times as hard.' He patted the sword at his hip. 'Not so good against arrows, and Afrique is a land of hunters.' Snaga looked back toward the gates. 'If I'm ever getting out of here it will be in a war party, a small army – a band of brothers, men bound to each other. No man's an island. Not even the ones that think they are. Especially not them.'

Harrac proved himself strong and fast, balanced in hand and eye. A year proved him hard enough of mind and spirit, ready to endure, ready to bleed. A second year proved him ready to kill.

Snaga sat with him one night, their backs against a baobab tree, away from the low fire set to draw in any remaining enemy. They had found the tribeless raiders at noon, a large band of men outcast from many nations. Camped without care, secure in their numbers. They called themselves sand-wolves. Jackals would be closer. Most carried hide shields, machetes, spears. A group of ten Laccoa broke among them having crawled through the scrub beneath grass mats. Snaga led them, laying about him with his heavy sword in a red carnage before running for the casca bushes that hid the rest of the Laccoa.

Harrac had waited among the bushes with his bow and his spear and his sword, a curved blade: only the Northman carried straight iron. He had crouched among his brothers, sweating. Each time the casca thorns pricked him it seemed that he heard his name spoken – Long Toe calling it as he had the first and only time it fell upon Harrac's ears. More thorn pricks, and other voices spoke his name – his father, Broken Bowl, his brothers, a chorus, all of them calling him home, calling him any place but there among the thorn bushes with the sand-wolves racing toward him howling for blood.

He loosed two arrows and brought at least one man down. Another died upon his spear, set into the ground, a longer thorn amid the casca spines. In the clash and chaos of blades Harrac had kept his head, the red heat running in his veins, all thoughts of fleeing burned away. There had been a joy in it. Aloor of the Nuccabi had fought beside him, fat and strong, a clever warrior without mercy. Three Stars of the Haccu had fought on his other side, tall, serious, turning to grey, a master of the sword. Three Stars had fallen, taken by a wild swing of a machete. Harrac's blade had all but severed the head of the man who killed him.

Now, sitting with Snaga against the baobab he felt sick. The visions wouldn't leave him – flesh laid open to the bone, men screaming, limbs parted from bodies, more blood that he had imagined possible.

'You learned a lesson here today, Firestone.' Snaga kept his eyes on the night. He spoke low, amid the whirr and chirp of the darkness. 'It's a lesson that will burn you, but if you hold it close it will make you the man you were meant to be. That's the first lesson – choosing what to hold on to, even if it scars, or marks, or changes, or ends you. We may not understand why we choose one thing to take close over another, but it is important that we do, and keep them tight. That faith makes us one with the gods.'

Only the night spoke, the endless, ageless voice of the dark.

'Do you hear me, Firestone?'

'Harrac.'

'What?'

'My name is Harrac.'

'Thank you,' Snaga said.

Three years proved Harrac ready to sacrifice.

'You should have gone to the king last year. You're a blooded Laccoa. Oomaran would have sent you home with cattle, or at the least paid you a handsome fee to stay.' Snaga scanned the bushland around them. Dust trails rose in several places.

'I wanted to see you go home,' Harrac said. The Snake-Sticks would find them soon. The bush offered many places to hide but the surviving Laccoa left a trail any skilled hunter could follow and they didn't have time to disguise it further.

'I was tracking raiders,' Snaga said, glancing back at Harrac. 'Not going home.'

Harrac watched the Viking and said nothing. As leader of the fifth Laccoa division Snaga had the right to make such decisions, but tracking Snake-Stick raiders for ten days had taken them far beyond prudence, out past the furthest reaches of the king-of-many-tribes' influence. Out to lands where even the Laccoa must tread lightly. The Snake-Stick raiders had led them into Ugand territory and set up an ambush with their allies.

Snaga grinned. 'I always said the only way home for me was with a band of brothers around me.' He looked around at the Laccoa. Their ranks were thinned but the core of their strength remained. 'We made it further than I expected. Another week and I could have shown you the sea!'

'I would have liked to see it,' Harrac said. 'But the gods were not with us.'

Snaga pointed to the east. 'You have the command, Firestone. Take the men and head back. If you reach the grey scrub you'll stand a good chance. When the Snake-Sticks come disperse and make separately to the great rocks we saw after the river.'

'It's a good plan.' Harrac sat back in the creoat bush and ran his whetstone along the length of his blade one more time. 'Why are you telling me to lead?'

'I'm going back along our trail to make an ambush of my own. You know what I can do if I get in amongst them.'

Harrac didn't argue. He knew where that led. He gathered the men and told them the plan while Snaga crouched a way off, scanning the bush. Nine of the Laccoa would not leave without arguing. Harrac sent them to Snaga and the big man held each by the shoulder, speaking softly to them, extracting a promise. They returned one by one. Hard men, killers, eyes red.

Harrac led the band away.

Snaga found his spot a few hundred yards back along their trail. The Snake-Sticks were close now, some still letting their dust rise to spook the Laccoa, others moving with more skill, almost unseen save for the occasional alarm cries of a kessot or the flutter of minta birds taking flight.

Snaga rolled under the skeletal branches of a thellot bush, letting the dust cake him, drawing around him armfuls of the ancient seedpod cases that lay in drifts beneath the thellot. Thus disguised, he lay in wait.

The hunting party came by presently, confident in their numbers, though stepping carefully so as to raise the dust only to waist height. Three slender, long-haired Snake-Sticks led an Ugand war-party, squat men with long thin spears and heavy clubs of knotwood. Three dozen in all perhaps.

Snaga rose silently and ran into the midst of them while a Snake-Stick tracker paused to study the confusion in the trail. The Viking loosed his roar only at the last moment when the majority had turned their heads, if not their spears, his way.

His heavy sword sheared through the neck of the first man he reached, ploughing on to slice the next from collarbone to hip. The thrust of his foot broke a man's knee. He drove his pommel into an Ugand's face then spun, arm stretched, scything his blade through every man within his arc. The dust rose about him, battlefield smoke, the dark shapes of men closing on every side. Red slaughter followed.

Snaga lay on the ground, head raised, resting on the leg of a dead Ugand. The Ugand dead sprawled on all sides, the dust spattered with their blood, reaching out in dark arcs in all directions, too much even for the thirsty ground to swallow. Close on forty men butchered, tumbled in untidy heaps, broken-limbed, red gore spread wide.

Three spears pierced the Viking, gut, thigh, chest. Harrac knew at least two of them were fatal wounds. His own leg had given out, perhaps broken, his eye closed by an Ugand club.

'You came back. I told you not to.' The blood around the spear in Snaga's chest bubbled as he spoke.

'Just six of us. Aloor is leading the rest back as you ordered.'

'How many . . . now . . .'

'Only me and you, I think. Some of the Ugand ran away.'

'They'll bring the other parties quick enough.'

Harrac nodded and pulled himself closer to the Viking, wondering if the other men of the Viking tribe were as deadly. He would guess that Snaga had felled twenty of the enemy by his own hand. Even with the spears in him he had fought on, snapping off the hafts – falling only when there were no foes left to stand against him.

'I—' Snaga coughed crimson. 'I'll tell you a Haccu secret.'

Harrac grinned. He hoped the Ugand would kill him quickly. 'You don't know any Haccu secrets, old man.'

'Harrac.' Snaga had never spoken his name before. He paused as if forgetting where he was. 'My other son is called Snorri. You would like him.' Snaga set a hand to Harrac's shoulder. 'You Haccu with your secret names.' He coughed again. 'But the old Haccu, the wise ones, know this truth.' His voice faded and Harrac leaned in to hear, wincing at the pain in his ribs. 'Your secret names are gifts, to share with those you honour or love – but it's your use-names, the ones young boys are so eager to shed, that say the most about you. The names you wear in full view, simple, ordinary, shared with friend and foe alike. That's where the truth lies. The stories behind them are the stories of where you came from . . . where you're going.'

Harrac saw the shapes of men moving through the bush on several sides now. He reached for his sword, dulled by use, the point snapped off, lost in some Ugand's corpse. 'I won't let them take me.'

'Find something worth holding to.' Snaga didn't seem to hear him, his eyes fixed on the sky, sharing the same faded blue. His fingers gripped Harrac's shoulder with surprising strength. 'Tell my boy . . . tell Snorri . . .' And the hand fell away.

The Ugand broke cover, screaming, and as Harrac struggled to stand a heavy net fell about him from behind. He tripped and fell, roaring. The first of the screaming Ugand reached him, spear raised to skewer him. Snaga's sword carved the leg from under the man. A second Ugand drove his spear through Snaga's neck but the Snake-Stick who had netted Harrac stepped over his prey to guard it.

Harrac lay unmoving, eyes on Snaga, now pierced by still more spears as if the Ugand couldn't believe so big a man truly dead. The Snake-Sticks would sell him north, a prize Laccoa, a fighting slave for some sultan's army or the blood-pits of a merchant prince. Snaga had said his life didn't end when they put chains upon him – Harrac too would endure. The net tightened about him and he said nothing.

Snaga had found him at the gates, a boy-turned-man, angry, with blood on his hands, and he had held to him. Perhaps to replace his own lost son, but there was no shame in that. Snaga had spoken of Harrac, offering guidance, but so often he truly spoke of himself, his own struggles, his own choices. Snaga had been right though. Firestone was the name that said most about its owner and Harrac had worn it without shame before those he loved. Both of them, Snaga and Harrac, were men who looked for something to commit to – something to guard – and once sworn to their cause both would die for it.

Harrac grunted as they lifted him in his net, the Snake-Sticks carrying him, hanging from a pole between four men, the Ugand whooping around, raising dust as thick as their anger. He watched until the bodies of friend and foe became lost. He travelled unseeing now, cocooned in the net, hemmed in by bodies. Perhaps it was like this to travel the oceans, swaying and bouncing with the waves. He had no knowing what lay ahead of him. Things as far beyond his imagination as Ibowen had been when he first walked from his village. Maybe there would even be snow. All he knew was that he would carry his name with him, Firestone. He had asked Snaga how it would sound in northern mouths.

'Kashta, my friend. That's how we would speak it. Kashta. It's a good name. Hold it close.'

Footnote

I enjoyed writing this one. We see the father of Snorri ver Snagason (from The Red Queen's War trilogy) and the Nuban as a young man. We see some similarities between the young Firestone and the young Jorg, and perhaps understand the relationship between them a little better.

Choices

'They say knowledge is power. But I know everything and have no power.' Jane gazed out across the dark lake. Her reflection burned there and the surface threw her glow at the cavern roof, each ripple written in light across the stone.

'You know everything that will happen. You could rule the world.' Gorgoth sat upon the shingle beach beside his sister, the water at his heels. 'Instead we hide among the roots of a poisoned mountain.' Jane almost never spoke. She hadn't answered a question in years, and though he loved her, her silence made him grind his teeth. To find her almost talkative filled him with both hope and fear in equal measure. 'Are you going to tell me where Alithea has taken her babies?'

'Did you know that it is impossible for me to be good or evil, little brother?' She looked up at him, her eyes full of sunlight, her skin like molten silver across which shadows flowed.

'That's not true,' he said. Time had burned its fingers

on Jane and left off touching her after her tenth year. Gorgoth stood twice her height and outweighed her ten times over, but still his older sister awed him. Among all the leucrota she alone was perfect, formed in Eve's shape, not a single deformity. Just the light that shone from her. He had always taken it for goodness – no matter what Jane had to say about it. 'You have choices.'

'I've seen the choices I will make. It's not in me to act otherwise. They are the right choices. But they were made before I opened my eyes to the world.'

'And Alithea?' Gorgoth asked without hope of an answer.

'You know why she ran.' Jane's light flickered and for a heartbeat the cavern's ancient night restored itself. There was a lesson there. Darkness is patient, always waiting for its chance, and swift to take it.

Gorgoth nodded to himself. 'I know.' The boys were changing too swiftly. Every leucrota changed as they grew – save for Jane – but if the changes came too swiftly the child would die horribly and that death would be dangerous for everyone around them. Gorgoth remembered his own changes, the thickening and reddening of his skin, the alteration of his face. At least the poison had compensated his appearance with great size and strength. He just had to look at his fellow leucrota to see the winning hand he had been dealt: no sores, no weakness, no limbs withered or twisted.

'I should go and hunt for her.' Gorgoth stood, the shingle clattering beneath him.

Jane said nothing, only sat, small and bright, beside the darkness of the lake.

A growl rose in Gorgoth's chest. 'Jane!'

Jane looked up, and Gorgoth's pupils narrowed to slits against the brilliance of her regard.

'She's our *sister*, Jane!' Gorgoth kicked a shower of stones out across the water, peppering the still surface. 'You must know how to help her . . . how to help our nephews.' If he found them they would be surrendered to the necromancers, an unholy exchange of doomed flesh to preserve the poisoned flesh of the leucrotas. If he didn't find them, they would die a slower and more painful death, alone in the dark, and some other leucrota would have to be sacrificed to the necromancers' hunger to save the tribe.

'Of course I know.' Her voice came closer to anger than he had ever heard it. 'I have known you would ask me since before you were born, brother. And I have no reply for you. Do you still think me good?'

Gorgoth turned his back on her and began to walk toward the distant tunnels that would take him deeper into the mountain. He paused as he reached the larger rocks. 'Yes, I think you good.'

'When I close my eyes, Gorgoth, every time I close my eyes, I see the future. All of it. And all of the past. A glowing structure of light and air that reaches through the rock, through the mountain, out to infinity. Endlessly complex. Whole. There is no "now" to it. Every part of it is a "now". And I could look at it forever.' She turned and Gorgoth's shadow swirled about him. 'And when I open my eyes I am reduced to this . . . speck . . . this "now", a point of no dimension travelling along a single thread in all that grand and beautiful chaos. And I come here for you, brother. For you and the others.' She fell silent and Gorgoth watched his shadow, wondering, feeling her light blaze across his shoulders. 'One day you will all see it too.'

'You never talk this much!' A sudden conviction seized Gorgoth and squeezed itself from his throat. 'You're going to die soon.' His eyes prickled.

'You're the soothsayer now, little brother?' She laughed. A warm thing. 'Go and do what you will do. Change is coming. For this mountain. For all of us.'

And Gorgoth stood in wonder for his sister had never laughed, not once in all her life, for laughter is a form of surprise.

Gorgoth took Hemmac with him into the deep caves. Hemmac's nose wasn't quite as keen as Elan's, but he was a lot quicker on his feet. Jane had once told Gorgoth the tribe had been named leucrota after the mythical monsters who spoke with a human voice. A cruel jibe from their enemies but less cruel than the spears and arrows that finally drove the leucrota to ground beneath

Mount Honas. The mountain had been bleeding poison from its veins since the Day of a Thousand Suns. Every stream that issued from it ran clear and deadly, no fish or weed braving its waters. No tree would grow within fifty yards of the banks. The toxins beneath the mountain had twisted the tribe, occasionally squeezing out a miracle like Jane, but for the most part delivering children who would sicken, deform, and often die. The bit that Gorgoth had never worked out was why his ancestors were known as leucrota *before* they were driven into the caves.

'This way.' Hemmac lifted his head from the ground and advanced on all fours, sniffing. The raised nodules all along his spine cast strange shadows in the light of Gorgoth's glow-bar. They followed the path of a long-vanished river that had chewed its way through the rock an age before man first climbed the slopes outside. In time the natural passage intersected a Builder tunnel. A bridge of poured stone had once crossed the passage to allow the Builder tunnel to continue without deviation, but it had fallen centuries ago and the supports were now a mess of broken stone threaded with rusting bars of steel.

'Up.' Hemmac nodded toward the Builder tunnel. The glow-bar's light glistened on the sores across the left side of his head. The glow-bar was always much brighter close to Builder tunnels. Inside the tunnels it burned so fiercely it almost equalled Jane at full flow.

Gorgoth scrambled up, his short talons finding purchase. From the Builder tunnel he reached down to haul Hemmac up behind him. They progressed then through the ordered labyrinth of the Builders. In places they picked their way across tumbles of fractured Builder-stone, fallen from the walls to expose the natural rock beneath, gouged by the teeth of some great machine. Here and there shafts led vertically to other levels both above and below. At one junction the poured stone had fractured to expose metal tubes filled with coloured threads and a low voice burbled endlessly from no particular source, its word blurred to the point where the meaning tantalized but could not be grasped.

'Body.' Hemmac sniffed.

Gorgoth tensed, his grip tightening on the glow-bar, anticipating the worst. He saw nothing ahead, smelled nothing, but Hemmac was never wrong. Two more turns and a hundred yards brought them to the ruin of a man, a desiccated corpse tucked up into the corner of the passage as if his last thoughts had been of a tidy death.

'Not one of us,' Hemmac said.

The corpse, ugly as it was, bore no deformity. An empty scabbard hung at the man's belt and he wore a padded jerkin sewn with iron plates. A soldier from the Red Castle perhaps. Occasionally someone would lose themselves beneath the cellars of Duke Gellethar's castle high on the shoulder of Mount Honas, but Gorgoth had never known one wander so deep before death claimed them.

'Mine.' He pulled the knife from the man's belt while Hemmac searched him for coin. A good piece of castle-forged steel was quite a prize. Gorgoth held the glow-bar aloft, eyes hunting for the missing sword.

When the dead man turned his head his neck creaked and dry skin fell away revealing darker meat beneath. Gorgoth backed away quickly, lip curling in a snarl of disgust.

'They came this way.' The dead man's voice emerged as a rasping, like leather over stone. 'The woman and two infants.' His lips split as they pulled back over yellow teeth. 'The young ones would be good tributes.'

Gorgoth raised his foot to stamp the dead thing into silence, then lowered it with a sigh. When Chella had first led her necromancers to the mountain the leucrota had fought them. It had gone poorly. Gorgoth's parents had negotiated the peace. The remnants of the tribe had not been in a position to resist Chella's terms.

Hemmac led on.

An hour later he paused again. 'It's bad ahead.'

Gorgoth could smell it now, the faintest sweet-sour hint. While a low level of the Builders' toxins pervaded Mount Honas, in some places they ran in veins or mouldered in hidden caches. The leucrota could survive high concentrations for a short time but their bodies would twist further to accommodate the new poisons. If Alithea had taken her young sons into such a place their changes would come still faster and still more powerfully. His sister wouldn't have done that though – she was desperate but not insane.

Five hundred yards later they found the source. The floor had given way in an area some five yards in length and crossing the width of the corridor. The glow-bar revealed a corroded pipe wide enough for Gorgoth to stand in, unbowed at over seven foot tall. The shattered top portion lay mixed with rubble along the pipe's bottom and through it all ran a virulent green trickle. The stink of poison curled Gorgoth's nose hairs. It made his eyes sting and his skin itch.

The collapse looked fresh, and if Alithea had fallen in with it then she would not have been able to manage the climb out.

'They're lost.' Hemmac backed away, the sores on his neck oozing in reaction to the toxin.

'They're my kin.' Gorgoth stood at the edge, hesitating as Jane had known he would hesitate. 'Go back, my friend. I will find them.' And, gritting his teeth, Gorgoth jumped, as Jane had known he would jump.

The glow-bar showed thirty yards of pipe ahead, and thirty yards to the rear. A rusty grating could just be seen where the shadows gathered. The boys might have squeezed through the gaps. Alithea could have broken through. But it stood intact. Gorgoth went the other way, bare feet splashing through the toxic stream.

Coughing and gasping, Gorgoth staggered on. Perhaps a mile, perhaps less. His chest ached, the poison burned in his lungs and his ribs seemed to be trying to burst free. Ahead a metallic thrashing echoed down the pipe, distant but growing closer. At last the pipe emptied into a large chamber, the floor flooded, a forest of columns supporting a flat ceiling. Gorgoth's light couldn't reach the far wall. The thrashing came louder here, reverberating through the room, the beating of swords on armour perhaps. Gorgoth dropped down into the still waters, relieved to find they reached only to his knees and that the poisons felt more dilute here.

Gorgoth waded toward the source of the noise. Islands of scum and rafts of decaying matter dotted the expanse of water between the pillars. Here and there thick chains hung from rusting rails on the ceiling. The glow-bar's light swung the shadows of the pillars all around as he advanced. When Gorgoth bumped up against Alithea's body it took him a few moments to understand that it had been a person, and several more to realize that it was his younger sister. The boom of his distress echoed back at him from distant walls and within a few heartbeats the thrashing sounds halted.

The first noise to break the silence was the keening of infants, faint but clear. Gorgoth started forward, splashing through the water, now thigh-deep, creating a bow-wave as he pressed on.

The forest of slim pillars marched off in all directions

with regular steps. In places the ceiling sagged danger-ously between them, dripping slime from dark cracks. In others it had partly fallen and rubble waited below the water to trip the unwary. Gorgoth made directly toward the cries of distress but didn't get far before the thrashing noises recommenced and drowned them out.

Fifty yards further in and the glow-bar revealed the source. The two small boys had scrambled up ropes of some Builder-stuff that hung from the ceiling. A collapse had exposed the veins within the stone where Builder-fire once ran. The boys now huddled together on a ledge in the cavity left in the roof by the falling stone. Below them paced a mechanism of silver-steel plates, built in rough semblance of a man, as the leucrota are. The thing stood somewhat shorter than Gorgoth and considerably less wide, trailing twists of wire below, hung above with strands of slime, some of its plates dented, others pitted as if something had eaten away at them. The eyes it fixed upon Gorgoth when it rotated its head toward the light were grey and multi-faceted, the hands it raised more complex than his own, fingers of metal or ceramic meshing and unmeshing. He had found the ruins of a similar servant once years before, though that was larger, and once Yongma had struggled back from an explora-tion of the deep tunnels with a silver steel skull almost a yard across, but none among the leucrota had seen one still living – if living were the right way to describe something made from cogs and wire.

Without challenge or cry the thing rushed forward, swerving around a number of heavy chains that trailed from a ceiling gantry. Gorgoth charged too, turning his shoulder and trying to toss the creature over his back. The impact was like being hit with a boulder dropped from a height. Gorgoth's weight and strength, unmatched among the leucrota, were nothing. He found himself flung back, the waters closing about him. The cold shock of the water and the hot agony of his arm combined to set him lurching to his feet. The glow-bar rested on the bottom close by, illuminating the area with an eerie greenish light that moved with the waves. The steel creature turned back toward him. Gorgoth tried to raise his arms in defence but only one lifted. He dived aside as his enemy charged again. It would not have saved him but the creature tripped on submerged rubble and its outstretched hands missed their target by inches.

Gorgoth found himself falling too and snatched at the hook on the end of one of the hanging chains. The chain came loose, pouring down through its housing to join him in the glowing water.

Cursing, Gorgoth surged to his feet and splashed to the pillar closest to the boys. Behind him the Builders' construct righted itself and started to follow. Gorgoth managed to keep hold of the chain and swung it, not at the monster but at the pillar. It looped around, the hook securing it to itself, and he raced on, using the chain as an anchor to allow a tight turn about the pillar. The construct pursued but proved unable to match Gorgoth's turning circle. Its feet went out beneath it and again it went sprawling with a splash.

Gorgoth halted, panting, and watched the creature break the surface again, water streaming from its armour. It advanced more slowly, hands raised. Gorgoth wondered if Jane had seen him die here, just as she had seen Alithea die, shredded by the implacable strength of those lifeless fingers. He rolled his shoulders, life returning to his numbed arm, along with pain. The chain he held ran for several more yards and the far end also terminated in a hook.

The creature leapt. Gorgoth swung the chain and twisted aside. His enemy hammered into the pillar with a stone-splintering impact but somehow iron-hard fingers caught Gorgoth's left arm and right shoulder. With a roar Gorgoth threw himself backward. If he hadn't been soaked and hung about with slime he would never have slid from the construct's grasp. Slippery as he was he only escaped by leaving skin behind, and because the creature's pursuit came to an abrupt end at the end of the chain now hooked around it. Red furrows oozed where the construct had gripped his shoulder. The machine itself recoiled toward the pillar, jerked back by its new leash.

'Run!' Gorgoth turned and followed his own advice. He ran in a desperate fury of splashing while in his wake the construct ground its gears and hurled itself after him. The sounds of Gorgoth's flight became lost in a deafening crash. The light vanished and the rush of water sent him sprawling.

He rose in darkness, spitting foulness, his chest agony.

He stood blind, listening. The pillar must have given before the chain did, and the roof collapse must have buried both the construct and the light. Pieces of the ceiling continued to fall, their splashes breaking the silence in irregular bursts.

'Are . . .' His voice, always deep, rumbled out deeper than he had thought possible. 'Are you there?' The boys had no names – you didn't name a child until you knew it would survive.

No answer.

Gorgoth stood, dripping. He had no idea in which direction the pipe lay. He moved slowly toward the next splash, huddled around the torture of his chest. His only hope was to find the glow-bar beneath the rubble. A distant hope.

His feet found what he took for the outskirts of the collapse. As he bent to begin his task a faint light broke out across the water. The two boys crouched atop the pile, thin things, ribs showing, spines knobbled, their skins stippled all over in scarlet and black, marked by the poisons. The older one held his hand before him and all across it the skin glowed like iron in a blacksmith's forge. An echo of Jane's own starlight, but carrying a heat with it, making the infant steam.

A fresh pang of agony made Gorgoth look down with an oath. His ribs were beginning to break from his sternum and push out from his skin. Builder poisons didn't kill leucrota, they twisted them. If he stayed here much longer he wouldn't recognize himself.

In the hot light Gorgoth got his bearings then staggered back toward the pipe. He said nothing to his nephews. They would follow or they wouldn't. He couldn't claim to have come to save them. The pain in his chest passed belief. Any more and he would dash his head against a pillar to make it stop. It was the sort of choice he offered the boys. A quick end sacrificed to the necromancers to pay the tribe's blood-debt, or a slow death, twisted by their own strangeness until it throttled them.

Scraping himself back over the pipe exposed his rib-bones: they broke free of the skin and reached from his chest like a monster's claw. The boys stood in the water below, neck deep on the shortest one, the taller one holding his hand aloft, still glowing. Gorgoth reached down and swung them up. He took the glowing hand and felt its searing heat. Gorgoth could run his fingers through the embers of a fire unblistered. The child felt hotter.

Minutes later the three of them emerged from the collapsed pipe into the Builder passage where Gorgoth had parted from Hemmac. If his sister had matched his height she could have escaped with her children rather than led them away to her death.

None of them spoke on the return journey. The

children strange and silent, the older boy's glow fading until in the last mile Gorgoth led them blind, only the patter of small feet to let him know he wasn't alone.

Hemmac met them at the west cavern, approaching with a pitch torch raised above him. 'Thought I sniffed you coming!' He peered as they drew closer. 'Alithea?'

'No.' Gorgoth shook his head.

'Jesu!' Hemmac stepped back when Gorgoth came into the light. 'It was bad down there.' His eyes roamed Gorgoth's chest. 'You ain't pretty no more, friend.'

'I never was.' Gorgoth met the man's eyes. 'Now it shows.' He had followed his sister on a monster's business and returned a monster. 'Where's Jane?'

'Where she always is.' Hemmac shrugged. Behind him, black against the dance of pitch-fires in the mouths of a dozen caves, the leucrota went about their lives. 'She's down by the lake.'

Gorgoth nodded and led on, taking the torch Hemmac offered. A few minutes later he trudged down the shingle to sit beside his sister. The two boys scampered around them, picking up stones, examining them, discarding them.

'You know what happened.'

Jane nodded. Her face showed no surprise at the changes in him. She had never known surprise.

'You know how I feel.'

'I know what you will do,' she said. 'I don't know how you feel, brother. I should like to know.'

'You were twice the elder boy's age before you showed any strangeness, Jane. And you barely survived the changes. You screamed for a year. Two of the tribe were killed when you flashed over.'

'This is all true.' Jane nodded. 'It is not how you feel though.'

Gorgoth took the castle-forged knife from his belt. He turned it in his hand. His fingers had thickened in the poisoned water, the skin had split and itched miserably. He let the blade catch Jane's light and danced it across the water. How did he feel? 'I am their father now. I am father to two extraordinary brothers whose potential for destruction is unmatched. I cannot keep them. *We* cannot keep them. But what father would ever allow the murder of his children, or raise his own knife to them?'

'You want to be a good man in a world that offers you no choices for goodness,' Jane said.

'Yes.'

'There's always a choice, brother.'

'But you said—'

'Knowing the future has taken my choices from me. I would never steal yours from you. Which is why I will not speak of what will happen.' Jane put a silver hand on Gorgoth's arm, tiny against the width of his muscle. 'But I am proud of you, little brother. Proud.'

'But—'

'Someone is coming, Gorgoth. Someone who will call

you brother when I am gone. Someone who will give you choices.'

Back in the distance an iron bell rang. It rang again beneath an iron hammer. The alarm! Gorgoth got to his feet. 'I have to go.'

'There are intruders in the valley. A gang of bandits. Road-men of the worst sort.' Jane stood. She smiled. She had never smiled. 'I will come with you.'

Footnote

Here we see some of Gorgoth and Jane's tale immediately prior to Jorg's arrival. This story echoes some of the tension in the trilogy about the dynamic between free will and knowledge of the future. How real are our choices? It also presents Gorgoth in a rough reflection of King Olidan's position, faced with similar choices. How much did Olidan know of his boys' future prospects? Did he consider them doomed by their nature and carrying the potential to ruin everything around them as they raced toward that end? Was he driven wholly or in part by Sageous? Or was he just a bastard?

No other Troy

'Why are we here?' Sir Makin asked, following me up the slope at a trot.

'I had a dream.'

Sir Makin snorted at that. So did his horse. But it was true. I had a dream.

There is a walled city that sits amidst the wideness of the River Lure on the Orlanth borders. It rests upon an island of bedrock and covers it so completely that the walls of the city wet their feet in the Lure's currents. They call it the City of Towers and it has never been taken by force.

The last time that the City of Towers changed rulers it was the people themselves that delivered it, overthrowing their lord and opening the gates to the Prince of Arrow. That is unlikely to happen again. The Prince of Arrow was famously good, and I . . . am not. In truth there is little to recommend me to the citizens within those walls. Lord Alstan, newly appointed by the hastily reinstated King of Orlanth, may be a greedy despot, but he is *their* greedy despot, a devil they know. All they know of me is that I am a devil. And that I have hastily uninstated the king, whose blood still shows upon the toes of my boots.

'We can't take that.' Lord Makin turned his horse from the ridge. 'Let's go home.'

'It *is* impressive.' I patted Brath's neck and let him chew the grass in front of us. Down across steep green slopes hatched with fields, across the sparkling waters of the Lure, the City of Towers rose, wrapped in its walls, as if it had been dropped into the river's midst. The early morning sun caught on its many slender spires, turning them to threads of gold, and lit the sandstone expanse of wall and parapet, making something precious that I might stretch out a hand and take. 'A thing of beauty.'

'We don't need it.' Makin looked back over his shoulder. 'Marten has had them bottled up for months already. In time they'll starve and open the gates.'

I could see the rows of tents where Marten's officers were stationed at the margins of woods to the east. Dotted across the landscape the concentrations of his troops and their lean-to shelters made ugly scars. To the west tendrils of smoke still rose from two blackened areas, farmsteads most likely, or villages.

'Bottled?' Marten hadn't the numbers to seal off so large a city. Even with the army at my back we wouldn't make a cordon so tight that determined individuals couldn't come and go. Still, Makin was right, they would starve given time. Hunger would be gnawing at them even now. 'Do you know why they're waiting, Lord Makin?'

Makin shrugged, clanking in his armour. 'It's what people do. People wait, even when the outcome is inevitable.'

'I believe you just described life in a single line, brother.' I allowed myself a smile. 'They're waiting because things may change. It's not safe to stand still in this Broken Empire of ours – not out in the open. Things change. They're waiting because they know that the tides may reverse and sweep us from their walls without them lifting a finger.' I pointed at the city while looking at Makin. Behind him the columns of my army snaked along the valley toward the river. 'That, Lord Makin, is a symbol of hope, a symbol of defiance. All across this land the people of Orlanth are talking even now about the City of Towers and how it holds its own against King Jorg. They will be making songs about Lord Alstan, songs that won't remember how many men of Orlanth lost a hand because they couldn't pay his taxes, or how he had his nephews throttled beneath his own roof. No, they'll be singing about a golden lord, proud among his towers, a man of Orlanth stone resisting the wind that blows from Renar's mountains.'

Makin took his helm off, running a hand up

through dark and sweaty locks. 'Lord Alstan has as many men-at-arms in that city as we have soldiers in the field. They say he's a decent tactician too. I'm not over-eager to fight him out in the open. Storming the walls would be suicide. If they want to wait until they're too feeble with hunger to do battle then that's all to the good!'

'It makes us look weak,' I said. 'It makes *me* look weak. And when you look weak the wolves come prowling. If we sit here for months, locked in place by our fear of those walls . . . the rest of the world will notice, and when we ride back to Normardy, Belpan and Arrow . . . those places will be in revolt. Fear is all that keeps them mine. Fear and certainty.'

Riders came up the slope, four of them, Rike the most obvious, hulking over his poor horse, jolting in that ungainly way of his having never learned any more grace in the saddle than your average sack of potatoes. They drew up alongside Makin, now returned to the ridge. Red Kent came across to me, Brother Emmer and old Keppen in his wake.

'It's big,' he said, sitting back in the saddle.

'Everyone says that.'

He shaded his eyes and gazed at the city. 'Those walls . . . what . . . ninety foot?'

'Give or take.'

'The river's running low,' he said.

I nodded. 'It's high summer.' The river *was* low though,

even for summer. Broad and muddy shores lay exposed, the water yards shy of its habitual levels.

'Walls like that need engineers if you're going to bring them down.' Brother Kent wiped the sweat from his brow, his skin near as red as his name. Only Rike burned worse than Kent. He frowned. 'Didn't you bring a crew of builders out of Hodd Town?'

'I did,' I said. 'And labourers.' I had a conscript force of three thousand workers, strong backs and semi-willing hands aplenty. Among them men who had built many of the most impressive castles to be found between the Horse Coast and the Quiet Sea. 'But they won't be coming. I have other work for them to do.'

'So . . . how in the hell are we going to take the place?' Brother Emmer rode in closer, chewing a toothpick in the corner of his mouth.

'And why?' Rike asked. Looming above me now. 'Let them starve. Loot the bones.'

I returned my gaze to the city. It took an impressive set of walls to make Rike suggest waiting when loot was involved.

'Time, my brothers, is the fire in which we burn,' I quoted. 'A king doesn't govern with troops. No army can suppress the unwilling people of an entire country. A king governs through authority, and that – whether it comes through fear or through adoration – needs to be earned if the throne in question is not one you were born to. This city is the price of the west.'

'I thought we paid that price when the Prince of Arrow broke his twenty thousand on your walls,' Makin said.

'That was the price of our freedom. To earn his dominions I need to do here what he couldn't do to me. I need to break the strongest fortress in his lands.' I knew it to be true. The six kingdoms that swore fealty to the Prince of Arrow would not swear the same to me simply because I wore the man's blood. They would go their own ways, divided by ambitious lords, usurped by lost heirs . . . unless I showed them something. Something spectacular.

That evening I had our tents pitched in the field in front of the woods where Marten had sited his headquarters. The man had taken to war. He had been a poor farmer but as a captain of armies he showed a brilliance for strategy and tactics seemingly absent when choosing which crop to sow and when to reap it.

Marten came to sit with me as we ate our lunch, laid on tables out in the trampled wheatfield. I sat with a view to the east, looking out across the sparkling Lure and upstream to where it divided around the city.

'It's not possible,' he said. 'The Prince of Arrow's twenty thousand would have broken here without the need for genius. Our four thousand would hardly get the bells ringing.' He looked tired. Four seasons of campaigning had hollowed his cheeks and put grey among the red stubble of his beard.

'We would need some kind of miracle,' I said. 'Some great work of magic.'

'Can you cast an enchantment on those walls?' he asked. Not entirely an idle question for in my time I had been filled to bursting with magics. And had very nearly burst.

'Enchantment is one burden I no longer carry.' I stabbed a small fish from my plate, a trout the cook had claimed, from the Lure itself, but if it was a trout it was the smallest I ever saw, as if the fish had shrunk with the river. It tasted good though.

'What about the lead casket?' Marten asked.

'Lead casket?' I paused to chew.

'That you've been carrying around for months on that rather fine piebald stallion,' Marten said. 'The men all think it holds some kind of wonder.'

I swallowed. 'Oh it does. Soil from Kane's Scar.'

Marten crossed himself.

'It's nasty stuff,' I said. Kane's Scar was Promised Land, still burning with the invisible fires from the Builders' war. I'd ventured into such lands in the Iberico Hills. No journey in such a place is short enough. 'But a little poisoned soil isn't going to bring a city down, now is it?'

Marten conceded my point with a shrug. 'I know why we're really here.' He drained his tankard and wiped the foam from his lips.

'You do?'

'She's in there.'

'She is.'

'You could just demand they send her out,' he suggested.

'There are other reasons I'm here too, Marten.' I picked two small bones from the corner of my mouth. 'My armies are not pushed here and there across the map by rumours of Katherine ap Scorron.'

'I'm sure Queen Miana would be pleased to hear it.' He pursed his lips and looked away. He knew he was safe enough to cheek me – though few men were. In any event he was part right. His three thousand were always due to visit the City of Towers. The thousand I'd brought with me from killing a king in Limoges though, those were a thousand launched by Katherine herself. I had seen her face in my dreams, and I had turned north.

'So, no magic, no miracle, we starve them out.' Marten reached for the bread. 'And as long as nothing happens that requires your forces elsewhere . . . the place will be yours by winter. Spring at the latest.'

'I didn't say I didn't have any miracles.' I pushed my plate back and rose from the table. 'Just no magic.'

I stood behind the good captain, still seated at table, with my brothers watching on and the bustle and clatter of camp all about us. I rested both hands upon his shoulders and we looked toward the city. 'The summer solstice is with us in three days. I want that city by then.'

'But—'

'You're going to need boats now the bridges are down. Get every rowing boat and coracle there is, upstream and down. I don't care if you have to send men twenty miles. If there are three planks lashed together, take them. If not, lash them together then take them. A thousand should do.' I smiled at Sir Makin. 'It's a good thing our army is quite small.'

The royal pavilion had been pitched near the top of the meadow, with banners flying above it, the black boar of Ancrath on Renar's red field. I say flying . . . in truth they hung limp in the hot and breathless night. Outside my table knights sweated in their mail, staring at the darkness, beyond them the tents and shelters of a thousand men and more, past that the patrols and scouts that any body of soldiery surrounds itself with, and further out still, the countless checkpoints, spotters, skirmishers, and spies that Marten had thrown around the countryside to throttle the city. And despite all those watchful layers, Katherine came unobserved to visit me in the hot confines of my canvas home.

'I'm dreaming,' I said.

'We both are.' She stood before me in a long, flowing dress the colour of poison, her face unreadable, red hair coiling about her head as if we were beneath deep and slowly moving waters. 'I told you not to come,' she said.

'And I told you not to stay.'

172

She narrowed her eyes at me. 'Must you break every good thing?'

'It is a beautiful city. I see now why they call it the Jewel of the West.'

Katherine shook her head. 'The people mean more than the elegance of a few towers. Take your war somewhere else.'

'When they open their gates to me, I will.' I meant it too.

'Lord Alstan will never surrender the city. I've seen his dreams as well,' she said. 'He will see the last child starve and still hold out.'

'Change his mind?' I suggested.

'I'm not Sageous. I don't have his skill or his lack of morals. In a way I'm glad I can't reach into Lord Alstan's dreaming and change his mind, because it means I don't have to decide whether I should or not.'

'And yet here you are in mine – seeking to do just that.'

'What are you doing here, Jorg?' Behind her the City of Towers rose in flames, the inferno coiling around its spires, the cries of the dying a thin and distant choir.

'Honestly?'

'Do you think you can lie to me?' Almost a smile on those lips of hers. The stuff of my dream swirled about us and she ran its threads through her fingers.

'I've never tried,' I said. 'And in truth . . . I came to save a young widow of my acquaintance. I'm going to take this city, soon, and when I do it will not be a safe place to be.'

She shook her head. 'The walls—'

'Walls are overrated. I'll be through those gates by noon tomorrow. I swear it.'

'You're m—'

But whatever my aunt might have had to say about my madness was lost in a shaking that brought down the towers behind her in a blaze of glory and dislodged me from my sleep.

'What is it?' I asked, the man's wrist in my grasp, my dagger half drawn.

'An assassin,' Makin said. 'Captured trying to approach the pavilion. He damn near made it close enough to cut a way in the back.'

'Good job I'm not sleeping in there,' I said. 'What time is it?'

'Near dawn.' Makin backed out of the two-man tent on all fours. If he'd stood he would have taken it with him and be wearing it like a dress.

I followed him out. 'Let's go and have a chat with the fellow then.'

Makin offered me a hand as I emerged, as if I were an old man needing help. I batted it away. He shrugged and stood staring out across the hundreds of similar tents surrounding us on all sides. 'You should have brought Grumlow. I hate this cloak-and-dagger stuff.'

I tilted my head and yawned. Brother Grumlow was

the closest thing I had to an assassin since we lost Brother Sim in the swamps of Cantanlona. 'Grumlow's a man for knives and fast work in tight corners. He would be wasted on campaign. I had something else for him to do.'

'For a whole year?' Makin started to lead the way to where they had the captive.

'For a whole year,' I said. 'I needed a carpenter.' In the east the sky started to shade toward pale. 'Did you never wonder why we didn't start here, Makin?'

'Here?' He glanced back, the lantern lighting his frown from below.

'Here. Orlanth.' Of the six nations the Prince of Arrow held before he led his strength to ruin in the Highlands only Orlanth and the Ken Marshes shared borders with my kingdom. Arrow had gathered his armies at the City of Towers before marching to face us in the mountains. Even now I could see the Matteracks as a blacker line serrating the eastern sky. The Haunt lay less than forty miles away, the border a mere fifteen. 'We could have rolled into Orlanth first. The city would have starved by now and been ours.'

We picked our way around the embers of campfires, navigating the detritus of soldiery, spears and packs tangled with guy ropes and the occasional sprawled drunk. They had the assassin in a corral, now free of horses, up by Marten's tent. Or at least the tent that looked most likely to have a general sleeping in it. Six of my men surrounded him. The man himself had been set on his knees, bound hand and foot. He looked up at my arrival, eyes hard and surprisingly blue in the torchlight.

The assassin wasn't much older than me, fair-haired, hollow-cheeked, clad all in black, his face darkened with soot. He'd have done better to mingle than to hide. Creeping around in the dark is a poor way to infiltrate any defence. Better to be invited in.

'Anything you'd like to tell me before I have your head cut off?' I asked.

First light found me on the riverbank, upstream of the City of Towers with a small band of regular troops, all seeming somewhat awed by my kingliness. That kind of worshipful behaviour, which comes with the wearing of crowns even if you don't have a string of military conquests to your name, is the main reason I kept my road brothers close. What Rike, Red Kent, Grumlow and the others might lack in manners, wit, eloquence, and aroma was more than made up for by the way they still considered me to be Brother Jorg, just *playing* the role of a king in order to pull off some manner of scam whose exact nature they weren't quite sure of but whose existence was in no doubt whatsoever.

At my behest the soldiers had secured a raft of decent size and had it ready out on the mud just at the water's edge, a good thirty yards out from the earthy ramparts of the riverbank. I rode Donatello out across the flats, the stallion's hooves sinking to the fetlock at each step. He spattered a bit but piebalds don't tend to show the dirt and he was still passably clean by the time I ushered him onto the raft.

I leaned around to look back at the soldiers, still floundering their way out to me. 'Hurry up! I've got a busy day ahead.'

Some came to load open baskets of bread, apples, and cured hams in lines across the downstream edge of the raft, others bearing poles with which to lever the precarious craft out into the current. Donatello proved remarkably docile where Brath would have startled and pitched us both into the river.

Four hand-picked soldiers remained on the raft, three to pole it, one to wave the flag of truce, white with a black dove upon it.

I glanced down at the flag-waver from my precarious seat on Donatello's back. At such an elevation every surge and dip felt like storm waves. 'Your name, soldier?'

'Argand, sire!' He looked up, seemingly astonished at being addressed.

'You know what stops men getting what they want, Argand?'

'No, sire!' He probably *did* have opinions but they were probably wrong, so I didn't press for them.

'It's fear of losing what they have,' I told him. And it's true. The more we acquire, be it gold, power, reputation, or love, the more we have to lose. Fear traps us. We build ourselves a cage. So here I was, risking everything, crown, reputation, my life . . . though that had been gambled on far smaller things many times before. Here I was, risking it all, for something I wanted.

The current gripped the raft and the Lure carried us on. From the banks scattered parties of my own troops watched us in surprise. If we'd tried this further upstream my own men would have feathered raft and everyone on it, but we were well past those defences. Ahead the City of Towers dominated the river. I could see the tiny figures of men at the walls. Perhaps they had seen us too. We were hard to miss, but there's nothing like watching the same scene week after week for blinding your eyes to what's before them.

The men with the poles angled us toward our destination, the broad, muddy beaches exposed at the foot of the great walls as the summer had drawn back the river. Ahead, one of the great bridges stepped across the river in a series of elegant arches, two of them tumbled now, their absence like missing teeth in a friend's smile.

By the time we drew close there were guardsmen aplenty atop the walls nearest to us, a veritable horde of them, bristling with bows, their shouts ringing out faintly across the water. The tolling of a bell began to sound. Marten had said my four thousand might not even get the men of the Towers to ring their bells but here I was managing it with just four. And a horse.

The raft ran aground with nothing but a faint squelch. At my nod the three pole-men started to throw the foodstuffs out into the river. I heard the groans from the walls high above us, turning swiftly to cries of outrage. At the bridge gates Towers men had begun to boil beneath the teeth of raised portcullises. The hams I had weighted to sink slowly. Much of the rest would wash up against the mud before long, and the hungry citizens would be free to grub for them.

I took the flagpole and rode onto the broad and stinking expanse of exposed riverbed. Moments later the soldiers had their poles in hand once more and were working to get back into the river.

I let the piebald walk up by the base of the walls where the beach turned stony. I took from his back a leather bag, full with what a hungry man might imagine to be a good sized melon.

Greedy for space, the city walls had in places been pushed out past the bedrock, their foundations sunk instead into the clay. Even so it would take an eternity of pounding with the world's largest trebuchet just to damage them.

Ahead of me my reception party, bristling with spears, was hurrying down the steps from the bridge to the quay below, now high and dry, surrounded by boats resting at odd angles on the shingle.

I dismounted. Being hauled off your horse never looks good and this was very definitely theatre. The men came churning through the mud, being too numerous to stick to the narrow stony strip close to the walls. As they closed the last few yards I lowered my flag of truce at them to ensure none of them got overeager with spear or dagger.

'Who's in charge here?' I demanded.

A red-faced captain pushed his way to the fore through the mud-spattered and gawking soldiers. 'I am. And who the hell are you?'

'Honorous Jorg Ancrath, King of Renar, King of Belpan, King of Arrow, King of Conaught . . . well king of a lot of places.' I tossed the flagpole aside. 'I'm here to discuss the terms of your surrender.' I raised the bag containing the assassin's head. 'Oh, and I've brought you something to eat.'

They stared at me then, the captain's mouth working but no sounds coming out. Eventually he managed to splutter, 'Nonsense!'

'I assure you—'

'Put this madman in irons.' He glanced toward the river where dozens of apples drifted by, swirling as they went. 'And for God's sake see what you can salvage down there!'

He had to call four of them back to hold me as the entirety of his starving command took off toward the water's edge. The first of those four to reach me grabbed the bag rather than my arms, his greed turning to horror as he opened it and dropped it almost in the same motion. The head rolled free and came to a halt in the mud, staring up at the captain with faint surprise.

Talk of clapping me in irons was of course just talk. Who carries irons with them? Let alone the necessary metalworking tools. Three soldiers began to manhandle me toward the steps, the fourth leading Donatello behind us. The captain cast a longing look out toward his troops wading in the Lure, thick with mud and cramming into their mouths whatever they could snatch from the current. With an oath he followed on behind Donatello, pausing only to retrieve the head.

And a minute later I was through the gates, walking the streets of the City of Towers, just as I had promised Katherine.

We gathered quite an entourage within just a few yards. The business of starving to death is a dull, if painful, thing and the people of Towers had had little by way of entertainment for months. News of an outsider, especially one throwing basket after basket of food into the river, spread quickly.

The people were an unremarkable lot, lean in their anger, dark eyes glittering in faces sunken with hunger. I watched the city itself instead. Tall houses of pale sandstone lined the fine broad thoroughfare whose cobbles I trod. Above their rooftops, in almost any direction you might choose to point your eyes, spires rose. Many of the slender towers reached remarkable heights, challenging the sky.

It didn't take long for the first clod of dried mud to wing my way, followed by stones. Anger is hunger's constant companion. Fortunately anger rarely helps your aim, and the first stone struck the soldier before me in the back of the head. I noted that rotten food did not feature among the projectiles. Nor did dung – there being an unusual absence of horses on the streets. Not so much as a cart-donkey in fact. Not even a scabby dog.

Nothing more serious than an old boot hit me before the captain had me bundled through the iron doorway of a large building resembling a fort and sporting an impressive pair of bronze scales above its entrance. A short corridor and a long search for any valuables I might be carrying led me to my cell. The door clanged behind me and I found myself in a chamber narrow enough that I could touch both walls at once. I had a cracked jug of water, a pile of soiled straw, and a high window crosshatched with sturdy bars.

I shrugged and laid my cloak across the straw before sitting on it. The place smelled of old urine and . . . not much else. Bars of sunlight lit the door and dust motes danced. I settled down to wait.

It took perhaps half an hour before the door re-opened.

'Who are you?' A tall man in half-plate, the captain bobbing about behind him, still flushed, though slightly less muddy.

'Jorg Ancrath.' I didn't get up.

'Jorg Ancrath would not put himself into the custody of his enemies.'

'I had a flag of truce,' I said. 'And a horse.' I shifted position. Straw can be awfully sharp, even through a cloak. 'I'd appreciate the return of both.'

'A madman. I told you!' The captain peered around the man's shoulder at me.

'You expect me to believe you're the boy-king?' The tall man raised an eyebrow.

I pursed my lips, irritated. 'When are they going to let up with this boy-king nonsense? I'm nineteen and married. I'm a good hand over six foot and I've killed more men than cholera. You'd think they could just call me "the king".' I shot him a sour look.

'And if you were the king, what would you be here for?'

'I told your monkey that.' I waved a hand at Red-face. 'To negotiate the surrender of the city. Though if I have to spend too long in this cell I'll be dictating terms rather than discussing them.'

Both men withdrew without a word.

An hour later the door opened again. This time the tall man was relegated to monkey and a blunt-headed lord in velvet jerkin and black trews filled the doorway. Large as he was though, he didn't fill his clothes. Even those eating from golden plates were going hungry.

The new man studied me as I studied him. He wore a thick gold chain of office across his chest and watched me from flat grey eyes with the look of someone accustomed to being obeyed.

'Who are you?'

'I'm Pipo the talking frog.' I returned my gaze to my hands, folded in my lap.

'What possible reason would Jorg Ancrath have for surrendering himself to me?'

'I heard this was a town where a talking frog could make an excellent living,' I said.

'The City of Towers will never negotiate with invaders!' He raised his voice, angry now.

'So you know who I am and why I'm here then,' I said.

'You're not the boy-king!'

I leapt to my feet and Lord Alstan nearly knocked his commander over as he jumped back.

'Enough with this boy-king nonsense!' I shouted. 'Christ! The next time I hear that phrase someone is going to bleed.'

Guardsmen clustered in the corridor behind Alstan. The lord himself had his dagger in hand, a wicked piece of steel.

'You're not him . . .' He didn't sound so sure now.

'I've ordered my troops to withdraw to the southern ridges as a sign of good faith,' I said. 'You just need to look over your walls.'

Lord Alstan backed into the corridor and slammed the door on me. I settled back to wait. 'Can't a body get a bite to eat round here?' I called.

Outside the door someone shuffled but made no reply. I'd had agents start setting warehouse fires over a year ago. One particularly resourceful assassin managed to get into the great grain store at the keep and soak large parts of it with river water. The ensuing mildew and sprouting rendered much of the reserve useless. It's always easiest of course to attack a city's reserves long before they feel under threat. Bands of raiders, some of them rivals to my own brotherhood of the road not so many years ago, had been well paid to drive off flocks, to trample crops, and intercept deliveries to the city. The net effect of all these actions had been far from a crippling blow, but together they had ensured that the City of Towers reached its current level of desperation far more swiftly than many would have imagined.

Thinking about being hungry made me hungry. I sat and stared at my boots. The decision to come to the Towers was, even by my own standards, a foolish risk. Makin and Marten would not have allowed it – which is to say that the force required to enforce my will in the matter would have irreparably damaged our relationship. I'd left explanations and orders for them on sealed scrolls with Red Kent. They didn't have to like what they read, just to do what I'd written down.

A year of campaigning sounds like a risky enough endeavour without marching into a city full of half-skeletons of your own making with just a white flag to hold them off. In truth though I had done much of my leading from behind, allowing myself to be persuaded by my advisors that the would-be king of seven nations would be a fool to storm into every battle, sword waving. Inevitably I would meet an arrow face to face and my legend would end two pages in, becoming merely a cautionary tale for young men convinced of their own invulnerability.

They were right, those wiser heads, Chancellor Coddin's and Queen Miana's among them – but the fact is that I hadn't felt as alive in those long months of campaigning, poring over my maps, issuing orders, watching the flames from a distance, as I did right here and now in a stinking cell at the mercy of my foes.

The door opened again, two guardsmen to the fore, swords bared. Between them, a little further back a woman in a long robe, veiled, her hair golden red within the confines of a hood drawn up over her head. Lord Alstan and the commander stood at her shoulders.

'Well? Is it him?' the lord demanded.

I stood, nice and slow so as not to spook the guards, spread my arms and turned in a circle. 'Is it me, Aunt Katherine?' I paused, a hand to each wall, and glanced at the stonework. 'I told you walls were overrated.'

She met my eyes, hers green and unreadable. 'It's him.'

'Good God!' Lord Alstan looked stunned, though quite who he thought he had before him this far into the game I had no idea. 'Seize him. Get some irons on the man! Take him to the keep!'

The commander took Katherine's arm as guardsmen bundled past her. Lord Alstan vanished quick enough. I guessed he'd heard what happened outside my gates at the Haunt.

I won't say I don't miss being able to raise death and fire to the ruin of all around me . . . but I had been a ship in the storm of those powers, driven before them, and destined to drown. My own resources might be small in comparison, but at least I owned them . . . as far as any man owns or controls himself.

I let my mind wander as the manacles were hammered in place and they dragged me to the yard behind the court prisons. From there it was a shortish wagon ride, hooded and hidden, to the great keep of Towers, the impregnable gaol where enemies of state were traditionally incarcerated before their execution. In the City of Towers hanging was the most common end for a criminal, but more celebrated miscreants were generally crucified, on the basis that it was the closest to Jesu any of them were likely to get.

Nobody came to see me that first night. I guessed Lord Alstan had some consulting to do. Also, if he was considering negotiating he would want it to be perfectly clear which one of us held the upper hand. Also he would probably like me to experience a little of the hunger I'd been subjecting the city to.

The manacles chafed, the chain permitting me to

reach the doorway but not go through even if it were open. The cell smelled no better than the last, a small drain allowing any sewage to trickle down the outer wall. And the stone felt cold despite the heat of summer. But all in all it wasn't too bad. I'd been in worse.

I slept reasonably well that night. They'd left me my cloak and it took the roughest edges off the floor. A dream of endless spires had me in its clutches when Katherine came wandering among them, taller than the highest of them, veiled as she had been when she came to my cell the first time.

'You could have brought your flesh and blood with you,' I said, gazing up at the slender length of her.

'The Towers keep isn't a place that welcomes visitors, especially not foreign aristocracy.' She began to dwindle, the spires reaching up around her. 'Especially not a foreign princess whose name has been blackened by false papers.'

'Ah yes,' I said. 'Sorry about that.' I had been carrying a scroll when I landed, sealed with my royal stamp, conveying both my regards to and affections for one Katherine ap Scorron. The tone, I felt, was warm. Perhaps a touch familiar. And it's true that a section in the middle might be taken by someone of a suspicious mindset as some kind of cipher. Perhaps a code hidden in lines of awkward poetry that didn't quite fit together.

'You must have known they would read it,' she said,

her voice growing distant now, lost as she was among the thicket of towers.

I started to run toward the spot she appeared to have been standing in, pounding the cobbles between towers taller than the tallest tree and so close together that a man might touch two at once with his outstretched fingertips as he passed.

'Why would you do such a thing?' Her voice echoed through the maze of towers. 'Lord Alstan suspects me as your agent. At the least he thinks you a foolish boy, smitten with me and that perhaps *I* return your affections.'

'I am.' I concentrated on her voice, turning left and right, narrowing the distance between us. 'And you do.'

'You're as deluded as Egan.' Nearer now. 'And at least Egan had Sageous to blame for the lengths his madness took him to.'

'All the world's a delusion.' I found her, dwarfed among the thick, clustered bases of the spires. Far above us their sharp points formed a thicket stabbing at the sky. 'You stand in a dream and accuse me of delusion?'

'It doesn't matter how tall you've grown, Jorg of Ancrath, you're still a child.' And in an instant we stood among the clouds, the spires a needled carpet around us, ankle-deep. 'You chase me like little boys chase little girls in the courtyard. Are you going to pull my hair and run away now?' She watched me above her veil. No part of her moved, only her eyes and perhaps her hair, still flowing in slow currents that remained invisible to me. 'I don't return your affection. I hate you. For what you did to my sister, to her child. For what you did to Galen and Hanna. For Orrin. Even Egan.'

'Orrin?' I said, seizing on the one murder I wasn't responsible for. 'The last time I saw him I was fourteen and lying on the ground where he'd left me bloody and beaten.'

'Sageous only used Egan against his brother because he needed someone to crush you . . .' She didn't sound particularly convinced about her accusation either. 'And now you're here, ready to burn and rape and pillage.'

'I'm here in gaol, Katherine. I came under a flag of truce.'

'So.' She fixed me with those eyes, emerald hard. 'Why did you come?' And in that place I knew I couldn't lie to her.

'To save you,' I said.

The next day nobody came. I sat in my cell and watched the sky through the narrow slot high above me. A guard brought water but no food. I doubt he'd be getting much to eat himself.

I passed the time thinking. As a pastime it's overrated. I should imagine those monks who spend their lives in quiet contemplation are quite insane by the end of the first month. That, or just deeply stupid.

In the east – which happened to be the only direction on offer – rainclouds were gathering, dark with threat. Storm clouds. They would be louring above the Matteracks. Over the mountainous border that the Renar Highlands share with Orlanth less than fifteen miles from the city. 'Share' would be a poor description of the current state of affairs. The border region, where the Lure runs its course through the deep gorges cut long ago as the mountains grew beneath it, is known as the Westfast. Lord Scoolar holds those lands in my name, his men hard as the rocks, skilled with both the crossbow and the shortbow. I would have liked to have brought them with me on my long conquest, but instead I left them to hold the border and to drive it forward to the very edge of the Matteracks.

'Jorg?' A hiss at the door.

'Brother Grumlow,' I said. 'How's life as a prison guard?'

'Fecking hungry,' he growled. 'Stomach thinks my throat's been cut.'

I grinned at that. I'd given Grumlow the best part of a year to get himself stationed at the Towers keep. I wasn't depending for his advancement on any talent for prison work Grumlow might own – I'd given him gold. Sufficient gold to bribe his way into pretty much any job of modest status he desired. The art though was to buy his way in with sufficient slowness that it seemed like regular everyday corruption rather than anything suspicious.

'Have you got the key?' I asked.

'No,' he said.

I waited.

'But I know who to knife to get it.'

'Good man.'

'So?'

'So what?' I asked.

'Should I? Get it?'

'Not today.' I lay back, my gaze returning to the window.

'Soon I hope. I want a decent meal. I'm skin and bones, Jorg.'

'And Lord Alstan and his captains,' I said. 'How did they dine last night?'

'I heard they set a fine table at the Lords' Spire last night.' I could hear the hunger in Grumlow's voice. 'Horse steaks thick as a child's arm, sizzling and running with—'

'I get the picture.' He was making me hungry too. I regretted the loss of Donatello. He was a good-looking beast, if a devil to ride. 'And Princess Katherine wasn't invited to dine?'

'The word is she's under house arrest,' Grumlow said. 'They say she's a foreign agent. The boy-king's whore!'

'All good then.' I stretched and yawned. 'Give me something to drink. Something sharp. And stay close. I imagine I'll be getting a visitor today. And sometime tonight we'll have the main event.'

Grumlow made no reply, only filled and passed back the water jug that I had left in the door hatch.

★　★　★

192

The tall commander came to see me as the light failed. The cell door banged open and there he loomed, with a soldier on guard to each side, and behind them, two gaolers.

'What is it that you want here, King Jorg?' Even now he sounded as if he didn't believe I was me. Perhaps when I blackened Katherine's name I undermined her credibility as a witness.

I studied the man. He had never introduced himself but I knew him to be Manos Targen, Lord Alstan's right hand and a capable field commander. 'To dictate the terms of the city's surrender,' I said.

He managed a thin smile at that. He didn't look well, sweat beading on a pallid brow. 'I have sufficient forces at my disposal to meet you on open ground and break your army,' he said.

'We both know that's not true, Manos. But you do have a good number of men under arms. Which is why you should surrender and join my forces. The alternative would see the Lure run red and leave Orlanth without protection after my inevitable victory.'

'I should just have you killed. Your armies would soon melt away once it was known that the great Jorg of Ancrath hung from our walls.'

'Renar,' I said.

'What?' His eyes had a glassiness to them that hadn't been there the day before.

'Renar. Jorg of Renar. My father is of Ancrath.' Manos wouldn't kill me – not any time soon at least – there were too many questions. Was I really me? Why had I really come? What advantages might be gained with me as hostage? 'You don't have the authority to kill me in any case . . . which does prompt me to ask where Lord Alstan is today?'

'Lord Alstan's whereabouts are not your concern.' The note of alarm in Manos's voice gave me all the answer I needed.

'When he's feeling better send him to see me,' I said. 'I'm not discussing the reasons for my visit with lapdogs.' I looked away to the faint glow of the sunset thrown across the ceiling.

'I could have the answers to my questions beaten from you.' Manos stepped back to let his soldiers come to the fore.

'Really?' I glanced their way. Behind the soldiers and Manos a pot-bellied guard held the keys before him on an iron ring, and beside him the other gaoler stood, hands folded behind his back, a smaller man, slight of build, a thin moustache hanging off his lip. 'If you send those two in against me I'll kill them both. Then you. Now run along.'

Manos shook his head, one hand across his belly as if it pained him. 'Madman.'

If he'd called me 'boy-king' I would have been tempted to pull the knife from my water jug and stand ready to stab any that advanced while Brother Grumlow cut them down from behind. But 'madman' I could let slide. It wasn't entirely untrue.

As they closed the door I saw a pink patch of Manos's scalp and there, swirling in the draft, a chunk of hair.

I sat staring at my boots. Imprisonment is boring. I'd collected the chunk of Manos's hair and twirled it into a thread. He wasn't, as far as I knew, a terrible man and I suppose a good man would have felt more remorse than I did over murdering him. I could weigh it up, the needs of the many against the needs of the few. Perhaps in the ultimate scales more lives would be preserved my way, more happiness guaranteed. But I'm honest enough to say that it was the needs of the one that drove me, and in a world where innocents died by the hundreds on any given day, and where justice was just something to be broken and burned, I doubted my own bloodletting would add much to the flood.

I fell asleep thinking of the bible if you can believe it. I thought of the flood that floated Noah and drowned the rest – sent by a loving God to wipe the slate clean. I thought of Nebuchadnezzar dreaming of a golden king with feet of clay. We all have our feet of clay. Even Achilles had his heel. And sooner or later a flood comes that will wash them away and leave us toppling into golden ruin.

'What have you done?'

Katherine came striding into my dream, still veiled, the waters of some great flood swirling around her thighs.

'Done?' I floated, gazing up at her.

'Alstan and his commanders – they're all sick.'

'They shouldn't have eaten my horse.' I drifted with the current. Katherine splashed after me, furious.

'The people are starving!'

'They didn't give Donatello to the people though, did they?' A moon-dark sky slid past above me. 'I came under a flag of truce to negotiate, and Lord Alstan slings me in gaol and eats my horse. It's the end days, I tell you.'

'How could you poison them?'

'Well, I must admit it was difficult. I've tried at least six times over the past year. And the sort of people who can get close enough to do it don't come cheap. But the man has tasters, and his stores are well guarded . . . he even pays a hedge-witch to hunt out those hard-to-detect poisons . . . The stroke of genius was using a live animal. Have none of these people read the *Iliad*? They stand besieged and yet they bring my gift horse through their impregnable gates, and not only do they look it in the mouth . . . they eat it. Common wisdom is that you poison dead meat. I poisoned live meat. The trick was in using soil from Kane's Scar – which is not easy to secure, I can tell you. It pervades the flesh and doesn't sicken the victim for at least a day. The nausea comes first, then hair loss, vomiting, diarrhoea, bleeding from the orifices, madness and death. The difficult—'

'I meant, how *could you* poison them?' A look of disgust on what I could see of her face above the veil.

I stood up, splashing, angry myself now. 'You think

Alstan would have faced me in "honourable" combat? You think it's different to cut him down with steel in my hand – to win because I happen to swing a sword better than he does? You think his death will be worse than any of a dozen sicknesses that sink their teeth into peasants in their huts every day?' In the distance a rumbling could be heard, a deep grating rumble as if the bones of the earth were breaking. 'Your head's still full of shining knights. Sir Galen. Prince Orrin of Arrow. You know what matters about your shining knights? Nothing! They're dead. They're dead because they didn't understand the world, because they thought that honour and fair play were some deep foundation on which existence rests. But they were wrong, Katherine. The world sits on feet of clay just like we all do, and any moment a flood can wash it all away.' In the darkness something huge was rushing toward us. The waters around our thighs began to draw away, swirling down as if they too wished to hide from what was coming. 'I'm the flood, Katherine. It's me. It's not a matter of good or evil. I'm not right, Alstan isn't wrong. None of that matters. Just who is left standing.'

The thunder grew so loud that even in her anger Katherine noticed it. She turned and her mouth fell open. A wall of water, its fury touched with starlight, glimpsed in one moment, on us in the next.

I woke with a start. It sounded like thunder rolling across the hills – but it wasn't a storm. Thin screams began to reach me, finding their way between the spires. The rumbling was too deep for thunder. I felt it through the stones of the keep.

In the gorges that the Lure has carved through the rising Matteracks, on land that is within my borders, there are both narrow places, and wide. There is a place called the Neck where a vein of obdurate granite allows the river barely thirty yards in which to pass. I've been there, stood upon the speckled pink of that stone and gazed back at the broad valley behind it. In my childhood William and I would dam streams at such points, watching small lakes grow behind our wall of pebbles and mud.

To dam the Neck had taken three thousand men nine months, guided by some of the finest castle-building minds of the Broken Empire. The cost had been ruinous. Just feeding the labour force required the spending of the loot from close on twenty cities. Keeping it secret had been a feat worthy of legend too. Lord Scoolar's mountain men had decorated slope and valley with the feathered corpses of over-inquisitive Orlanthians for month after month. The measures to prevent word leaving camp on friendly but loose lips were similarly draconian.

The lake behind my dam had taken nine weeks to fill and reduced the mighty Lure to a trickle. Children build not for the ages but to knock down. Men are just larger children, haunted by different needs, but at their core the same instincts rule. I doubted there had been many tears when the equinox approached and the scheduled time for collapsing the fruit of all that labour drew near.

How far the flood would travel, and how furious its arrival would be after a descent of fifteen miles from the mountains I had no sure way of knowing. Experts offered opinion of course – but in the end it was just words. True, the land offered no real chance for escape between the City of Towers and the Neck. The Lure cut itself a deep valley and its flood plains opened out west of the city.

An unimaginable weight of water had rushed west, faster than any horse, rolling great boulders amid the white fury of its advance. I hoped Marten's men had dragged their boats to high enough ground.

The door opened. Grumlow stood there with a red knife in one hand and a black key in the other, his lantern on the floor beside him.

'Let's go.' I held up my manacles.

He came in, taking hammer and bar from the bag at his side. He had been a carpenter once, Brother Grumlow, who turned his carving skills toward flesh when his own flood bore away the world he'd known. A blacksmith would have had me free more quickly but Grumlow wasn't slow. Minutes later we both left the cell – the corridor outside still empty despite the echoes of hammer on metal rattling down its length.

Grumlow paused by a barred window at the end of

the corridor and, on tiptoe, took in the scene outside. 'Doesn't look any different.'

No wall as thick as those of the City of Towers would fall to the rush of mere water, at least not at such a distance. Perhaps if the gap had been a mile the walls would have caved, the spires fallen with elegant despair. What brought the City of Towers to its knees was greed, hubris if you like. Here and there the walls strayed from the bedrock to snatch a few more yards from the river. Not everywhere, not often, but often enough for the architects I paid to inspect them to note the weakness. The city had its own feet of clay, and in those places the mad tumult of my flood undercut them, carrying away those foundations and the black yards of river clay beneath.

In perhaps half a dozen places the walls followed the terms I dictated and surrendered to the flood. Maybe less than a hundred yards of breach opened up, each with its own stepped ramparts of rubble leading conveniently up to it from the river. It wasn't Katherine's face that launched a thousand boats – I had always intended to break the City of Towers – but it was her who had me sitting chained in the midst of it all. And it was Katherine that saved untold thousands of lives. Having failed in my earlier attempts to eliminate Lord Alstan and his commanders, I had resigned myself to a pitched battle at the breaches and to fighting our way down every street. In the end though, my foolishness had set Alstan's officers in their sickbeds along with their lord, leaving the troops leaderless, without anyone to rally their morale and turn their astonishment to defiance. In such a battle desperation would have had Alstan bring Katherine bound and gagged to some high place and led him to test the truth of the rumours. A different kind of desperation would have led him to the same place if I'd starved them out – and in the end I would have had to choose between the city and her life.

Marten and Makin attacked on two fronts and within hours the city lay in our hands. The largest body of Towers' troops had surrendered beneath my own flag of truce, liberated from the high court stores to serve its intended purpose once again.

'You mad bastard.' Makin found me in the King's Spire, watching the view from Lord Alstan's high seat, a moon-dark city lit by innumerable small fires. He came at me as if he hadn't yet decided whether to hug me, hit me, or pitch me over the balcony into the long fall.

I shrugged. 'I was never built to last, Lord Makin. You should know that by now.'

He faltered at that, a yard from the throne, eyes bright with sorrow. 'No good thing is,' he said. 'No wild thing. No thing that burns bright.' He wasn't thinking of me. A lost child haunted him. All of us have our ghosts that follow at our shoulder. Pause for a moment and they catch you up.

'You're letting them go?' I asked.

'As you ordered, anyone that wants to leave gets a boat,' he said. 'Though why I don't understand. The opportunities for ransom . . .'

I waved the suggestion off. Katherine would be gone into the night. No good thing was made to last and certainly nothing as tenuous and ephemeral as that which hung between the two of us, never more real than when denied, but I wasn't ready to kill it. Not yet. Not this day.

'And where is the captain—'

Marten pushed his way in before I'd finished asking after him. He wore the day – soot, mud, blood – all smeared across a torn grey cloak.

'Jorg of Ancrath . . .' His mouth worked, seeking some insult large enough to cover the enormity of my stupidity. And failing to find one settled for that eternal question that never fails us. 'Why?'

And I gave the only answer I had in me. 'What other Troy was there for me to burn?'

Footnote

I get messages about the Broken Empire books. Lots of them. Most are back-slapping and much appreciated. Writing's a solitary job and it's great to get an atta-boy. Some are of the 'Why didn't' variety, and the most common of those are (to paraphrase) 'Why didn't Jorg do a boss-battle with his father?' and 'Why didn't Jorg and Katherine get together?' The answer in both cases is complex as the books weren't planned but came off my fingertips essentially full-formed. However, part of the answer, is definitely: Because these books are different. Many readers <u>expected</u>

those things to be delivered, almost as if the genre demanded them. And how could they ever be anything but an anti-climax?

Moreover, much of Jorg's story is about shades of grey, about how life often doesn't deliver us what we want, or need, or feel we deserve, no matter how skilled we may be at taking it. Not only is revenge an empty meal no matter what temperature it's served at, it is also a meal that is not guaranteed to us outside of storybooks, no matter how valid our claim or desire for it.

Similarly in matters of the heart, just because it's a story the writer has made no pact with the reader that any love, romance, or obsession will ultimately be requited. Life is messy. Circles are left unclosed. Words remain unsaid. Temptations untried.

I wanted, even in a story of swords and sorcery, to say something true. How could I do that by lying to you?

The Secret

The moon shows her face and Sim crouches, low to the ground. On the castle walls, on the high towers, a dozen pairs of eyes hunt the darkness of the slopes outside, but only the wind finds Sim, tugging at his cloak, keening in his ears. He studies the battlements, the sheer expanse of stonework, the great gatehouse hunkered above the heaviest of portcullises. When the time comes he'll be fast. But now he waits. Sinking the teeth of his patience into the problem, watching how the guards move, how they come and go, where they rest their eyes.

'Every good story tells at least one lie and holds a secret at its heart.'

The young man kept his head so still as he spoke that Dara thought of the statues in her father's hall. She watched his lips form the words, her gaze drawn by their motion amid the stillness of his face. All part of the storyteller's art, no doubt.

'The secret of this story hides in darkness, trapped behind the eyes of an assassin.'

Dara let her gaze stray from Guise's mouth to encompass the rest of him, slight within his teller's tunic, buttoned to the top, his velvet tricorn rakishly askew, features fine, the light that had first lit her up still burning in those grey eyes.

'Sim, they called him. Perhaps it was his name. Assassins wear such things lightly. In any event Sim had been his name since the brotherhood took him in.'

'A brotherhood? Was he was a holy man?' Dara knew the pope kept assassins – the best that money could buy.

Guise smiled. A true storyteller doesn't bridle at questions. When questions are not welcome the story will not allow its audience to speak. 'A holy man? Of a kind . . . He offered absolution, dealt in peace. Steel forgives all sins.'

When Guise smiled Dara's heart beat faster and the lingering worry retreated. If her father discovered she'd sneaked a man into her rooms, a mere commoner at that, he would double the guard – though she doubted the walls would hold more soldiers – have the bars at her window shackled together so no illicit key would open them, and worse, he would talk to her. He would summon her before the chair from which he spoke for all of Aramis and treat her not like a child but worse, like an adult in whom his trust had been misplaced. She would have to stand there, alone in that echoing expanse of marble, and explain the knotted curtain pulls she'd lowered as a rope, the alarm she'd had Clara raise to distract the guardsmen from their patrols . . .

'Brother Sim took his work seriously. The taking of a life is a—'

'Was he handsome, this Brother Sim?' Dara stretched on the couch, a languid motion, hot and sultry as the night. She felt sure a storm was building, the treetops in the gardens had been thrashing in a humid wind when she opened the window for Guise, rain lacing the breeze. It would break soon. The distant thunder would arrive and make good on its threats.

Dara half-rolled to face the storyteller. He leaned forward on his small chair, the story scroll unopened on his knee. Around his wrist he wore her favour, a silk handkerchief, embroidered with flowers and tiny glass beads.

'Was he handsome? Was he tall, this Sim?' she asked.

'Ordinary,' Guise told her, 'unremarkable. The kind of face that might in the right light be anyone. Handsome in one instant, in the next forgettable. He stood shorter than most men, lacking the muscle of a warrior. His eyes though – they would chill you. Empty. As if he saw just bones and meat when he looked your way.'

Dara shuddered, and Guise unrolled his scroll, fingertips floating above the characters set there, dark and numerous upon the vellum, crowded with meaning. 'To find out why Sim watched those walls we have to journey, first many miles to the east, and then back through the hours and days until we find him there.' Guise raised his voice, though still soft, for the guards outside the door mustn't hear him, and as he lifted his hand from the page, the story bore her away.

Brother Sim waited, for that is what assassins must do. First they wait for their task, then for opportunity. The brotherhood had made camp in the ruin of a small fortress, amid the wreckage and char-stink of whatever battle had emptied it. Sim had sought out the highest tower, as was his wont, and sat upon the battlements, staring at the place where the road that had brought them became compressed between sky and land and vanished into a point. His legs dangled above a long drop.

'A name has been given.' Brother Jorg spoke behind Sim. He'd climbed the spiral stair on quiet feet.

'Which name?' Sim still watched the road, leading as it did back into the past. Sometimes he wondered about that. About how a man might retrace his steps and yet still not return to the place he'd come from.

And Brother Jorg spoke the name. He came to stand by the wall and set a heavy gold coin beside Sim. In a brotherhood all brothers are equal, but some are more equal than others, and Jorg was their leader.

'Find us on the Appan Way when this is done.' He turned and descended the steps.

Assassination is murder with somebody else's

purpose. Sim reached for the coin, held it in his palm, felt the weight. Coins hold purpose, bear it like a cup. A murder should always carry a weight, even if it's only the weight of gold. He turned the coin over in his scarred fingers. The face upon it would lead him to his victim.

Sim rode from the fort, beneath the gutted gatehouse, his equipment stowed, his weapons strapped about his person. The brothers saw him go and made no comment. Assassination is lonely work. They each feared him in their way. Hard-bitten men, dangerous with a sharp edge or a blunt instrument, but they feared him. Everyone sleeps after all. Every man is vulnerable.

Sim slowed his horse to a walk and set out along the trail that would bear him to a larger way, and thence to the Roma Road that led to Aramis. There was no haste in him, no eagerness. The assassin requires no passion – his work is not artistry, simply efficient. The very best assassin is no warrior, he doesn't achieve his ends through skill at arms. Instead he must know people, he must understand them, intimately. Sometimes it's the people who stand in his way whose skin he must inhabit, sometimes the victim themselves.

Sim found an apple in his pocket, wizened but still sweet, and took a small bite, leaving a precise wound. The catch of course is that knowing the full depth of any human, knowing their hopes and frailties, the hurts of their past, the tremor with which they reach for the future . . . that knowledge is akin to love.

'Do you think that's true, Guise?' Dara asked the question into the pause the young man left. 'Because who knows people better than a storyteller?' She drew herself up on the couch so that she sat opposite him, their knees almost touching. 'You make your living telling our tales. And so many of them are about princesses . . . you must know *us* very well.'

They shared a knowing smile, close enough now that Dara could see the rain's moisture still clinging to his hair. Dara laid her hand upon his knee. She could guess how this night's story would end. She had invited him to her chamber for more than old tales. Guise set his fingers above the symbols on the scroll, and began to speak again, not looking down but holding her gaze, as if he could read the story by drawing the words up through his hand.

'Sim sat and waited and watched, as he had sat and waited and watched on each of ten previous nights, sometimes at the walls, sometimes in the city that washed up around the barren mount upon which the castle squatted. Always he listened, learning what could be learned, presenting a new face to each night, seeking his way in.'

Dara frowned. 'This Brother Sim came to Aramis to

murder the man whose face was on the coin?' She shot Guise a sharp look. 'My father—'

'Or some grandsire of his, my princess? Or perhaps just someone who might be found wherever the king might be? Or maybe Hertog the Second, that fearsome warlord who died in mysterious circumstances and whose brother, Jantis, inherited Aramis's throne three centuries back? Jantis proved somewhat inept in the business of armies and wore the crown for just two months before your family disposed of him upon the battlefield . . . Give the story space and it will tell itself.'

Dara settled back, embarrassed at her outburst. Had she spoiled the secret – was the story how her line came to reign in Aramis?

'We were discussing love, Princess Dara. The perfect assassin, the one who can reach anyone, anywhere, needs to know his target intimately, and such knowledge breeds love. So there lies a dilemma. The perfect assassin needs to be able to kill the thing he loves – or rather to understand the emotion but not let it stay his hand.'

Sim never stayed his hand – always seized his moment. When some alarm within the castle turned the guards from the battlements he advanced to the base of the wall, swift but smooth. He threw his padded grapple and the thin rope snaked out behind it. Within heartbeats he was climbing, drawing himself up along a line chosen after long inspection toward a section where he stood least chance of being observed.

Arms burning, he reached the battlement and crossed the parapet on all fours, quick as an eel, kicking free the grapple behind him and dropping into the tree he knew stood close to the wall at that spot. Below him the gardens seethed in the newly-risen wind. The castle walls enclosed several acres of garden, set to trees, shrub and bush, capturing a manicured hint of the wildwoods in which the nobility of Aramis so loved to hunt.

Sim waited, high in the arms of the elm, waited for whatever commotion had drawn the guardsmen's attention within the walls to die away. The wound on the heel of his palm had started to bleed again. He'd killed seasoned veterans without taking a scratch and somehow let a church librarian slice him with a letter opener. A half-inch lower and it would have opened the veins in his wrist, cut tendons perhaps. He touched his fingers to the wound and while he waited, cradled in the treetop, he let the recollection of the incident unfold behind his eyes.

The librarian, Jonas, had proved useful in the end – providing maps from the days of the castle's construction and reading out the legends in a tremulous voice. A fair exchange all told. And when his store of information ran dry they sat looking at each other, the young man and the old.

'Brother Jorg said he might teach me to read,' Sim told the churchman, folding the ancient map and slipping it into an inner pocket. 'But he says a lot of things.' Sim withdrew his hand and turned it over to reveal the short throwing knife on his palm, below it the cut Jonas had scored across him which still bled. It had been instinctive, a lashing-out in fear as he turned from the table bearing his correspondence and a paperknife only to be surprised by Sim standing at his shoulder. 'It's a beautiful piece isn't it?' Sim turned his hand to let the candlelight slide along the blade. The weapon felt good in his hand, familiar. Strange to take comfort in the sharp edge of a little cross-knife, an instrument of pain and death . . . but he supposed the crosses that the faithful took their own comfort in were symbols of an instrument far crueller than his knife.

Sim slipped the blade between his middle fingers so an inch protruded like a gleaming claw, and with a swift motion cut Jonas's throat. He caught the older man's head then, and held it, despite the thrashing, whispering into his ear, loud enough to be heard above the gurgles, but quiet enough that only they two would share the words.

'What did he say?' Dara slid from the couch to sit at Guise's feet. His suede boots were streaked with mud from his journey through the gardens.

'That's the secret, princess.'

'You will tell me though?' She looked up at him, arching her brows.

Guise met her gaze. 'Of course. Before the end.

Nobody's story should end with the secret untold.' He returned his eyes to the scroll before him. The low rumble of thunder reached them, vibrating in Dara's chest.

Sim waited in the tree, ripe with a purpose that was not his own. Many years before, his mother had tied all his purpose to a single coin, a lifetime ago, back when he'd been too young to know he was being sold. The brothel had taken him and held him until that day when the brotherhood came with blood and fire and, seeing in him a different value, took the boy into their number. He'd been fourteen when they gave him a new life, and in the years since he'd come to accept a leader's direction to replace his own spinning compass. Though for each death he took a coin, perhaps hoping in some deep and unspeaking recess of his mind that the coin his mother once accepted would find its way to his hand, and give him back to himself.

When Sim's moment came he dropped, cloak fluttering behind him, two feet striking the back of a guardsman's neck. The man fell nerveless into a bush while Sim launched himself onto the second guard, punch-knife in hand. In a heartbeat only Sim remained upright. He dragged the second man into the bush that had received the first and, while all around him the leaves seethed beneath the wind, Sim whispered the secret to the men as their last moments came and went.

Beneath the shelter of the tree Brother Sim changed into his disguise. By the time he'd done up the last button a cold rain had begun to fall and the dark gardens bent and dripped. He advanced on the tall towers, the royal apartments, pausing only to set in place his equipment within the shrubs that marked the gardens' perimeter.

'You didn't just come here to tell stories did you, Guise?' Dara moved her hand upon the young man's knee, feeling the firmness of his thigh. A flicker of lightning lit the room, mocking the lamps' illumination for a second, and burning in the storyteller's eyes. Three times in the past week she'd seen him in the houses of nobility, declaiming from the petty-stage to entertain the diners. Something about him had drawn her gaze, an almost delicate beauty, and he'd returned her frank attentions with something ambiguous, something more tempting than lust or admiration. At Lord Garzan's presentation of suitors Dara had paid more mind to the storyteller than to the lordlings and minor princes her father had invited to seek her hand. Her father might have grand politics at the front of his thinking – alliances waiting to be sealed. Dara however had more immediate desires to satisfy and felt if she were to be sacrificed into some arranged marriage she may as well have a little fun first.

She'd thrown Guise her favour when his story ended and sent her maid Clara to arrange their current assignation. The maid had returned looking as flushed as Dara felt, and confirmed that Guise would dare the walls for a chance to meet the princess if she would provide sufficient distraction to give him the opportunity to reach her without being filled with spears . . . And here he was, in the flesh. Firm beneath her hand and far more real than stories. Far more interesting. Thunder rolled outside, deep-voiced and raw. She leant closer still. 'You came for more than stories.'

'I did, princess. I'm not just here to tell stories, no.' Guise took her hand in his and stood from his chair. 'It was on a night like this, in the gardens of this very castle, that Brother Sim murdered his way toward the high towers of Aramis.' He led her to the window where he'd clambered into her chamber not an hour before. 'Bloody-handed Sim came, leaving the bodies of half a dozen men in his wake.' Guise slid an arm about her shoulder and she shivered beneath his touch as he guided her to stand beside him and watch the rain fall through the darkness. He held out his other hand to catch the drops, steering her gaze.

'Is that— Is there—?' Something caught her eye, still adjusting to the dark, something among the vegetation flailing beneath a storm wind . . . something darker . . . almost . . . man-shaped. A lone guardsman?

'I—' Lightning flashed again and amid the shocking green Dara saw a black figure, ragged and tall, half-emerging from the bushes that stood between the inner court and the gardens. The crash of thunder drowned her scream. 'Oh God! It's him!'

215

'What?' Guise stepped back, staring at her. 'What did you see?'

'Someone— Someone's out there.' She clung to his shoulder, heart thumping.

Someone pounded on the door, scarcely louder than the thunder in her chest. 'Your highness?' The handle rattled but she'd bolted it earlier, before Guise climbed the rope.

'Tell him,' Guise whispered. 'If you saw someone.'

'I'm fine,' she called out. 'I— I saw a man in the grounds, not a guardsman or one of the staff. I got scared.' She sat in the chair Guise offered, trembling in her limbs and unsteady.

'I'll order a search, princess.' The guardsman's voice through the door – Captain Exus. 'I'll leave Howard to guard your chamber. Please set the main bolts.'

'I'll do it,' Guise whispered, and he hurried to push the two heavy bolts home into their housings. From beyond the door the sound of boots on stairs as her guardsmen hurried down to initiate the hunt. Dara felt safe now. The door would keep an army at bay and Howard would take some getting past too.

'I think the story's over.' Guise returned to her, easing the tension in her shoulders with an expert touch.

'But you never got to the lie or told me the secret,' Dara said, craning her neck to look back at him, behind the chair.

Guise shook his head, a sad smile on his lips. When

he passed the cord beneath her chin she thought for a moment that it was a necklace, a gift.

'I'm the lie.' A moment later the cord tightened choking the question off her lips. Her hands went to her neck and all thought narrowed to a single aim, a single goal, to draw another breath. And into that moment of silent, terminal panic Sim whispered the secret.

Sim crouched behind the chair, safe from any clawing hands, hauling on the curtain cord until Dara's struggles ceased. Even then he kept the pressure, rising with the cord knotted between his straining hands. He knew how long it takes to kill someone in such a manner. The garrotte would have been quicker, but bloody, and his escape would be safer if he kept clean. In any case a wire seemed wrong for so royal a throat. Silk seemed . . . apt . . . for nobility.

Eventually Sim let the cord go, allowing the princess's corpse to flop forward, hiding her purple face, blood-filled eyes, protruding tongue. He took from his bag a copy of the royal servants' tunics and hose, changing into it quickly but without haste. He removed Dara's favour and hid the wound on his wrist beneath the cuff of his new uniform instead. A long blonde wig and a touch of rouge delicately applied with the help of a hand mirror to achieve the desired effect, and Sim looked every bit the serving-girl. Disguise had always come easy to him. His childhood had served him well: when your sense of self is taken it grows easier to become someone else, when you sell affection it becomes easier to both understand love and be unmoved by it. The brothers had seen the killer in him at fourteen – he wondered how people less used to murder managed not to see it until it was far too late.

Sim straightened and went to the door. A device of one water bladder dripping into another acting as a counterweight had raised the rag figure amid the bushes. It would not take long to find and the guardsmen would return soon enough.

A drop of oil applied to the heavy bolts allowed each to be drawn back without alerting the guard outside. A couple more oil drops for the hinges and Sim set his four-inch punch-spike in hand. He pulled the door open in a smooth motion and drove the steel into the back of Howard's neck, bringing him down in a clatter of useless armour.

Once Howard had been hauled into the room Sim collected the dining tray from Dara's chamber and closed the door behind him. The tower guard were thinned by Dara's alert; and, suitably attired for one wishing to pass unremarked along the corridors of power, Sim took his leave.

He had served his purpose, the coin's purpose, Brother Jorg's purpose. Brother Jorg whom he both hated and loved. Brother Jorg who found direction everywhere he looked, as if it bled between each word he spoke. And, with his task complete, once more Sim had a free choice of path. As free a choice as ever he'd been given in his eighteen years.

Half an hour later, on a dark and rainswept highway with a good horse beneath him, Sim made his decision, pulling the reins once more toward the Roma Road that would bear him east and south toward the Appan Way, toward his brothers, toward another coin, another duty, toward the clarity of purpose in a world so lacking in direction.

In his wake, torn and flapping in the mud, the story scroll, its incomprehensible symbols smeared by rain, words and meaning running together, soaking away.

The story is done. Be glad that it wasn't yours and that for you the lie is still untold, the secret still unspoken.

Footnote
Although the plot here is more complex than some of the other stories in this volume, the story itself is fairly simple. If there is any depth it's in the nature of leadership, where the value of certainty is often held higher than the need to be correct.

Escape

In Orlanth there's a popular song that will get you killed if a kingsman hears it on your tongue. Properly the punishment is just the standard one for sedition of any flavour. The aforementioned tongue is cut out. But that will kill a man often as not, what with the blood loss, the choking, and the likelihood of infection. Even so, sing 'The Merchant's Gold' too loudly or in the wrong place and it's likely a kingsman will just put his sword through you then cut your tongue out as an afterthought.

The 'merchant' referred to in the chorus is, strictly speaking, a count, but as verse three points out, Count Merren purchased his title, and a merchant who purchases his title is still a merchant. Verse four is the killing verse, though. It says that Orlanth has a king, but that it also has an owner. And that these two titles are not held by the same man.

'Othello! New meat for you.' Sorrel Tarn at the doorway, ledger in hand, inkstains on his fingers.

Kashta looked up from his sword, polishing rag still in hand, whetstone on the table before him. He had carried the new name they gave him for many years now and whilst, like the chains he once wore, it had never become comfortable, it no longer chafed. They had never asked his true name nor would he have given it if they had.

He returned sword to scabbard, checked his uniform, and followed Sorrel from the barracks room down through the long corridors of Count Merren's fortress palace to the training yard behind the guards' stables. His years in the count's bodyguard had built Kashta into a formidable warrior both in physique and skill. Heads turned as he passed and he wore his reputation with a degree of pride.

Sorrel led the way out into the blustery day. It had taken longer for Kashta to adjust to the cold of these northern climes than it had to become accustomed to their barbarous customs and terrible food.

'More Moors.' Sorrel waved a hand at the two young men shivering before them, both hugging themselves against the wind. Five of the gate guard watched on though both men stood in fetters. 'All yours.'

'Gratitude, Sorrel Tarn.' Kashta inclined his head toward the little scribe as he strode away across the courtyard. To the scribe any man with a brown skin was a Moor. Most in the count's employ shared his ignorance though some had it that they were all of Nubia, as if Afrique were an island inhabited by a single people.

The pair before Kashta were not of any tribe he recognized. The tall one bore ritual scars but in no pattern Kashta had ever seen, circles of radiating lines, each ring of a different size and seeming randomly placed. The other man stood broader, darker-skinned, and wholly unmarked save for an old wound stretching across his ribs.

'Do you speak the Empire tongue?' Kashta asked them, with little hope. They would have been sold from the Afrique coast to merchants of the Horse Coast or Port Kingdoms only weeks before.

'A little.' The taller one with circle scars. He looked perhaps eighteen, a man of his tribe but a young one. The other stared without comprehension.

'Do you speak his tongue?' Kashta nodded to the other.

'No.' The boy shook his head. 'We both have a few words of Hutsi.'

'They call me Othello,' Kashta said. 'I am commander of the count's personal night guard. I will oversee your training, and if you prove yourself in all the required ways, you will serve to protect our master too.'

The boy's eyes widened in surprise. 'I am River-Stone, he is Oltoo.' He glanced around as the gate guard took their cue to leave. 'Why would the chief of such a place want me to keep his enemies from him?'

'Follow me.' Kashta led the way, setting off around the perimeter of the training ground. A squad of wall guards was entering from the west gate to train under Gremmon, one of their captains. The two young men shuffled along behind in their chains. Kashta imagined they were exchanging glances. River-Stone perhaps sizing him up from the rear, considering how easy it might be to fell him with a blow to the back of the neck. He had that kind of fire in his eyes.

Kashta took them to the blacksmith. The forge lay in an outhouse in the trade yard. Both the new purchases watched everything with wide eyes, seeming to be constantly amazed. Kashta had been the same when they had brought him to the fortress, though his journey had taken him several months and through the hands of half a dozen masters. The count's man had bought him from the fighting pits of Verdone and Kashta had arrived at Fort Merren with the unhealed cuts of several knives marking his body.

'You're thinking what's to stop you running if they unchain you,' Kashta said to River-Stone as the smith struck off Oltoo's fetters.

River-Stone shrugged. 'Also I wonder why this rich man needs me to guard him when his stone house is full of warriors.'

Kashta nodded. The same questions had plagued him when he had been brought in chains to the count's fortress in the hills. The answer was of course that Count Merren had many enemies. There's nothing the aristocracy dislike so much as the idea that sufficient coin will buy a place among their ranks for anyone, no matter if they were born in a sty.

'The count's personal guards are all slaves whose homes lie very far away. It means we have no family that can be threatened to turn us from our duty.' Every man of the guard depended wholly on Count Merren, their lives forfeit if the count should be killed. None of them had lives beyond the fortress walls, nothing for the count's enemies to get their hooks into.

River-Stone's fetters fell to the stone-flagged floor and he stepped away, bending to massage his ankles. In places the flesh had been rubbed raw. Those were new scars the boy would wear to his grave, declaring him a slave in a universal script.

'What stops me now?' River-Stone straightened. He was tall, taller than Kashta, long limbs lined with the hard corded muscle of a bushman used to running for days on the trail of game. His kind would wear the prey down rather than out-race it. He waved a hand at the courtyard beyond the smithy. 'I can climb these walls.'

The smith grunted and put away his hammer, shaking his head. It was the smith who broke those who the count felt in need of the most severe punishment. Merren didn't keep a torturer or an executioner, he just set his smith to the task with a hammer, sometimes a hand or a foot, sometimes ribs or a jaw. For those who had to die it could be a quick blow to the head, or something that sent a message, and involved the breaking of many bones, one after the other.

'What keeps you here?' Kashta asked. 'I could tell you what will happen when you are caught, and trust to the fear to hold you in place. But that would be foolish for young men have too little fear.' He started back out into the yard, waving for Oltoo to follow. 'Come!'

'What then?' River-Stone hurried after him. 'Why do you stay, brother?'

Kashta halted in the rare, weak excuse that was all the north had to offer as sunshine. 'I am not your brother, boy.' He pointed to the trade gate. 'The world lies beyond those doors. Where would you go?'

Half a lifetime ago the Snake-Sticks had taken Kashta as a slave, bearing him wounded from the ruin of his foes. Most of those taken by the Snake-Sticks were sold within a couple of hundred miles of the place that they had been born to people not unlike their own. Often set to labour in fields or to tending cattle or goats. The tribes hadn't iron to waste on slave-chains, or walls to keep them in. What held the slaves was the simple fact that they were lost and that they were different. The Snake-Sticks would sell a plains slave in the hills, a forest slave in the plains, a mountain man in the desert. A land whose secrets are not known to you will not feed you. A land whose tribes bear different scars, or no scars, or wear their hair just so, or pierce their bodies with copper bands . . . such a land will always know you as a slave and every spear will turn against you.

River-Stone regarded the gates, his lips searching for an answer.

'Where would you go?' Kashta repeated. From what he had seen of it, in the Broken Empire a man of Afrique was as far from home as Salash from the desert would be among the Haccu, Kashta's own people.

'Somewhere!' River-Stone spat the word. 'I would go somewhere. I do not plan to grow old here with you, old man.'

Kashta shrugged and walked away toward the barracks, knowing he would be followed. The boy's words were hot and foolish. Even so, they stung him.

In the weeks that followed Kashta oversaw the new recruits' training. Watching from the walls when off-duty as Sergeant Wrexler put the boys through their paces with the regulars. Kashta would take over if either lived up to the expectations of the agent who had purchased them. Oltoo demonstrated strength and courage but seemed clumsy with sword and shield. He also lacked the fire Kashta looked for. Some might call it killer's blood. The difference between the hunter and the farmer. He would be sold away to some other master. The nations of the Broken Empire held few slaves, though many of their peoples seemed little different to Kashta, held by chains of poverty and imposed duty. Even so, there was a market for the peoples of Afrique among the aristocracy, for they were regarded as a status symbol in many of the southern kingdoms. Oltoo would find a place.

River-Stone on the other hand had all the talent promised by the agent. He took some time to adapt to the sword, having fought with spear and knife before, but the boy had an instinct for combat. He fought with a smile. When knocked down he got up and fought with a crimson smile. The boy was strong, but most of all he was fast, and speed counts.

A month after River-Stone's arrival Sergeant Wrexler delivered the boy to the Sword Cloister, a small courtyard close to Count Merren's personal rooms. Kashta had the night-watch training. The day-watch used the same yard to train during the night. Apparently the count slept better with the clash of steel filtering through his windows.

'River-Stone.' Kashta raised a hand to halt the others, a dozen men from as many nations.

'Othello.' The boy halted in their midst, wrapped in the padded grey armour of a trainee, longsword at his hip, blunt but still a deadly weapon.

'The sergeant tells me you've stopped holding your sword as if it were a spear,' Kashta said.

River-Stone showed his teeth. 'Try me.'

'I will.' Kashta couldn't help but smile back. Something in the boy woke his old fierceness. 'But first; what is the night-guard's most important weapon in defence of Count Merren?'

River-Stone twisted his lip, clever enough to know that the question was a riddle, but not seeing the answer. 'You will tell me that it is not the sword.' He set his hand to the hilt of his blade. 'Or any work of iron.'

Kashta nodded. He pointed the outer two fingers of one hand at his eyes. 'We watch. We know this place better than any hunter knows his ground. We look, we listen, we sense any change, any thing not in its place or time.' He covered his throat. 'Your voice can summon a hundred swords to your side. Better a poor swordsman who sees trouble coming than the best of blades who walks into it.'

River-Stone nodded, his gaze lifting briefly above Kashta's head to skip across the rooftops. Kashta had noticed that about the boy, always looking up. River-Stone was trouble coming, there was no doubting it. Kashta should send him on his way with Oltoo. Sell the trouble to someone else. But sometimes, just once in a while, you see trouble and you run to greet it.

Kashta drew his sword, the metal ringing as it left the scabbard. He swung at River-Stone, a wide blow, signalled by every muscle to give the boy time. Even so, many of the count's guardsmen would struggle to stop it without formal warning.

River-Stone drew and interposed his blade, counter-attacking in the same motion. Kashta struck away the attack, hard enough to make the boy's fingers sting. River-Stone shot him a speculative look then dropped to the floor, sweeping his leg towards Kashta's ankles. Kashta adjusted his footing, bracing against the blow and withstanding it. At the same time he moved his sword to aim at River-Stone's chest, the point an inch from the boy's breastbone. River-Stone moved to block, but realizing he was too late he let his weapon drop.

'Good.' Kashta reached down to haul River-Stone to his feet. 'Inventive. It nearly worked.'

'You never know what will work until you try.' River-Stone offered that smile of his, half humour, half bite.

'And your plans for running?' Kashta asked.

'You were right about that,' River-Stone said.

Kashta nodded, feeling an unexpected twinge of disappointment. 'Go spar with Mai T'uii.' He pointed to the easterner. The man came from so far away that none in the fortress even knew the names of the first dozen lands he had passed through to reach them.

Later in the barracks Kashta pointed River-Stone to one of the empty bunks. 'We live well here, boy. We eat better than most in Baletown down the road. We're rarely called to action. In ten years three have died on the training yard. Only one man was hurt defending the count, Ferro the Slav. A small cut. The count laid gold coins the length of the wound and Ferro only wished it had been twice as long! There's ale at festivals. Women too.'

River-Stone said nothing, only gave the smallest of shrugs and let his gaze flit to the light filtering through the shutters. It was nothing, just the reaction of a boy who knew little more about the world than which leaves to wipe his arse with. But somehow Kashta went to his own bunk frowning, feeling for the first time in a long while that the life he'd just described was less than he desired.

Kashta dreamed of a cage of golden bars in which he sat with the other warriors of his tribe, feasting on an untold wealth of meat, rich, dripping, bloody . . . They ate and ate but still he was hungry, and on every side his brothers and the boys he had grown with chewed at their bones with a kind of desperation and a false good humour. For a moment Kashta put his bowl aside and watched . . . and all the time the bars drew in closer and closer still, with only the empty laughter escaping.

It took another month for River-Stone to earn a place in the night guard, to be equipped with uniform and armour befitting his status, though still with the white bands of a trainee and a junior. Kashta had to argue the boy's case with Sir Gromtal personally, stating that in terms of potential River-Stone had no equal among those brought to the fort in the past decade and more. 'It will not be long before he can best some of the others on the yard.'

Sir Gromtal had pursed his lips, narrowed a cold blue stare, and nodded. 'On your head, Othello. On your head.'

River-Stone ran three days later. Kashta and Mai T'uii were assigned to the band of six guardsmen set to hunting the boy down. The six, led by Sir Gromtal, included Isaak, the count's best tracker and Yomtof, a houndsman directing three hulking bloodhounds.

'Why did he run?' Mai T'uii asked. The easterner had been taken into chains late in life but had never once complained about his station in Kashta's hearing. The man had no gods but his ancestors and held a great belief in fate. Which was lucky, for Kashta wasn't sure that any of the count's men could stand against Mai T'uii in a fight. 'You put your name behind him, Othello. Has he no pride?'

'A different kind of pride.' Kashta put a hand to Mai T'uii's shoulder and followed the houndsman from the great doors of the fortress out into the cold bluster of the day. The sky lay mountainous with cloud, a high sun thrusting its spears through any chink found, and the world below promised only trouble.

'Pray we find the boy, Othello, and swiftly.' Sir Gromtal eyed the horizon sourly. He was a small man, but tough, of an age with Kashta, dark hair already peppered with silver, known among the servants for acts of petty cruelty. 'Count Merren will not take kindly to the discovery that one you vouched to guard him has fled his walls.'

River-Stone's trail lay across the ridge of the Jostler Hills, Little Skirid, Big Skirid, Derry and Maltop, all in a row pointing south and east. 'He's heading for Hentris,'

231

Kashta told Mai T'uii. They walked together at the back, conserving their energy behind the eagerness of the guardsmen. Runaways were rare and always cause for excitement.

'Have you been there?' Mai T'uii asked.

Kashta shook his head. 'Only to the count's estate outside.' Hentris lay three days off if you took the best roads. Orlanth's biggest city after Limoges. In such a place even a man as markedly different as River-Stone might hide away. The boy hadn't been persuaded against running by Kashta's speech. He'd been persuaded to wait and learn more before running. Kashta shook his head but a faint smile clung to his lips.

The hunting party covered the ground swiftly but mile after mile came and went without sign of the boy. Runaways were normally ill-prepared for the elements, short on supplies, and lost. River-Stone was probably well equipped on all fronts, having spent his weeks at the fortress collecting both the information and material he needed. As his tiredness grew toward exhaustion and sore feet began to blister Kashta found himself hoping not that they would sight their quarry but that he would elude them.

They spent the night in a farmhouse, the farmer and his family exiled to their own barn. Sir Gromtal woke in a foul mood, his curses and speculation upon both Kashta and the boy's fate growing more venomous by the mile. 'Count'll have the smith take a claw hammer to the slave's hands and feet. Show him on the wall for a month before finishing the job.'

Rain came and the houndsman cursed, the bloodhounds sniffing at the mud in confusion. Isaak could find no trail either.

'We know where he's going,' Sir Gromtal said at last. 'We'll take horses in Leffy, ride ahead on the City Road and watch for him outside Hentris. He'll come through the forest to the west rather than along the highway.'

Kashta had to agree it was a sound plan. As fullfledged members of the count's guard he and Mai T'uii were both competent riders, able to escort the count when he wished to travel swiftly between his various estates and business interests. It took an hour to reach Leffy, marching north up the Dorlon Valley. Sir Gromtal secured the necessary horses with a generous use of the count's name and miserly application of silver coinage.

They rode hard, Sir Gromtal increasingly seeming to take River-Stone's escape as a personal insult. The bloodhounds failed to keep pace and Yomtov the houndsman fell back with them, promising to rendezvous with the band on the forest trail outside Hentris. Another of the guardsmen was left in a hamlet with no name, his horse having thrown a shoe. But four guardsmen and two night-watch reached the garden-lands of Hentris with Sir Gromtal. They would be more than enough. The knight had them settle to wait for the fugitive. Their numbers would offer River-Stone no chance of escape.

They sat, eyes upon the trail, crouched in the dripping undergrowth, hour after hour, moss-clad trees standing sentinel on all sides. Sir Gromtal waited further back, sitting on a fallen log, scowling at the greenery.

'He might take another way.' One of the guardsmen.

'He might,' Kashta agreed. He hoped the boy would choose a different path. Part of him wished that he too had chosen a different path years ago. Like River-Stone he had waited, harbouring thoughts of freedom, planning escape. Months had passed with him balanced on the edge of that precipice. And by degrees the comfort of his prison had drawn him back from the brink.

'Chances are he'll come.' Albert, an older guardsman, crinkled around the eyes, rain dripping from the rim of his helmet.

Kashta crouched, shivering, warmed by memories of his childhood sun, baking the mud huts, casting short dark shadows. The boy who had earned his name on the ghost plains hadn't seen this future. He would have laughed at the suggestion that he might accept invisible chains in place of those of iron. If Kashta were to go back through the years and speak to the young man newly returned to the village wearing the fresh scars of his name – if he were to tell him of life within the stone halls of Count Merren, that fierce young warrior would declare him to be a different man, a ghost who had come back to haunt the wrong person. He would paint himself with the blood of an ox, marking his chest with the many eyes of the dust gods, and send this current Kashta back to his fate with scorn.

River-Stone kept them waiting the best part of half a day. Kashta and Mai T'uii were stretching their legs when the shout went up. The two guardsmen who spotted him, angry at the inconvenience of it all and overconfident in their numbers, stepped out into his path immediately. Both were bleeding on the ground by the time Kashta reached the trail. Sir Gromtal could be seen further along the way, chasing after the other two members of his command who were hard on the boy's heels.

Kashta and Mai T'uii set off after them at a steady jog designed to eat up the miles if need be.

River-Stone could have outdistanced all of them were he fresh but two days and a night of constant travel across unfamiliar ground had sapped his strength and the cold had got into his bones. After a quarter of a mile following deer paths into the untamed forest Kashta heard the clash of blades. He picked up speed, leaving Mai T'uii in his wake. Two hundred yards on he jumped a stand of hook-briar, and crashed into a natural clearing where River-Stone held the two guardsmen at bay.

Kashta watched as River-Stone applied the lessons hammered into him back on the training yard, keeping his guard up, not being drawn but counter-attacking at moments of his own choosing. He faced the older guard, Albert, he of the crow's-feet and smiles, puffed from the chase, and Rolon, a large man, but slow. Of Sir Gromtal there was no sign other than a crashing in the thickness of the undergrowth to the left.

'Step in . . .' Kashta found himself saying. The boy had the aggression but he tended to keep his distance, a lesson learned with spear in hand. 'Step in.'

River-Stone stepped in. He drove his sword entirely through Rolon's chest, left it there and spun the man into Albert, leaping into the tangle, a knife in hand.

Only one man got up. River-Stone, his dagger dripping crimson. He bled from a cut down his side, blotting into padded armour around the slice through it. Albert had proved he had teeth despite his years.

Sir Gromtal broke from cover, roaring, sword in hand. He reached River-Stone before the younger man had properly found his feet. Instead of leaping away River-Stone took the initiative and threw himself at Sir Gromtal's feet, skewering the left one to the dirt with his knife. The knight's roar took on a different tone but he kept his focus, stabbing down, trying to impale the boy as he rolled away. Twice his sword drove into the earth before River-Stone cleared his range, but the second attempt sliced a deeper wound across the escapee's other side.

Sir Gromtal pulled the knife free and glanced at Kashta. 'What are you waiting for, damn you?'

Kashta expected the boy to run. They would track his blood through the forest and find him sitting with his back to a tree miles on, the fight having dripped from his veins. Instead River-Stone flung himself at Gromtal, diving beneath a wild swing. They went down together. A thrashing of limbs, shouts that seemed neither human nor animal but necessary consequences of the violence. Moments later Gromtal rose, unsteady, River-Stone lying in a dark and unnatural twisting of limbs. The knight panted, pale-faced, his mail splashed with scarlet.

'Little bastard . . . had some . . . fight in him.' He leaned back against a tree.

'His name was River-Stone.' Kashta didn't mention that he'd stood a foot taller than Gromtal. He crossed over to stand between the knight and his fallen opponent.

'I don't care . . . what the bastard's name was.' Gromtal heaved another breath. Kashta couldn't see if he were injured or just exhausted. 'He was just a slave.'

Mai T'uii entered the clearing, sword in hand, his steps cautious, left leg painted crimson where the hook-briar had punished an earlier lapse in vigilance.

The runaway lay curled as if sleeping. Rolon and Albert sprawled to either side, limbs thrown wide, their bodies bloody. Sir Gromtal stood with his back to a tree, leaning as if to rest. A long sword kept him there, skewered through his chest.

'You should go.' Othello's deep voice rumbling out behind him.

Mai T'uii made no attempt to face the man at his back. 'Why?' They both knew what question he was asking.

'Sometimes the heart speaks to the hand,' Othello said. 'If Gromtal had not called the boy "just a slave" I think we would all be walking back to our horses together.'

'You should come with me, old friend,' Mai T'uii said. He sheathed his sword. He didn't think the man he called Othello would run him through from behind, and he didn't think if he were allowed to turn that his friend would be able to defeat him sword in hand. Mai T'uii understood his duty, it ran through him and wrapped his bones. He had sworn to Count Merren and it didn't matter if that oath had been forced upon him. Even so, he sheathed his sword and did not turn. 'River-Stone killed the knight. We will return to our duty.'

'And you should come with *me*, old friend,' Othello replied. 'A man can buy a title but he can't buy another man. All he gets then are words saying that he owns you. I have my own words and they say I own myself.'

'Come back, Othello,' Mai T'uii said. 'These lands are not ours.'

'No.' Othello sounded a different man, neither happy nor sad, just changed. 'River-Stone is dead and my hands are red with his blood. Whatever his years he was a man not a boy and he has taught me a new thing. Or taught me to remember an old thing that I already knew. Either way some of his blood runs in my veins now.'

'What will you do?'

'I will try a new road. Find new brothers. Learn these lands and their ways. In time I will turn my feet south and walk until I reach the sea. My home calls me, Mai T'uii. I hear the drumming circles. I see distant skies.'

'May your ancestors watch over you, brother.'

And Mai T'uii waited, listening to the sounds of the Nuban's departure fade into distance. At the last he caught the strains of 'The Merchant's Gold', rumbled out in the Nuban's deep voice, a man now free to choose his own direction and sing whatever song he pleased, provided he lived with the consequences. The notes diminished beneath the quiet of the trees and Mai T'uii finally stood alone in the forest with only dead men and his own regrets for company.

Footnote

We're all prisoners of something. Sometimes it takes someone else to show us the chains we've become accustomed to. But the decision regarding what, if anything, to do about those chains is only ours.

Know Thyself

'Honour thy father.' The words echoed from the throne as Gomst approached, hurrying the length of the black carpet that stretched from doors to dais.

Gomst passed the last pair of table-knights and stood before the king of Ancrath. Clergy, no matter their station, do not bow to crowns, but Gomst felt the pressure on his shoulders even so. He kept his gaze on the bottom step, waiting to be acknowledged.

'*Honour thy father.* This instruction constitutes ten per cent of all the commandments that God himself felt fit to hand down on tablets of stone, does it not?'

Gomst raised his eyes to the king now. 'It does, your highness.' He decided against adding 'and thy mother'. King Olidan looked to be the sort of man who would not take well to sharing honour.

'I have two sons who would benefit from further education in such a commandment.' Olidan sat back in his high throne, not sprawled, but at ease. An iron circlet bound the blackness of his hair, rubies set there, bloody in the torchlight. The eyes that watched Gomst beneath it were winter-blue.

'All men benefit from such instruction, highness.' Gomst resisted the continuing urge to bow. The bishop had called the appointment a reward for good service, but beneath the weight of Olidan's gaze Gomst was beginning to feel that perhaps it had been a punishment.

'My eldest son has vowed to murder me, priest. What do you think to that, eh? What sentence would the church prescribe for such treason?' The king leaned forward in his chair now, as if it were just the two of them, perhaps in the snugness of the confessional.

Gomst opened his mouth, hoping that an answer might appear, but none did. 'I . . . I understood your sons to be infants, majesty?'

'The eldest is six. The other four.'

'Corinthians 13:11. *When I was a child I spake as a child.*' Gomst raised his hands. 'Even our Lord had a time for childish things and childish thinking.' Gomst felt himself walking a labyrinth of knife edges. He wanted neither to fail whatever test was being set nor to give offence. Olidan Ancrath was not a man you offended without consequence. 'Perhaps I misunderstand, highness. A boy of six years is surely no threat?'

'This child of six stole from the royal treasury.' The king rose from his throne. 'He didn't wander through a carelessly open door. He descended the walls of the Tall Castle and broke through the bars of a window too narrow for any man.' The king turned to study the wall to one side of his chair. His fingers traced a scar in the stonework. 'My son threw a hammer at me. It missed my head by the width of a nail . . .' He paused as if remembering the incident. 'Thou shalt not steal, thou shalt not kill, thou shalt honour thy father. My boy, Jorg, broke or attempted to break three of the ten in one day.' The king returned his gaze to Gomst. 'I will confess, priest, that I possess small understanding of what it is to be a father. My own offered precious little instruction in the matter. After the theft I taught the boy a lesson. A harsh lesson, but necessary. Now the child believes himself at war with me. This is a belief I could have beaten from him, but for his mother's sake I have commissioned the services of an expert to instruct him more gently. I warn you though, Father Gomst. I expect Jorg to have come to his senses the next time he is brought before me. Or I will not be pleased.'

Gomst swallowed. 'May I ask the nature of the lesson you taught your son, highness?'

'An eye for an eye, that's what your bible says. The boy took from me. I took from him.' King Olidan frowned.

'Not—'

'No, not his eye. I killed his dog.'

Father Gomst settled into his quarters that evening, a small room close to the royal chapel. He would instruct the faithful in the castle church out in the compound but for the king and his family the chapel served. Like his room the chapel too was small, and although well-appointed, with sufficient gold upon the altar, the place had an air of neglect about it, the dust thick upon the pews.

The last incumbent, Father Hermest, had succumbed to a winter flu two years earlier and it seemed his ghost had been considered sufficient moral guidance for the Ancraths up until the king's recent epiphany that religion might actually be useful in controlling his apparently murderous offspring.

Father Hermest had left nothing to mark his decade of service save an abundance of incense packed into a large cupboard in Gomst's room, a bible, and a sampler on the wall bearing the instruction 'Know thyself'.

Before he lay down in his narrow bed Gomst went to bolt his door. The sampler caught his eye. Two words. *Temet nosce.* They said it was Socrates who had first uttered them, though who could say after such a span of years? Socrates had died for honour: he had drunk his draught of hemlock and gone to the shores of the Styx long before Jesus was birthed of a virgin. *Know thyself.* Sound instruction for men of honour perhaps, but poison when poured into the ear of the ignoble. Gomst knew too much of himself for his liking.

Morning found Gomst shivering beneath his thin blanket. He put on his priest's robe and stood once more the impostor, claiming the authority of the almighty whilst knowing himself a fraud at every moment, weak, impure, unworthy.

He broke his fast in the great hall, dining with Friar Glen, a brother from the monastery out in Vieux who had been brought in after Father Hermest's death to keep order in the castle church until a replacement arrived.

'I'm to see to the princes' religious instruction, brother.' Gomst brushed crumbs from his beard and reached for another roll. 'Where might I find them at this hour?'

'Those two devils? You'll need the patience of an angel there, father. And a stout cane.' The friar made an ugly smile as if imagining applying that cane himself. 'They should be with their nurses up by the queen's quarters, but most likely you'll have to join in the hunt for them. The dungeons might be able to hold them but I'm not even sure about that.'

Whatever else Friar Glen might be he proved a good teller of fortunes. The princes weren't with their nurses and half the castle guard were engaged in a desultory search. Father Gomst found himself co-opted into the effort and traipsed about the upper floors with a guardsman named Geffin who suggested that the boys would be discovered when they felt like it and not before.

'Probably around lunchtime.' Geffin turned over a chair cushion in the queen's parlour, as if Prince Jorg might be hiding beneath. 'Unless they managed to steal food too.'

Gomst slipped away after an hour and returned to the steps that Geffin had said led up to the roof. The view from the heights of the Tall Castle's keep would offer an unparalleled panorama of Ancrath and give Gomst a better feeling for the layout of the rest of the castle.

With everyone roaming the keep in search of errant children nobody thought to oppose the new priest's exploration and Gomst set off up the spiral stairway that would take him to the battlements. He got up two turns of the stair before fetching up against a heavy iron gate with a formidable lock. Gomst puffed out his disappointment and was about to descend when he noticed half a bread roll resting on a step beyond the gate. One step higher and the turn of the spiral would have hidden it.

Gomst took hold of the gate. No matter how good at ratting a castle's cats may be, no dropped food will lie unmolested for long. He pulled and the gate swung toward him on oiled hinges. Gomst went up.

The top of the tall castle sported a bell-tower, a water tank, an observatory, and three mouldering siege machines of a sort that Gomst couldn't name. No sign of the missing boys. The keep itself had been a work of the Builders. Various more recent dynasties had squatted in the structure since God's judgment had wiped the Builders' pride from the world, along with their lives. The Ancraths had been the ones to add battlements to the truncated building but the walls did little to tame the wind at this elevation. Gomst went to lean against the stonework and stare out across Crath City. To the south the River Sane snaked its way silver through the urban sprawl. Gomst could see the Cathedral of Our Lady down beside the waters and the Cathedral of the Sacred Heart up on its hill. To the west the city surrendered to salt fens and the brown vastness of the Ken Marshes where the rising sea had finally abandoned its march inland.

After half an hour Gomst turned from the view, eyes watering from the wind. He wandered across to the bell-tower that stood precariously at the front edge of the square keep, older than the wall and interrupting it. A large iron bell hung in the belfry some forty feet up. Gomst came up to the door, craning his neck to watch the tower scrape against a grey and moving sky. He pushed the door, a weathered collection of planks, and it swung open. With a shrug he followed up the creaking wooden stairs beyond.

Immediately Gomst reached the top of the steps he saw the rope, tied to the stair-post and straining out over the low guard wall. Gomst edged into the belfry, which was open on all sides with the bell taking up most of the space. If it swung it might knock him over the guard wall to a messy reunion with the roof of the keep. He inched around to where the rope went across the wall at the front of the tower and peered over.

A small, dark-haired boy stood horizontally about a yard down, feet braced against the outer wall, the rope around his chest. He faced down over the drop of two hundred feet or more to the courtyard before the keep's main entrance. The child had his head raised a little, as if looking out toward the stables block opposite rather than at the scene directly below him.

Gomst debated whether to speak. If he startled the boy he might slip and possibly come free of the rope harness.

'I heard you on the stairs.' The boy made the decision for him.

'What in God's name are you doing out there, Prince Jorg?'

'I'm trying to kill my father. In my name, not God's. William is going to signal me when he sees him coming. He's not to wave the flag until Father draws level with the Belpan armour standing in the hall. Then if I let this rock go it should hit him just as he comes out. If I waited to see him it would be too late.'

Gomst hadn't seen the rock, hidden as it was by Jorg's body, but he could see the tension in the boy's arms, held beneath him. 'And what do you think will happen if you succeed? You'll be a murderer! Do you know what they do to murderers? Do you know what happens to them in Hell?'

'I'll be king,' Jorg replied, still calm, focused on the distant windows above the stable stalls. 'I will pardon myself.'

'God won't pardon you, Jorg!'

'Kings rule by divine right. I read that. If it is my right to sit on the throne then God has to approve how I got there.'

Gomst considered the rope. Would he be strong enough to haul the boy in? The child was supposed to be six. He didn't sound six. He looked bigger than a six-year-old should too. And what if he struggled, dropped the stone and killed someone, or worse, slipped out and left Gomst holding the rope that the king would hang him with? He took hold of it with both hands.

From the stable-block window a red cloth fluttered and suddenly Gomst was hauling on the rope with all his strength. Jorg came up with a strangled cry, still clutching the rock he had intended to drop on his father. Gomst grabbed the boy under one arm and heaved him into the belfry, clutching the rope with the other. They fell together, Gomst panting, Jorg furious. The boy found his feet and raised his rock overhead. Gomst, who had been relieved that the child had had the presence of mind not to drop his missile when hauled up the wall, now reversed that opinion rapidly.

'Who are you?'

The anger on the boy's face, combined with the size of the stone he had hold of, quite unmanned Gomst.

'Gomst! F-father Gomst!'

'Why are you dressed like a priest?' The boy frowned and lowered his weapon.

'I am a priest.' Gomst's voice lacked conviction. He sat up and brushed at his robe. 'I'm to instruct you and your brother.'

'To save our souls?' Jorg seemed unimpressed. He set the rock down and sat on the wall, his back to the empty yards below.

'I just saved you from killing your father. If you'd dropped that stone and missed then the very best you could have hoped for would be being sent away to a monastery. Probably on some desolate rock. Did you want that?'

'I wouldn't have missed.' Jorg scowled. 'But living out in the wilds surrounded by brothers doesn't sound much fun. William is pain enough by himself.' Jorg pinned Gomst with a dark stare. 'He won't be happy you stopped me.'

'He's *four*! He will have forgotten by tomorrow.' Gomst got to his feet. It made him feel better, towering above the child.

'Not William.' Jorg shook his head. 'He won't give up. Father killed our dog. We have to kill him now.'

'And how will that help? Will it bring the dog back?' Gomst went to the steps, hoping to lead Jorg from the tower or at least get him off the wall. Looking at him balanced there in the wind made Gomst's stomach turn. 'It won't make you feel better. You might think it will, but it won't. Vengeance is mine, sayeth the Lord. Vengeance is God's, Jorg. Not because he is greedy, but because he is *saving* us from it. Taking upon himself a cancer that eats those who try to hold to it.' Gomst shook his head. 'Killing your own father. I ask again: how will that help?'

Jorg dropped into the belfry. 'It would stop him killing more dogs.'

Gomst tried another tack. 'You could stop stealing instead.' Guilt was a weapon the bishop favoured and though Gomst recognized its power he always felt dirty when wielding it. 'Was it not your sin that prompted your father's actions?'

The boy scowled and looked down. In the hand he had taken from his pocket he held a tuft of brownish fur bound with gold wire. 'I'm not without sin. But that stone I was about to cast wasn't the first one.'

'Your father taught you a lesson about right and wrong, prince. A hard lesson, but kings often teach hard lessons. The king knows you will sit on his throne one day and if you are not strong enough to keep it then someone will take it from you . . .' Gomst put a conviction into his words that he didn't feel, the same conviction with which he delivered the sermons that so long ago ceased to hold meaning for him. To save the child from disaster he must dress up the actions of a monster as something reasonable. A mental shrug. Gomst had told bigger lies for worse reasons. One could hardly rise in Roma's church these days without a crooked tongue.

'If you kill your father it will be a stain on your soul your whole life, Jorg. And what of your mother? Will it make her happy? How would she look at you then?' Gomst had no insight into Queen Rowan's marriage but he suspected that her relationship with King Olidan was as much of a mystery to young Jorg. The bond between their parents is hard for any child to fathom.

'William will do it by himself.' Jorg frowned.

'He's *four*!' Gomst threw his hands up. 'Olidan's table-knights can fend off a four-year-old!'

'He won't always be four,' Jorg said.

Gomst stared at the boy before him, six years in the world, looking closer to nine, speaking as if he were twelve. 'He's like you? This brother of yours?'

'Worse.' Jorg started down the stairs.

Gomst met William that evening. Gomst had turned Jorg over to the castle guards and the errant youngest prince had been discovered an hour later then returned to the care of his nurses, four tough-looking women with no-nonsense expressions. The one who now opened the door to Gomst's knock appeared to be rather harried by the responsibility of keeping two small boys where they were supposed to be.

'Prince Jorg! Prince William! The new priest is here to see you.'

William, golden and cherubic, trailed his dark-haired brother as he came across for the introduction.

'Father Gomst.' Jorg nodded and stepped aside, revealing William who stood clutching a rag doll, albeit that the rags were satin and velvet.

Gomst sank down on his knees to be on a level with the young boy. Seeing the child for himself, he found it hard to believe Jorg's claims. 'Prince Jorg, good to see you. And Prince William, pleased to make your acquaintance.' Gomst shot a quick, doubting look in Jorg's direction.

In response Jorg snatched the rag doll from William and yanked its head aside to reveal the point of a meat skewer gleaming amid the satin.

'Oh no, Prince William!' A nurse crossed swiftly to take the doll from Jorg. 'Not another one!' She extracted the six-inch skewer and put it into an apron pocket where the metal-on-metal chink suggested she might have a significant collection of similar implements.

Gomst returned his gaze to William and frowned. 'Did Jorg not explain to you how bad it would be to hurt your own father? Didn't he tell you about the lesson he had to learn?'

'Father killed my dog.' The boy's brows knitted in a scowl.

'I told him,' Jorg said. 'He won't listen. He said *I* needed the lesson but *he* lost his dog.'

'I see . . .' Gomst rubbed his chin, finding himself unwilling to look away from William. It doesn't do to offer the other cheek to a furious infant with a talent for hiding sharp objects about his person.

252

'I told him he wouldn't be king even if he killed Father,' Jorg said. 'I think that made him even angrier.'

'I *will* be king!' William turned his glare on Jorg.

'It's me that will be king, and not just of this castle!' Jorg faced the boy, ready to fight. 'King of the whole world!'

Gomst got to his feet. 'This really isn't helping. Come with me, both of you.'

Waving the nurses aside, Gomst led the two princes from their quarters, down the steps, across the next floor, down more steps, then more steps.

'Where are we going?' Jorg tugged at Gomst's robe.

'The catacombs.'

'Don't want catacombs, want Justice!' William stopped in his tracks.

Gomst frowned. 'Justice? I don't—'

'Our dog, Justice,' Jorg said.

'Oh.' Gomst considered a lie but settled on evasion. 'Well we're going where they put the dead.'

Both boys followed without further questions. Gomst had discovered the catacombs on a map tucked into his predecessor's bible. Father Hermest had annotated it with the identities of those lying within the current sepulchres along with the chambers provisionally reserved for living members of the family.

In the basement they passed the kitchens where a fat cook in a floury apron waved at the princes, addressing them with none of the proper deference.

'That's Drane,' Jorg said. 'He gives us pastries.'

'Well he has no business doing so.' Gomst found the way down into the wine cellars, opening the door with a key that Friar Glenn had given to him, accompanied by the advice that copious Ancrath red would help deal with the stress of tending to the princes' souls. Gomst had brought a lantern with him and now turned up the wick, letting the flame light their way.

The route led along avenues flanked by barrels and eventually down more steps. They entered the catacombs through a doorway paved with mahogany planks. The ironwork suggested an enormously thick door had once stood there, but no sign of it remained.

'Can you smell them?' Jorg sniffed.

'Who?' William asked.

'Dead people!' The prince made his voice waver as if telling a story of ghosts and ghouls.

A surprising length of corridor and several turns at last brought them to the vaults in which the Ancraths waited out eternity. None of them had been waiting particularly long yet. Gomst led the way past half a dozen chambers to the end of the long vault where a black marble tomb displayed in gruesome relief the armoured likeness of the skeleton of the man beneath.

'This, my princes, is the last resting place of your great-great-grandfather Caine Ancrath who took these lands and this castle from the House of Or. He died at the age of forty-nine.'

The two princes came in close. Before Gomst could protest Jorg had hauled himself up onto the lid, to stand on the carved skeleton.

'Prince Jorg! That's hardly seemly!'

Jorg ignored Gomst and reached down for William's outstretched hand. 'Baby!' And pulled him up.

Gomst straightened his robes then raised the lantern to afford the boys a better view.

'So, you know where Caine Ancrath's bones have been these past one hundred and fourteen years . . . but where has his soul been?'

William shrugged.

'Over there?' Jorg pointed to a nearby tomb whose lid depicted a well-proportioned queen.

'In paradise!' Gomst raised his hand to clout the boy around the head, then lowered it, recalling that the head belonged to a prince. 'In paradise, cavorting with angels and feasting on ambrosia!' He paused. 'And where would it have been had he murdered his own father – for *whatever* reason?'

Both boys narrowed their eyes at him and made no answer.

'He would have spent those years in torment in the fires of Hell!' Gomst moved the light below his face to lend it a demonic aspect. He would scare the sin out of William Ancrath before the child grew too old to be saved. 'Burning in a lake of fire with no prospect of ever escaping. That, boys, is why you must obey the

Lord in all things and cast sin aside.' He fixed Jorg with his stare, hoping for an ally. 'And what is the biggest sin of all?'

Jorg frowned. 'Fornicating with camels?'

'No! And where did you hear that?' Again Gomst had to lower his hand halfway to strike the boy.

'It was in the bible.' Jorg clamped his jaw shut. Defiant.

Gomst swung his glare at William. 'Killing your father is the greatest sin.'

'What *are* camels?' William asked.

Gomst's hand decided the matter for him. He smacked the youngest prince around the head, hard enough to topple him from the tomb. A moment later he pulled Jorg from atop his great-great-grandfather and started to march off, dragging the boy with him.

'It's for his own good! We need to put some fear into him. I can't say what King Olidan will do to the child if he's caught coming at him with a skewer. But it will be much worse than this! Your father is not a gentle man!'

Jorg came tripping along behind, not trying to wrench his hand free.

Gomst glanced back. He could see Prince William in the thickening shadows at the base of the tomb, sitting up and rubbing his head. 'Your brother will come running after us soon enough,' Gomst said. 'He won't stay there in the dark.'

Gomst's confidence in his statement began to waver as he reached the far end of the vault without any sounds of distress or pursuit. He turned back but could see nothing save darkness.

'He can still see our light,' Jorg said.

Gomst hesitated, uneasy, his fingers still stinging from where he had slapped the boy. Any normal child would have run after them, sobbing and terrified by now. He gritted his teeth and led on, around the corner and back down the long corridor. After fifty yards he stopped. 'We'll wait here.'

'You shouldn't have hit him,' Jorg said. 'You'll be his enemy now.'

'It was for his own good.' Gomst bit off the words, exasperated at finding himself having to explain his actions to a child.

'It wasn't for your good.' The lantern light gave Jorg's face a sinister cast that Gomst would never have thought to see on a six-year-old. 'You're my enemy too now.'

'Me?' Gomst bridled. 'Why for God's sake?'

'You hit my brother.' Jorg sat down, his back to the wall, and said no more.

Seconds stretched into minutes and minutes stretched beyond Father Gomst's ability to judge. He sat beside Jorg to save his legs. His imagination ran in circles, the explanations he would offer to the king if something had gone wrong, the route he would take to escape Ancrath, the sanctuary he would seek at the cathedral . . . And all the while these thoughts circled the image of a small blond child alone in the dark, lying in an ever-spreading pool of blood.

'He must be hurt!'

'He wasn't,' Jorg said. 'I saw him get up.'

Gomst opened his mouth again but said nothing. The walls seemed to press in from all sides. The dank air offered insufficient substance to his lungs. And the darkness crowded about them, thick with ghosts, not of the Ancraths silent in their tombs, but of the unquiet hordes who had fallen to their swords.

At last, with the lantern's flame starting to flicker, Gomst stood. 'We have to go back.'

'He's beaten you,' Jorg said.

Gomst bowed his head. It was true. 'I'm a priest,' he said. 'We play the long game.'

They retraced their steps, turned the corner, walked back down the length of the vault past the empty archways to chambers where more dead Ancraths lay, and the chambers where King Olidan and Queen Rowan would one day take their final rest.

The lantern's flickers revealed the child crouched ghoul-like upon the black bones of Caine Ancrath. William raised his head to them, slowly, as if about to reveal a face from a nightmare rather than that of a cherub.

'I like it down here,' he said.

'Time to come away, Prince William.' Father Gomst held out his hand.

'If Jorg is going to be king of all the people up there . . . I could be king of all the dead,' William said. 'Then I wouldn't have to kill him to be king. And we could both be kings.'

Gomst found his outstretched hand trembling. There was such a certainty in the boy, as if some far older spirit watched from his eyes. 'There's no king of the dead, William. Come with us.'

'Is that why Father killed Justice?' William asked. 'Did he send him ahead so that he would be waiting for me? Waiting to help me?'

Gomst felt a weight upon his shoulders then, heavier than Olidan's regard, heavier than the Tall Castle towering above him fathoms high. A simple lie. A simple lie to save a boy from his father's wrath.

'Is it?' William asked.

'Yes.'

And Gomst led both boys out of the darkness.

On the stairs, with William falling behind, Jorg whispered, 'You lied.'

Gomst made no reply. Lies are soft and accommodating. The truth is hard, full of uncomfortable angles. It rarely helps anyone. Jesus said *I am the way, and the truth, and the life. No one comes to the Father except through me.* But in the Tall Castle only one father mattered and he was neither Gomst nor God.

Gomst knew himself well enough, and the truth was: lies were all that might save him.

Footnote

In the Broken Empire books I gave you Father Gomst through Jorg's eyes, and although Jorg learned to see more as he matured we never really saw into the man. I never thought of Gomst as hero or villain, though certainly young Jorg saw him in unflattering terms. The idea of weak men representing ultimate authority interests me, and Gomst is an example of that. A man with many flaws, an average sort of man with a goodish heart, and the job of representing the ultimate power . . . People often ask me if I see myself more as Jorg or as Jalan (from my Red Queen's War trilogy). Sometimes I think as an author, representing the ultimate power in my fictional worlds . . . I'm more of a Gomst!

*Finally, an extra tale for you featuring Prince Jalan Kendeth,
the star of The Red Queen's War, a trilogy set in the Broken
Empire which crosses paths with elements of Jorg's story
while telling one that is all its own.*

Three is the Charm

I woke in the bed of Abigale Monici. Or rather
half-way between it and the floor. That left me with
just enough time to anticipate the pain of hitting the
ground but insufficient time to do anything to prevent
it happening.

After the impact I lay there groaning.

'Come back to bed, Jal.' A murmur from above. 'It's
not even noon yet.'

'Noon?' I levered myself up onto all fours and glanced
longingly at the contours offered beneath silken sheets.
'Hell.'

The amount of time spent putting on a pair of trousers is inversely proportional to how late you are. Being
potentially very late it naturally took me several minutes
to struggle into mine. Somehow a simple activity that

I've performed most days of my life, often several times a day, became a stupefyingly difficult feat of dexterity in which my defiantly undextrous feet refused all attempts to push them through the two tubes of cloth. I fell over backwards at one point, destroying an elegant washstand and prompting a sleepy complaint from Abigale, along with a delicious rearrangement of the aforementioned contours.

I fled the scene and hastened from the balcony into the Monici gardens, something of a wild tangle sprawling over several acres of an estate purchased in better days. I make no apologies for the way I live my life. Actually, that's a lie. I make lots of apologies for it. But I don't mean any of them. I probably should have said goodbye, but then I probably should do a lot of things I don't. The important thing is—

'Darin?' I spotted my elder brother before he saw me and pulled my leg back over the estate wall. Returning by inches, I peered over at him as he walked on, oblivious, along the street outside. He appeared to be making for the estate's main gates. I dropped over, landing on quiet feet, and ran in the opposite direction. Of my two brothers Darin is the most bearable but I don't like him to know what I've been up to.

I'm not normally up to much of anything before noon, but this weekend in addition to appointments at the racetrack, card table, and fight-pits, I had a scavenger hunt to contend with. The hunt was the brainchild of the young Duke Gottenberg, a senior member of Vermillion's most debauched secret society, the Hellfire Club, of which I was of course a fully paid-up member. Well . . . a member at least. Among the items on the list were Judge Loreno's silver-stitched eye-patch, a salt-cellar from the table of crime-lord Maeres Allus, bedding three members of any royal family, a wooden leg, an elephant seal, dancing with the Dowager Countess of Momford, kissing a lord . . . it went on. An assortment of random tasks and acquisitions, each of which would earn the contestant a number of points commensurate with their difficulty. In addition to a sizeable prize for ticking the most boxes there were numerous side bets placed on individual items from the list. The smart money is always in the side bets.

I slipped away into the well-heeled streets of Old Vermillion, pondering what business Darin might have with Lord Monici. He wouldn't be trying to sneak a kiss. Darin disapproved of the Hellfire Club wholeheartedly. Could he have come a-courting? The Monicis were hardly marriage material. I supposed that technically Aldo Monici was a prince, which would allow his daughters to call themselves princesses, but the family had fled their tiny kingdom in the time of Aldo's grandfather and were never likely to return, unless they fancied decorating stakes outside the usurper's palace.

★   ★   ★

I made the royal racetrack by noon, just barely, panting and cursing as I elbowed my way through the crowds to reach Bent Gotti's stall.

'Mr Clip-Clop to win. Twenty in crown gold on the nose!' Shouted over a row of heads.

'You don't have twenty in crown gold, Prince Jalan.' Bent gave me a dubious look.

'Twenty, I say.' I pushed an old merchant to the side and slapped both hands on the counter. 'You know I'm good for it.'

Bent shrugged. 'On the horse's nose and on your head. Maeres Allus is collecting your IOUs.'

'There won't be an IOU, my good fellow. I'm going to win!' I turned away with my slip and resumed the elbow dance, this time bound for the stands. The win was a certainty. Abigale's father owned the horse and a few pertinent facts about the stallion had slipped out during the slipping in and subsequent pillow talk. From his performances in training on their estate out in the sticks this was more like robbery than betting.

I paid my silver and took a place in the grandstands where a prince might rub shoulders with a merchant but certainly not with a pauper. That's when I saw her. Penelope Monici, resplendent in a velvet gown of dark burgundy down which the narrow fall of her pale hair made a striking contrast. Penelope was the youngest of the Monici sisters and doubtless here to see her father's horse triumph. She appeared unattended so I wove a path to her side.

'Jalan?' She blinked her surprise at me.

'You were expecting another prince?'

'I'm sorry.' A radiant smile. 'I was just speaking with Martus. I think he's gone to place some bets.'

'Martus?' I made a scornful face. 'He's an oaf. You and I both know the youngest sibling is always the pick of the bunch.' I sidled closer, then, with an arm around her slim shoulders, steered her toward the far end of the track. 'I do believe your horse is due to run any minute now. I have high hopes for Mr Clip-Clop.'

Penelope gave me the sweetest smile. 'It would be nice. He deserves a win after all his recent ill-health.'

'Ill-health?' My question was lost beneath the swelling roar as the horses moved toward the rope. 'But I heard that—'

They were off! By the third lap Mr Clip-Clop was a good ten lengths in front of the rest of the field. Sadly he'd only done two laps.

At the end I stood there holding my drooping betting slip amid the cheering crowd, watching the winning jockey celebrate and waiting for my horse to finish. Clouds and silver linings as they say, though. Apparently I looked so forlorn that young Penelope couldn't help but take pity on me. She proposed an early luncheon and we hastened off before Martus's return. My older brother being something of a blunt weapon and guilty of overtopping me by two inches and several years, I felt no pang of conscience at abandoning him to the luck of the races.

I say *young* Penelope, but at nineteen she lacked just two years on me. She had a certain wide-eyed innocence about her, however, that reminded you she was the baby of the family. I learned how misleading that look was on the carriage ride back to the Monici mansion.

We both dined well though very little food was involved. I left the mansion by a bedchamber balcony for the second time that day and crossed the grounds somewhat wobbly-legged. I had intended to meet my regular cronies at Madam Lau's for cards and wine that afternoon but Penelope proved herself something of a chatterer during the unlacing and lacing portions of our encounter. Normally I let such stuff wash over me but when she started on about her rich cousin Ferdini and his poker games I paid attention. As a card player, certainly as a player of my considerable skill, you learn to listen carefully to any account of the personal habits of a potential opponent. You never know when it might come in handy. And having lost a fair bit of money to the man the previous year I was keen to gain any edge I could. It also occurred to me that Ferdini employed among his chain of betting interests one Bent Gotti, bookmaker at the royal racetrack. So technically the man had already robbed me today.

★   ★   ★

266

'Prince Jalan! Have you been running?'

'Me?' I sucked in a breath. 'Nothing of the sort. A gentleman strolls!' I wiped the sweat from my brow. 'If I'm guilty of exercise it's of an entirely different sort.'

A knowing laugh ran around the table.

Actually I *had* been running. Nearly all the way from the Monici mansion. I'd spent the last few minutes recovering with a glass of wine downstairs before coming up to the cardroom where I knew Ferdini would be gambling with his friends.

'Would you like to join us?' Ferdini waved at two of the men to make a space. He was a fat man in his thirties, an ugly fellow whose blood relationship to the Monici sisters took a significant amount of imagination to accept as truth.

'Me?' I pursed my lips in surprise. 'Well. I suppose I could sit in for a hand or two.'

'It's a twenty-piece buy-in,' Ferdini gestured to the golden pile of coins at the middle of the table.

'Of course.' I patted my pockets, finding no jingle, then dropped one of my pre-made IOUs on to the pile. I have an artisan on Ink Street make them up, in crimson to remind everyone I'm the favoured grandson of the Red Queen.

I sat with them for the next three or four hours, my fortunes waxing and waning with the flow of the cards. I'd played cards with Ferdini before, of course. And lost. We held each other in cordial disdain as knights who

267

meet at the lists and knock each other from their horses might. I'd had quite a few occasions to wager with the man. We even had a side bet on the Hellfire Club scavenger hunt, one I'd made whilst drunk and had regretted bitterly ever since. On that front, though, circumstances beyond my control and that I like to call 'natural justice' seemed as if they might be conspiring to deliver me victory.

'How's the hunt going, my prince?' Ferdini asked after a particularly galling hand. 'Danced with the dowager yet? Secured an elephant seal? Or perhaps you've succeeded in the matter of our wager.' He scoffed into his wine.

'I'm working on it.' All the time I kept my eyes fixed firmly on Ferdini's smug, pudgy face. Earlier, Penelope, bracketing demonstrations of a wicked inventiveness I would never have imagined her to possess, had let slip an interesting observation. She had mentioned that when playing games with their cousin back in the days when all of them truly were innocents, the sisters had discovered that they could always tell when Ferdini was lying to them.

'He touches his nose with the back of a fingernail.' She had laughed like a tinkling bell. 'Just like this.' And demonstrated.

'Too rich for me.' The fourth our group of six players folded as the pot in front of Ferdini mounted. I was left as the sole contester. More than two hundred in crown gold rode on the turn of his cards. My own hand was a strong one. Not unassailable, but strong. Jacks and queens.

'A good hand then?' I stared at Ferdini, my face offering him nothing.

'Perhaps.' He gave nothing back, his features a mask.

'Let me think.' I looked at my queens again.

'Be my guest.' He set the back of his nail to his nose. Just a momentary touch, unconscious.

'All in!' I pushed forward all the coins that remained from my IOU.

I walked to the Blood Holes. A decision forced upon me despite the rain as I lacked the money for a carriage. Ferdini had been holding aces. The bastard.

The men on the doors knew me and let me in despite my bedraggled appearance. I dripped my way into the main hall, finding myself enveloped immediately in the sweat and smoke and stink and din of the place. Nobles in their finery strolled around the fight floor, each close-pressed by companions, a ragged halo of hangers-on beyond that: hawkers, beer-men, poppy-men and brazens, and at the periphery, urchins ready to scurry between one aristocrat and the next bearing messages by mouth or hand.

I slouched around, hunting my good humour, while the roar of the crowd fought to swallow the cries of men fighting down below. At last I let Ochre reel me in. It was my lucky pit, in as much as I'd lost less money betting on its fights than I had at the other three main pits.

I'd almost made it close enough to see down to the combatants when a terminal grunt rang out, the cheer went up, and a woman, turning suddenly from the rail, crashed into me, nearly taking me to the floor.

'Why, Prince Jalan, you're all wet.'

The woman, Adora, eldest of the Monici sisters, had hold of my shirt front in both hands and seemed disinclined to let go of it. The fights inflame some people like that, filling them with fire and passion.

'I like my men wet.' The thrill of the kill had clearly overwhelmed Adora's senses. With her dark hair in wild disarray, for reasons I was never entirely clear upon, she looked as if she might be dangerous to refuse.

I allowed her to drag me off to one of the curtained alcoves that ring the great hall. The alcoves are usually reserved for private discussions concerning fighters and betting thereupon, also for the consumption of wine between the main contests. Adora's plans involved the table but allowed no time for wine or conversation.

I rolled from that table some while later feeling rather bruised and checking my backside for splinters. Adora hurried away through the curtains without so much as a parting kiss, saying that she had to see Unan the Goth fight. Her friend, Rilo, had told her to expect an upset!

Since Rilo Diago was a close friend of the Terrif brothers who ran the Blood Holes, and since I'd never heard of Unan the Goth, I hastened out after the departing man-eater to see if there might still be time to lay a wager upon the new fighter.

I could hear them calling the audience to the rail for the Unan versus Shi-Otta contest. Shi-Otta was a veteran of scores of fights, including at least a dozen death-matches. The odds would be heavily stacked in his favour whoever this newcomer was. Only moments remained to me. Hilo Mills stood close by, another of that damned Ferdini's bookmakers but the only man who still had his board up on the fight.

'Twenty on the Goth to win!' I lunged toward him. 'You know I'm good for it.'

'The Goth? Unan?' He drew the words out as if all the time in the world remained to him.

'Fighters enter!' Shouted from across the hall.

'Yes, damnit, the Goth!'

'Twenty?'

'Twenty!'

'Gold?'

'Gold!'

'Done!'

I had been. Unan the Goth was a weedy fellow with a hollow chest and strangely short arms. I never got to see him fight. He was dead before I'd made it halfway across the hall.

★   ★   ★

The Hellfire Club was a welcome sight after a day of heavy losses. The club hid beneath a warehouse facing the Selene and was given over to the storage of wine. I stumbled in through the towering doors under the watchful eye of the club wardens, and on past row upon row of stacked casks, Normardy reds in the main with whites from Orlanth. The steps down to the cellars looked unimpressive and uninviting, remarkable only in their number. At the bottom of the flight however, along a short corridor, around a corner and through a door, things were very different. The long, barrel-roofed hall of the Hellfire Club had seldom been so packed. All the rich, bored wastrels that Vermillion had to offer gathered in one place to brag about their exploits. A chaotic sea of colour lapping up against the dais where the young Duke Gottenberg held court, ready to score the scavenger hunt. He had a mind-sworn truth-teller by his side lest any claim be doubted. And every claim would be. The truth-teller was a dour-looking bald fellow named Merton who was, from past experience, unamenable to bribery.

I'd got a scant ten yards through the throng when Ferdini intercepted me. People parted before the advance of his rotundity like the water before a barge.

'Jalan! My prince!' He clapped a hand to my shoulder, and only with great restraint . . . and a sensible fear of the consequences . . . did I prevent myself from breaking his overly familiar wrist. Instead I gave him a broad smile.

'You look happy, my friend!' He clapped my shoulder

again. 'Unusual for a man who has lost so much gold in one day. What was it? Twenty at the track. Twenty at the table. Twenty at the pits. A tragedy! But . . . some must lose if others are to win!' He patted the fat coin purse at his hip.

'I'm smiling because you owe me thirty pieces of gold, Ferdini! I succeeded with item thirteen on the list. Three princesses in one day. Your own cousins.'

'Ah.' He nodded sadly. 'I shall reduce your debt accordingly.'

'You're not going to take me before the truth-teller?' I asked, fearing the answer.

'I believe you, my friend. They are girls of considerable appetite.'

'Damnit! You were in league with them all along!' I smacked my fist into my palm. I should have known! I had assumed that it couldn't be a set up because Ferdini stood to lose so much gold if I succeeded . . . but when I totalled up the losses I'd earned following the false tips I'd been fed, they proved to be twice my winnings. 'Oh well . . .' I smiled a rueful smile. 'Such is life.'

'So magnanimous in defeat!' Ferdini said. 'A true prince among men, to smile when you have emerged so very far behind in the game.'

I parted my hands. 'It has to be said that the day held rewards other than monetary ones.' I allowed myself a brief mental glimpse of Abigale beneath the silk, Penelope spread across a carriage bench, Adora rising above me

on that table. 'Three princesses are their own reward.'
I started off toward the duke's dais. 'Besides . . . I believe
that item thirteen was worth a dozen points all on its
own. That's more than most of the others put together!
You'd have to drag a fucking elephant seal down those
steps to beat me! And as the winner I shall enjoy claiming
my three hundred in crown gold!'

Triumph quickened my stride and I left Ferdini open-
mouthed in my wake. I'd had three of Vermillion's finest
beauties and was going to earn hundreds in gold for
doing so. Not bad for a day's work!

I was somewhat surprised to find all three women in
question standing just in front of the duke when I got
there. Surprised and rather pleased to see them again.
They really were beauties! 'Ladies, if you'll move aside
I'll be with you in a moment. I'm here to claim my
prize.'

Duke Gottenberg slouched back in his chair and
looked me up and down with a dubious eye as if princes
were ten a penny. Which, although there *are* quite a few
of us in Vermillion, was a significant undervaluing. '*Your*
prize, Jalan?'

'Put me down for item thirteen. A gentleman can't
go into names or specifics of course . . .' I turned and
gazed pointedly at the sisters. 'But I think you'll find
baldy here agrees with me.' I nodded to Merton.

'But I kissed a lord!' Abigale pushed past me as if our
tender moments had meant nothing to her. If I had been

274

less occupied looking down her dress I might have been hurt.

'So did I!' Penelope pushed past on the other side.

'I danced with the dowager duchess!' Adora chimed in from behind me.

'Yes, yes,' I tried to keep any irritation from my voice but I did want my three hundred. 'All laudable achievements, ladies. But one-point achievements that my number thirteen towers above.'

The three of them spoke as one. It was most uncanny. 'Jalan, Darin, Martus. We all got number thirteen too.'

'My . . . brothers?' I took a step back. 'But . . . that's . . .' I wasn't sure what it was. Damned unsportsmanlike for sure. 'You're all wh—'

'As bad as you,' Abigale said.

'Except one point ahead,' Penelope said.

'And much richer!' Adora reached for the prize coffer.

And that was how I lost two bets, a game of cards, *and* three hundred more in crown gold between a morning and a night.

Still . . . It wasn't a bad day.

Footnote

Jalan Kendeth is a very different character from Jorg. He's a coward, a womanizer, a hedonist utterly lacking in ambition. He's a liar and a cheat. Jorg would also lie and cheat, but for very different reasons.

The main thing Jorg and Jalan share is that they are both princes living in the Broken Empire at the same time. On occasions they meet, and those were fun scenes to write.

That's all I have. Fourteen tales returning us to the Broken Empire, shining a light in dark corners, lifting the odd rock, colouring in some of the outlines sketched in the books. Thanks for coming back for more!

And if you've read The Broken Empire trilogy and The Red Queen's War trilogy then please accept my wholly unbiased recommendation that you pick up Red Sister, *first entry in the Book of the Ancestor trilogy. It's an unrelated story in a new setting, but I think it's some of my best work. So please give it a try!*